FINDING OUR WAY

by Peter Stipe

FINDING OUR WAY
Copyright © 2019 by Peter Stipe

This book is a work of fiction. Names, characters, businesses, organizations, places, events and incidents either are the product of the author's imagination or are used fictitiously. Any resemblance to actual persons, living or dead, events, or locales is entirely coincidental.

For information contact :
Blue Fortune Enterprises, LLC
Lavender Press
P.O. Box 554
Yorktown, VA 23690
http://blue-fortune.com

Cover photograph by Peter Stipe

ISBN: 978-1-948979-29-0

Second Edition: November 2019

For Debbie

My muse and best friend

Table of Contents

Finding Our Way

I WAS SCARED. IT WAS a terrifying time of confusing social and political changes, of race riots, and open drug use. Above it all, there was the war. Every night the news told us that we were winning, but the newsmen also gave us pictures of the fighting in Asia and listed the dead. The dead soldiers were my age, and when I graduated from college, I would be eligible for the draft.

I didn't know what to do about the war. The politicians told me why we were fighting but it made no sense to me. I could really only run. I was fast, and so I ran on my college track team. That gave me the chance to run along the river through Boston for an hour or two each day. It wasn't much, but it was all I had until I met Maggie. Maggie made the difference for me back then.

At first, it was Maggie's hair that got me. To see it was like looking into a fire. There was a wildness, a brilliance to it, unlike anything I had ever seen. Light and colors flickered and flamed. Later, during the winter, when we had been dating for a while, we stopped in the midst of a walk on a cold afternoon for a moment. I pulled her close to me to kiss and noticed that the color of her hair exactly matched the fox fur on her coat collar.

I met Maggie on the first day of my Renaissance History class in the fall. I had enrolled in the class for two reasons. I needed the credits to graduate on time and then go to graduate school. Grad school would give me a draft deferment for one more year. I also believed that by studying a period of history like the Renaissance, so full of social and cultural changes, I might find answers. I looked for any clues to help me cope with the tumult I felt every day. The war was being waged on the other side of the world, but people rallied against that war right down the street on Marsh Plaza in front of the chapel. It didn't seem to make any difference. The war went on and on. I was helpless to stop it.

I got to the classroom early and took a seat next to the window so I could watch the people pass by outside on Commonwealth Avenue. Professor Schulman's lectures were notoriously boring. I would have to sit through his class but at least I could daydream by looking out the window.

Professor Schulman arrived exactly at noon, placed an old three-ring notebook on the podium, opened it, and began reading to us. I took notes but soon focused more of my attention outside the window, watching the parade of denim clad, long-haired hippies on the sidewalk. The door to the classroom opened quietly and quickly closed. Professor Schulman stopped reading to us.

"Young lady, you are late," he announced, looking down over his half-lens glasses toward a seat by the door. In it sat a small girl, her head down, her face hidden by a mass of curls, not blonde, not red, but some color in between, filled with light.

"Yes," she answered, not looking up.

"This is Renaissance History," he said. "The class starts at twelve sharp."

"Yes," she said again, head still down, but the hair moving as she nodded.

"You will be here at twelve noon from now on."

"Yes."

Professor Schulman turned back to his notebook and resumed reading from it to us. I kept on taking notes, but I couldn't stop watching the girl and her hair, wondering if her face was as beautiful as it would have to be to keep pace with the hair. For the full hour she never seemed to look up from her notebook and rarely turned her head. Late in the class she paused for a moment. Seeming to sense me staring at her, she turned. Our eyes met. And as suddenly as it had happened, we both looked away and down at our notebooks.

The class ended, and the girl scooped up her books and hurried out of the room. I chased after her through the crowds in the hall outside, hoping to get a closer look, to see her face again, maybe even to meet her.

I caught up to her at the end of the hall. She paused suddenly and turned to face me as though she had expected me to be there. I stopped, red-faced, breaking into a nervous sweat. She was a tiny girl, barely five feet tall. Her eyes were a pale blue, as vivid as her hair. Faint freckles crossed her nose. She had the face of the Venus in that Botticelli Renaissance painting; "Venus on the half-shell" I had always called it. And here she was face to face with me. She smiled. I was stunned. I was lost.

"Hi," she said. "I'm Maggie. I saw you in Professor Schulman's class a few moments ago."

"Yes." It was all I could say. Even choking out the one word was an effort.

"God, I'd better not be late on Wednesday. I don't want him to grill me like that again."

"No, better be on time." I wasn't usually at a loss for words when I met a girl, but this was different. Inside my head, I screamed. *Talk to her! Talk to her!*

"Anyway, now I know where to park, so I shouldn't have a problem. But I probably will need coffee to stay awake next time. God, he does drone on and on, doesn't he?"

"He sure does."

Come on. Talk to her! Say something!

"Well," she said. "I've got to go get lunch. See you Wednesday?"

It was a question. I had to answer. "Yep, see you Wednesday."

Then off she went, bell bottom jeans flapping at her ankles, past the anti-war signs, out onto the street with the other students, the peace people with petitions, and the Black Power activists.

It took me a few moments to gather myself. I stood, dumb and dry-mouthed, in the middle of the hall. Then I moved on to lunch for myself, and off to track practice in the afternoon. But all I could think of was Maggie.

On Wednesday, fifteen minutes before the class, I walked into the room with two paper cups of coffee. I took the seat next to the door where she had been and placed one of the cups on the desk next to me with two creams, two sugars, and a stir stick next to it. I prepared the other cup for myself; one sugar and one cream. Students began to arrive, noted the seat next to me with the cup on it and took other seats. With five minutes to the start of the class Maggie came in. She saw me and the coffee on the desk and gave me a smile that floored me again.

"For me? You remembered! Aren't you sweet."

"I didn't know how you like it," I said. "I got sugar and cream for you. You'll have to fix it for yourself."

"One sugar, one cream. What's your name?"

"David. Are you a history major?"

"Yes. I guess. I'm pre-law, and history is a good basis for law. How about you?"

"Yes, history. I was going to be an archaeologist, but I've decided to become a history teacher and a coach. It's a draft deferment. Besides, if I can teach better than Professor Schulman, I could save a lot of students from a slow and painful death."

With that it was noon, and Professor Schulman walked in, opened his notebook, and began to read to us. Maggie and I took notes. But we also wrote notes to each other in the margins, leaving them where we could each read the other's messages. Near the end of class I wrote, "Do you have plans for lunch?"

She wrote back: "No. Do you?"

"Not yet. I'm thinking of going to the deli across the street. Want to join me?"

"Yes."

That was our first date. I usually finished lunch by 1:30p.m. and went to track practice by 3:00p.m. But that day I talked with Maggie until 3:30p.m. Later, I lied to my coach that I had gotten hung up with my class work. I ran alone for an hour, energized with thoughts of Maggie.

We had lunch after class again on Friday. I told Maggie about my family, that my father was a professor at the University, that my family lived in Wellesley outside of Boston, that I lived in the dorm because my track practices kept me on campus too late to get home each night. She told me about her family, part of a large Irish family scattered all around Boston, that she lived in Newton as an only child with her mother and father, and that she waited tables some evenings in a restaurant to help cover her tuition.

At one point, she said, "Wellesley. That's the next town over from Newton. It's not far at all from where I live. We should get together sometime."

I got the clue. "I go home on weekends if I don't have a meet to run in. Maybe we could get together this weekend."

"I would love that," she replied. "Where do you live in Wellesley?"

"Just an ordinary neighborhood near the center."

"Oh, there's nothing ordinary about Wellesley," Maggie said. "It's a lovely town. Beautiful homes. I'm sure your house must be pretty nice."

"I'm not in one of those big pretentious mansions. We're just ordinary people. My dad's a professor. We're not wealthy. We don't have all the big-time airs like some of the people in town."

"You don't have to apologize for living in Wellesley," she said.

"I'm not apologizing. But some people make a big deal about their money. They act as though it matters."

"There's nothing wrong with money," answered Maggie.

I explained, "Money *does* matter, I guess. But it's not that big a deal. As long as I make enough to live on and be happy after I graduate, that's all I want."

"What makes you happy?" she asked.

"Right now? Being here, having lunch with you."

"You're so sweet to say that. But what will make you happy after you graduate? What do you want to do? You said you want to be a teacher?"

"Yes, I'll probably teach history in a high school and coach track. But I'll have to go to a year of grad school to get certified to teach. If the draft gets too close, I'll find something else sooner to get a deferment. But I want some sort of job where I can make the world a better place."

"Oh, the world's not so bad. We're young. We're alive and healthy. We can do anything we want to when we graduate. Why do you want to teach?

You could do anything. You could make more money with some other job." Maggie seemed genuinely puzzled that I would choose a job that might never give me a big income.

"Come on, Maggie. There's the war. There's the civil rights movement. There are so many things. You walk across this campus and you see all the people with all the causes they're fighting for. I don't know what I can do to fix any of it. But at least I've got to try. You live in Newton. That's a pretty wealthy town, too. You know what money is like, just as much as I do, coming from Wellesley. And you've got to see that there are good people and bad people who've got money. Money's not that important. It's not the answer. Doing something to change the world is. That's what matters."

"Well," she replied. "I admire you for your convictions. But I can do all that 'save the world' stuff and have a good income too. That's why I want to be a lawyer. I can fight injustice and get rich all at the same time."

Maggie and I ate lunch together after class three times each week after that. We began getting together on Saturdays as well. On the weekends I usually stayed in my dorm, ran in a cross-country meet in the afternoon, then met Maggie in the evening. She had a car and I didn't, so for most of our dates, she picked me up at the dorm or at my house in Wellesley. She would drive us into the city and we would ramble around Boston or Cambridge together.

It was easy when she met me at my dorm. I waited in the lobby or out on the street until she came by. The first time she picked me up at my house it was different. My house was a basic cape on a side street. Maggie parked at the curb and came to the front door. My parents welcomed her into the living room and stood formally, side by side, to meet her.

The living room was crowded with antique furniture and a piano. I hadn't played for several years; not since I had begun to spend most of my time out running. But my sheet music, Haydn, Mozart, and Shubert, still lay on the piano. Time magazine, Scientific American, and Agatha Christie paperbacks cluttered the tables.

Maggie came into the living room cautiously, being careful of what she said, trying to make a good impression. My father stood there grinning like a kid when he met her. I knew he'd always had a thing for redheads, even though my mother was dark-haired. From his reaction it was clear that he saw in Maggie some of what I did. But then, most men were captivated by her when they met her. He was no different.

"How are you, Maggie," he said. "It's great to meet you." He shook her hand and continued to grin.

My mother's reaction was more reserved, though polite.

"David tells us you're in his Renaissance History class," she started. "That's such a marvelous time in history. So much great art and science. How do you like it?"

"It's okay," answered Maggie. "The professor's a little too dry, but the topic is interesting."

"Isn't the art from that time elegant, Maggie? Which artists do you like?"

"I like the Dutch Masters, but they're from a period a little later than the Italian painters. We haven't studied them yet."

"David tells us you're pre-law. I expect Renaissance History will be useful for you in law."

"I guess. I'm interested in international trade law."

"And you're from Newton? What does your father do?"

"He works in the city." That was all Maggie would say about her family.

After meeting my parents, we went out to her car and headed for Boston. I tried to explain my parents. "Well, now you've met them. I hope my mother didn't scare you off with all her questions."

"Oh, that's all right. I hope I passed her test. What was she looking for, do you think?"

"My mother probably wants to be sure that you're up to her intellectual standards. She's not convinced that all college students really care about intellectual things, and it's important to her if you do. I expect she'll be fine with you. And if not, I really don't care. You're seeing me, not my parents."

"Okay. But I must say that you've got a beautiful house. A wonderful neighborhood, lovely furniture and everything."

"It's not a big deal," I replied, remembering our earlier conversation. "You should see some of the other houses in town. My house is really pretty much average."

"Well, I think it's wonderful. You should be proud of where you come from."

Maggie and I sat together in a coffee house near Harvard Square. It had an inexpensive cover charge I could manage, and the music was always notable. We were crowded so close together our knees touched beneath the tiny table. Three steps below street level, we could see the legs of people passing by a window. The air was smoky. A man sitting next to me leaned over and said, "This place is fantastic! The people they get here. In the past few weeks we've had Gordon Lightfoot, Judy Collins, Tom Rush. Tonight it's Joni Mitchell. Next week James Taylor. Or is it Livingston?"

He leaned away from me and we all clapped as a thin, plain woman walked onto the stage carrying a guitar by its neck. She set the guitar on a stand, no more than ten feet away from Maggie and me, sat at a piano and leaned forward, her dark blonde hair falling straight as rain and hiding her face.

Without a word of introduction, she began to play the piano. Then she sang, her voice as pure as a sterling silver bell. After the first song, she stood from the piano bench and continued with her guitar. She sang of her rapturous love of men she had lost. Of the heartbreak, of the joy, of her anger, her despair. In that small room with the low stage, her presence was palpable. I could see the bitten cuticles on her nails as she played. With her so close to us, the ragged intensity of her emotions almost moved me to tears. I'm sure that Maggie must have felt it too, because she hugged my arm and beamed her radiant smile.

Maggie and I sat transfixed through the whole set, holding hands as we listened. Joni never made eye contact with the audience, looking inward at the feelings that had inspired her songs. When she finished, she turned quietly and walked off the stage through the applause, her guitar still slung over one shoulder.

After the show we went to a German-toned restaurant in Harvard Square and got a booth. Maggie and I talked for hours about the war and other problems. Mostly I talked and she listened, chin on her hand, beaming at me. I told her of my dreams for the better world I imagined we could both have in just a few years. It was so apparent to me that Maggie and I would make a difference.

"Together," I told her, "we really can change things. Me with my teaching to help shape the minds of the future. And you as a lawyer to hold the people who don't get it accountable." Maggie smiled back at me and nodded.

Mostly, when I was with her, I sat enthralled, just looking at her, soaking in her beauty. Her hair cascaded around her face, an unbelievable riot of curls. I noticed that the bones of her face and cheeks were tiny, and that her eyebrows and eyelashes were bronze, matching her hair. Her body was small as well, not the classic Playboy centerfold body that college boys in the sixties believed every man should want. I was a captive anyway. On many occasions, I said to myself, "Damn! I can't believe a girl like this is with me. Just look at her! People all around us are looking at her. And she's here with me. How can it be that I'm dating a girl like this? How lucky can I be that a girl like Maggie chooses to be with me?"

I believe she was as taken with me as I was with her. I remember her laughing most of the time and listening intently to everything when we talked. She seemed to place value on everything I said, and that made me feel very, very good.

In December, after we had been together for several months, I finally asked her to come see me run in a track meet. She knew I was on the track team, but we hadn't really talked about my running. I had run cross-country races all fall, but that's not much of a spectator sport. With cross country, most of the action takes place out of the spectators' sight on trails in the woods. The indoor track season is different, a contained world where the races are run on small tracks close to the spectators.

"Maggie," I said, "we're racing at Harvard tomorrow evening. Could you come see the meet and watch me run?"

"Sure, David. I'd love it. Do I need a ticket?" Hockey was the big sport in town and tickets were hard to get. I had gotten hockey tickets from a friend, one of the players, a week earlier and had taken her to a game at the Boston Arena.

"No. This isn't hockey. You don't need a ticket. Just come over to the Harvard field house and walk right in. You just hang out during the meet. There really aren't seats or anything. And you need to know that I won't be able to spend much time with you. I'm running the mile and the two-mile. Please understand that if I don't spend time with you, I'll still know you're there, and I really would like you to come. Anyway, you need to see this side of me."

"I'm sure you'll be marvelous! You must be good to be on a college team. I'll try to come if I don't have to work. I'll see if I can rearrange my hours at the restaurant and be there."

The Harvard field house was an old brick building with a dirt floor and a tight, twelve laps to the mile cinder track around the perimeter, square, with slightly banked corners. Walking to the starting line for my first race, I looked around the field house. I hadn't seen Maggie and had begun to doubt that she would come. I pushed her from my mind and focused on the race ahead.

I stood on the starting line, shivering slightly and breathing the dank, damp, air. It smelled of dust and sweat. In the infield, the weight guys competed, their shouts echoing off the hard walls when they threw. The thirty-five pound weight, a big iron ball with a steel triangle handle, tumbled through the air, thudding as it hit the dirt, its handle clanking. Sprinters warmed up in the outside lane of the track. The starter's gun cracked.

Three Harvard runners set out with me right behind. The leader, a tall, lank, aristocratic English runner, set a pace much faster than I could sustain, but I had to cling to the pace or be left behind. A red-headed runner clipped along flatfooted in second, his long hair flapping around his shoulders. The third Harvard runner, a rock-and-roll type from New Jersey, was just ahead of me. They carried me through the quarter. My breath began to come in loud wheezes. I felt no fatigue, but I simply couldn't run any faster.

In the third quarter I began to fade, dropping a stride behind the three Harvard runners, then two, then three. Desperately, I fought off the runners behind me and maintained loose contact with the three leaders. I finished as I had started, in fourth place. I felt hot, a bit light-headed, and a little nauseous. I couldn't have willed myself to go a step faster, but I wasn't really tired. I walked awkwardly onto the infield of the track. *The two mile starts in just over an hour. I'm winded now, but I'll be ready.*

"That was beautiful!" Maggie appeared out of nowhere, came up to me, and wrapped her arm through mine like I was her escort at a formal dance, not a sweat-soaked runner. She walked on the infield dirt with me.

"Yeah? You saw me lose. They kicked my butt."

"But you looked beautiful. I never knew you could run like that. It was amazing."

"I'm not fast enough for the mile," I explained. "I can run all day, but I don't have that kind of speed."

She stretched up and gave my hot cheek a kiss. "Oh, you're fast. Maybe a couple of the Harvard guys beat you. But I don't care. You did great!"

I gave up trying to explain that I had lost and that it mattered. She honestly didn't seem to care, and I didn't want to dwell on it. We talked a few minutes more and then I told her I had to get ready for my second race. I got into my sweats and retreated into a quiet corner to concentrate. The meet went on. I saw several other runners, my teammates and friends, go up and chat with Maggie, and she brushed each of them off. I went to the starting line for the two-mile, elated that she was there, she had come to see me, and she wasn't paying attention to anyone but me.

I ran the two-mile desperate to show Maggie what I could do. A tiny, goofy Harvard kid and I broke away from the rest of the race at the mile. With a half mile to go, I took the lead and pressed the pace as long as I could, trying to break the Harvard runner. He tagged along on my shoulder till the last lap. Then he darted past me and won.

Ashamed, I stood on the infield holding my sweats. Maggie came to me and said, "Two races! And you almost won that one."

"Yeah, but I lost again. That's what I mean about not being fast. I had it, but I just couldn't hold on."

"But the guy who beat you didn't run in the first race."

"No, I know, but he still beat me."

"I don't care. I think you did great. You're so intense when you run. It's incredible to watch you."

And for the second time that night she kissed me. It still astonished me to be with her. I watched her as she left the field house, her golden hair flashing.

The meet opened up a new side to my times with Maggie. Before the meet, we talked about Professor Schulman and Renaissance History. And of course we talked about the war, and the demonstrations and rallies, and about my draft status. And we made plans for each weekend. Now she was full of questions about my running. How did I train? What did it feel like to run a race? She seemed to believe I was a better runner than I knew I was. I didn't care, just as long as we were together.

Once, sitting in a shop off Kenmore Square having coffee, she asked, "David, you're such a good runner. Could you make a living from your running? I mean, teaching is fine, but you could be so good as a runner. There are professional athletes in other sports. Is there anything like that for track runners?"

"Not really. There are old rules about amateurism. I could get under-the-table prize money. And sometimes they pay excessive travel expenses if you go to a race someplace. But it's not enough to live on. It's not a career."

"Then why do you do it?"

"I don't know. I just like it. And I guess I *am* pretty good. After I graduate, I won't be chained to the short track races and I can run the longer road races. I might do okay in the marathon."

"But won't you make money for doing that? Even in big races like the Boston Marathon?"

"No, not much. But I like training. And racing. I just like running."

"What's the point if you don't make money at it?"

"I get to find out just how fast I really might be. That's something, isn't it? To discover just how good you can be at something. To find out how fast you can run a race?"

"I guess. But I still think you could find some way to make a living at it."

"Look at it this way, Maggie. The world is nuts. There's the war and everything. Nothing really makes any sense. Doesn't running for an hour or so every day make as much sense as anything else? Doesn't it make sense to see if I can cut a few seconds off my times? Doesn't it make as much sense as becoming a teacher or a lawyer?"

"But don't you get awfully tired?"

"I'm tired all the time. But I'm also a little stronger and faster every day. I'm better now than when I met you a few months ago. Look, I can't end the war or change the world all by myself. But I can make myself into a pretty fast runner. It's about the only thing I can do where I can make a difference right now."

"How does running make a difference?"

"Maybe it doesn't really do a thing to save the world," I admitted. "It's like this. I have some control over my body and the way things are when I run. They line us up and start the race. And if I get to the finish line first, I win. Nobody can deny that to me except maybe a few other runners who are a bit faster than me. I don't really have any control over the war, or the draft, or racism, or all the other terrible things that are going on in the world. But for a few minutes each day, when I run, I have a little control over my own destiny. It's the only thing where I really have any control over what happens to me."

I first went to Maggie's house in February. I borrowed my parent's car and drove to her house to pick her up.

Newton is an unusual town. It's tucked in between the affluence of Wellesley and Weston, and the city of Boston. Parts of Newton are notably wealthy, not unlike their prosperous neighbors. Others are clearly middle class. To the south are the working-class Boston neighborhoods of Roslindale and Mattapan. The bordering neighborhoods in Newton are typically middle-income suburban.

Maggie's house sat on the edge of Roslindale. It was a ranch on a slab foundation. A waist high chain-link fence surrounded a small backyard. A short driveway led alongside the house, and, though the front door looked formal, the snow on the front walk wasn't shoveled. It was clear that people used the side door directly off the driveway. I went up two wooden steps to the side door and knocked.

Maggie's mother opened the door and welcomed me into the kitchen. She was tiny, like Maggie, with Maggie's electric blue eyes. Her hair was reddish, but tipped with some white.

"You must be David," she said, bustling about, fussing with her hair. "Maggie's told us so much about you. You're from Wellesley, right? Come on in. Maggie's still getting ready. She'll be out in a few minutes. Would you like some coffee? A drink?"

"No, I'm fine."

Her father sat at the kitchen table with a white mug of coffee. He was a short, thick man with a receding crew cut. He didn't stand, but leaned back in his chair, looking directly at me, assessing. Then he reached out his hand to shake mine. "I'm Frank." His hand was as thick as my forearm. I felt the bones in my hand shift in his grip like the ribs of a bird.

He began. "Maggie tells us you're quite the runner."

"I guess so. I'm on the track team."

"I used to run," he said. "In high school. Catholic Memorial. The 440. Have you ever run the 440?"

"Yeah, but that's a little short for me. I'm a distance runner."

"You run the mile?"

"Yeah. The mile, the two-mile. Cross country in the Fall. Steeplechase sometimes in the Spring."

"You ever break four minutes for the mile?"

"No, I'm not that fast. I'm more of a distance runner."

"The mile's a long distance race. What's your best time?"

"Four twenty-four."

"Oh." He was unimpressed. "So, what are your plans after college?"

"I want to be a teacher. And a coach. I'll probably go to grad school for a year. That'll get me certified to teach, and it might get me a draft deferment, too."

"You're not one of these anti-war peaceniks, are you?"

I knew I was on shaky ground. I thought I might be in love with Maggie, his daughter, so I wanted to be in good standing with him. But it was obvious that he didn't have any love for the anti-war movement. I chose my words carefully.

"Whatever we may think about the war, I'm not sure that I would be a good soldier. I don't know if I could kill someone, and yes, I'm afraid of getting myself killed by being out there and being unwilling to fight."

"I fought in the Pacific. I didn't want to go either. But I did it."

"Daddy, lighten up." Maggie had on a white, ribbed turtleneck, tight, highlighting her tiny torso. Her hair flowed down below her shoulders. I stood next to her father, feeling foolish, transfixed as I watched her shrug into her pea-jacket.

"That was a different war, daddy. This is different. David's a good guy." She scolded her father gently and leaned down to give him a small kiss as he sat at the table.

He stood up and gave Maggie a hug and a kiss. "He's your guy, Maggie. If you like him, I'm okay with him, too. Just take care of yourself, you two."

I shook his rough hand again and Maggie and I left.

"I'm sorry about that," she apologized. "He fought in the war, and now he just gets crazy when he sees all this anti-war stuff on the TV."

"That's okay. I just hope he's okay with me. But you've never really seemed all that committed to the anti-war movement yourself. You've never really told me where you stand on it. It was good to have you come to my defense back there."

"Well, it's like I said. You're a good guy. And you're my guy. If you don't believe in the war, then, neither do I. Daddy'll be fine once he gets to know you better."

We got back to Maggie's house late. Quietly, we slipped into the kitchen. The rest of the house was silent and dark. I realized that this was the first time we had ever been truly alone at the end of a date. We never went inside my house at the end of an evening. My parents always waited up for me to be sure I got home safely, so it would have been awkward. And in that era, girls weren't allowed inside men's dormitory rooms. We kissed at the end of each time we were together, and we hugged, but things never went further. Aside from some clumsy fumbling in her car outside my dorm, we had never had anything close to a physical relationship. She whispered to me, "We need to keep quiet so we don't wake my parents. Let me put on some coffee."

She started the coffee. "Come see our living room."

Maggie stood at the doorway to the living room and reached in to turn the lights on for me to see. The formal living room had a white carpet and a large, thick sofa, covered in plastic. Two wingback, upholstered chairs were also in plastic covers, and a large vase of silk flowers sat on a coffee table.

"Very nice," I said.

"Oh, I'm sure you've seen better, living in Wellesley. We don't have the antiques like you do in your house."

"It's beautiful," I repeated.

Maggie went off to hang our coats on the backs of the kitchen chairs and to fix our coffee. I tiptoed into the living room and sat in the middle of the sofa. The plastic squeaked beneath me. I expected Maggie would join me with the coffee in a minute or two. I could only dream where things might lead with us sitting together on the sofa in the dark, quiet house.

Maggie came back and found me. Standing in the doorway she said, "There you are! Come on out of there. I've got the coffee ready in the kitchen."

I got up, puzzled, and joined her in the kitchen. We sat facing each other on wooden chairs, across the corner of the kitchen table from each other with our cups of coffee. Our knees barely touched, but I felt electricity. We were alone, yet it was hardly more intimate than if we were still in a Cambridge coffee house.

"Wouldn't we be more comfortable in the living room, Maggie?"

"This is fine. We don't go in the living room much. This is where I always have my coffee. Let's just stay here."

I leaned over and gave her a kiss. Her mouth tasted of coffee and sugar. She shifted forward in her chair, hugging me, her hair brushing my face. My hands shifted from her back to her shoulders, feeling her delicate collarbones. Then soft flesh. She dropped her face onto my shoulder and sighed.

"You'd better go. We can't wake my parents."

"Maggie, I love you."

"Yes, but you have to go."

I kissed her again, dragged myself away from the table, and went home. I didn't know as I left that it would be the only time I ever went to her house or met her parents.

Spring came. On the first warm day, Maggie and I picked up subs and headed to the Charles River bank to picnic. Leaving the campus, we passed another anti-war rally. A tall student wearing a baggy army jacket with patches shouted into a bull-horn. A militant professor in a tweed jacket stood next to him. A crowd of several hundred students surrounded the pair, chanting slogans in response to prompts from the bull-horn. Something had happened in Cambodia and big rallies were planned all over Boston.

Maggie and I settled onto the grass of the riverbank and unwrapped the subs. Behind us people strolled and jogged along the esplanade. In front of us a shell stroked by, swiftly, moving with the current, the coxswain's cadence coming to us over the water.

Maggie started. "God, won't these anti-war people ever give it a rest? Day after day, week after week, it's the same thing. Lyndon Johnson, Eugene McCarthy, Bobby Kennedy. It doesn't make a difference who's President. I just wish the stupid war would hurry up and be over."

"But that's just the point, Maggie. Johnson didn't know what to do about it, so he's not even running for another term. At least McCarthy and Kennedy are talking about getting us out of there as soon as they're elected. Nixon's likely to be the Republican candidate, and who knows what his plan is."

"Then I like the Democrats. Kennedy's a good guy. I'll vote for him. My parents always have."

"But what if he loses? People are dying every day over there."

"Nobody I know," said Maggie. "I don't want to talk about it. I don't even want to think about it. I'll be in law school here next year, and I just want to get on with my life."

"But that's just it, Maggie. I'll be in grad school next year too. Studying to be a teacher. I'll be draft bait. Do you ever worry about me getting drafted?"

"Not really", she answered. "You'll be a graduate student next year. And then you'll teach. You'll get a deferment. I know you won't have to go."

"I don't know," I said. "They had the lottery, and my birthday, my number, is in the middle. I could get drafted. They might not defer grad students next year."

"Oh, I can't imagine you getting drafted. And if you did, it would only be for a year or two. You'd be fine. I can't let myself worry about that. I just can't."

"Maggie, it could happen. And I worry about it. Sometimes I dream about it at night."

"You dream about it? What's the dream? Are you fighting?"

"Yes. No. I don't know. I don't want to be there, and I don't want to fight. But in the dream, I'm there, I think."

"This dream, David. You sound like you've had the same dream several times." She was intrigued, but she looked a little concerned, too. For the first time.

"Yes, I've had the dream a couple of times a week for maybe a month. Sometimes I'm in a thick forest that I think is the jungle. Sometimes it's in tall grass, maybe a rice paddy. But it's the same dream."

"What happens?" Maggie turned to me and rested her hands on my forearms. She looked into my eyes, caring suddenly, trying to read me.

"There's a guy. Vietnamese, I guess. He's Asian, anyway, and he's wearing only black shorts. But he's holding a machine gun. His back is toward me, and he's turning slowly, looking, searching through the trees or the grass, maybe for me. I've got a gun, too, and I've got it pointed at him with my finger on the trigger. I've never held a gun in my life, let alone aimed or shot one. But in the dream, I'm pointing the gun at this guy, and my finger's on the trigger. So, the guy keeps on turning, and looking. And finally, he sees me."

I stopped and looked up into Maggie's eyes. I could feel my eyes starting to tear up, so I looked down at her hands. I took them and held on tight. It was the only way I could hold myself together.

"So you shoot him, right?" Maggie almost begged me to shoot him, not to be shot in the dream.

"I don't know. That's always when I wake up. I don't know what I do. I don't want to shoot him. That's murder. And I don't know if I could do it. And if I could, I don't know if I want to find that out about myself. But I also don't want to get shot by him."

"But you'd have to shoot him. God, David, you couldn't just stand there with your gun pointed at him and let him kill you. You've got to shoot him."

"I don't know. I imagine him living in a house in a village nearby. He's got a wife and maybe kids. I don't know him, and I've really got no reason to kill him. How could I do that?"

Maggie began to sense my dilemma. But it didn't help.

"If you got drafted," she said, "I know you'd be a good soldier. Maybe a great soldier. I know you'd be fine. I can't imagine you any other way. You'd probably end up a hero. They'd give you a medal, I'll bet."

"I don't know," I answered. "I really don't know what I'd do. I don't even know if I'd go."

"Well, what would you do if you were drafted? Being in the army's not the worst thing in the world. Look at my dad. He got through it. Forget about that dream of yours. It's just a dream. That's all it is. It's not real."

I lay back on the lawn, having finished my sandwich. "I don't want to go in the army, Maggie. I don't want to kill people. And I certainly don't want to get killed. Look at me. I'm just a skinny distance runner. I'm not exactly the kind of a guy you'd want defending your country. And I'm not even sure that this war has anything to do with defending the United States anyway. If we win the war, how are we better off? And if we lose, do the Vietnamese take over our country? Of course not. So why are we even fighting?"

Suddenly thoughtful, Maggie asked, "If you got drafted, isn't there something safe you could do so you wouldn't have to fight?"

"I guess so. My coach knows some people with the Navy, and he's already said that he might be able to get me special duty where all I do is train and run races for the Navy."

"Well, there you go, then." Maggie seemed pleased that it was so easily settled.

"It's not that simple, Maggie. I don't even want to be a part of the military in any way. If I do that, I'm still showing support for the war."

"You wouldn't become a draft dodger would you? You wouldn't run off to Canada or something? I don't want you to go to Canada with me stuck here in law school in Boston. I hoped you'd still be here next year with me."

"No," I answered. "I'm not running off to Canada. And I don't want to be a draft dodger. I don't plan to go underground or anything. I just don't know what I'd do if I were drafted. I don't want to go to the war, and I don't want to break the law. I don't know."

In a moment Maggie's face took on a set look I'd never seen before. "I hate all this talk about the war. It takes the fun out of everything. I know you'll be fine. We'll both be in grad school next year. After grad school you'll become a teacher, and teachers get a deferment. You don't have any reason to worry, David."

"I hope you're right. But I don't know."

"You'll be fine. You'll become a teacher. And I'll become a lawyer. Together we'll have plenty of money. We'll get a great house, maybe out there in

Wellesley near both our parents. Don't worry about the war. We'll both be fine."

I liked that she talked as though we would always be together. "I hope you're right," I said.

Maggie pushed the thought of the draft away. "Let's talk about something else."

She rolled next to me as I lay on the grass. I pulled her tight to me, feeling that she was braless beneath her peasant blouse. Her hair fell around us, sheltering me from the sun.

"All I really want is for it to end," she concluded. "I don't want to lose you. To Canada or to Viet Nam. And I get so tired of all these demonstrations. The only rally on the campus here that's made any sense to me was that guy who came and spoke about birth control and handed out the pill and condoms. And he got arrested."

"Birth control and condoms. Now there's something we might want to discuss," I said, happy to change the subject. "That's something maybe we should think about."

Maggie smiled coyly. "And why would that be?"

"Make love not war, Maggie."

"Well, all right! But not here on the riverbank in front of everyone. Maybe this weekend?"

My heart pounded. My God, I was as much at a loss for the next thing to say to Maggie as I had been on the day I met her. I just smiled. She rolled on top of me, straddling me, and kissed me.

"What do you see in a guy like me, Maggie," I asked. "I'm not rich and I'm probably never going to be rich. I'm only a running fool who hates the war. And you don't really see the problem with the war."

"It's your eyes," she replied. "I like your eyes. And your intensity. You really seem to care about things. About the war, and your running. And about me. I like that. I guess I love that about you."

"Well, then. Let's plan something special for this weekend," I said.

"What do you have in mind?" She smiled, flirting with me and with all the possibilities.

"I don't know," I lied. I had a pretty good idea what I hoped would happen. But not a clue where to start.

"Okay, you need to come up with a plan then."

"Listen," I offered. "There's supposed to be this huge anti-war thing over at Harvard Saturday afternoon. Let's go over there and watch the circus. Hear the speeches. It'll be fun. And maybe when you attend a rally like that you will begin to understand why I care so much about this. Then we could go get dinner and find someplace afterwards to be alone."

"The being alone part will be easy," Maggie said, ignoring the importance of the rally I had invited her to. "It's my parent's anniversary and they're going away for the whole weekend. We can go to my house for dinner if you'd like. I'll pick you up before noon for the thing at Harvard and you don't have to go back to the dorm until Sunday night if you don't want to."

I spent the rest of the week counting the hours till the weekend. I bought a pack of condoms. I was ready.

Saturday came and Maggie picked me up. She smiled when she saw me toss a small duffle into the back seat. "Clothes for tomorrow," I said.

She drove us over to Cambridge. We parked near Central Square and walked up Massachusetts Avenue to Harvard Yard. Maggie was dressed for peace; bell-bottom blue jeans, a denim shirt, and a shiny, new metal peace symbol on a leather thong around her neck. Her hair fell free around her face. She glowed with anticipation. She was magnificent.

There was already a large crowd when we got to Harvard, spilling out of Harvard Yard into the street. Large banners, hand-painted in red on bed sheets, were paraded through the mobs. Marijuana smoke drifted. Spontaneous anti-war chants started. "Peace Now!" "Revolution!" "Hell no, we won't go!"

Someone started to sing. "All we are saying, is give peace a chance." People began to clap with the song. Other voices joined and I saw that Maggie was among them, singing.

She turned to me and dazzled me with her smile. "This is nice. You said it would be fun but I didn't realize how much fun it was going to be. I'm glad we came."

I kissed her and turned with my arms wrapped around her to listen as the first speaker started. He was a tall, thin guy with long blond hair and wire-rimmed glasses. He stood at the base of John Harvard's statue, supported by the crowd. He began to rant against the war, against racism, against big business, against the oppression of women.

"He seems to be against everything," said Maggie. "What is he for?"

"Probably he's for putting an end to all those problems. Can you really blame him?"

"No, but how does he plan to change things?"

"Good point. Do you have any ideas?"

Maggie shook her head and turned back to the statue as a new speaker took the bull-horn and started. This one was an angry black guy wearing a beret. He told the crowd that the war was a racist government plot to send all the young black men to Asia where they would kill Asian men and get killed themselves. It seemed a little far-fetched and conspiratorial to me, but it carried an anti-war message and the crowd cheered. Maggie joined in, clapping her hands and shouting slogans.

As the third speaker, a Harvard professor, began to speak, some noise began near the gate into Harvard Square. The edge of the crowd had pushed into the street, blocking traffic. Helmeted police pushed into the crowd with clubs, crushing them back through the gate into Harvard Yard. People screamed and began to swing back at the cops.

As we watched from the back of the crowd, Maggie grabbed me and shouted, "What's happening?"

"Something's going on out in Harvard Square. I think the cops are trying to get the crowd off the street and back in through the gate."

Near us, someone pulled a brick out of the sidewalk where the roots of an old elm tree had heaved the brick paving apart. He looked at the old brick, worn smooth by centuries of academic footsteps, and shouted, "This is for you, pigs!" Then he threw it up over the top of the crowd into the rank of police.

Now the cops were swinging their sticks at the crowd. The professor stopped his speech and began trying to calm the crowd. "People, people!" he called into the bull-horn. "We're for peace, not violence! Remain calm! We don't want to bring the war home to Cambridge. We want to end violence. We don't fight war with war. We want to end the war with passive means!"

Nobody listened. People were pushing back, shouting at the police. Maggie looked stunned, frozen in place. People started running away from the police, heading toward a gate at the far end of the Yard.

"Come on," I shouted at Maggie. "Let's get out of here. This isn't looking good."

She stood still, staring at the milling, running mob. A small metal can, the size of a soft drink, tumbled through the air over the crowd, trailing gray smoke. It clattered to the ground a short ways from us and began to roll. Now I, too, stood baffled, watching the can as it rolled, smoking, closer and closer. The breeze shifted as people ran and a patch of smoke blew at us. I gagged and grabbed Maggie. "Run," I shouted. "It's tear gas! Run!"

We were out on the street now, running. Cars had stopped and people all around us were running, too. Maggie flew past me, her bright hair streaming behind her, her tiny body pumping hard, driven by adrenaline. Even in her sandals, fear had her outrunning my track-trained legs.

I caught her and, when we were several blocks clear of the chaos on the campus, I pulled her to a stop on the brick sidewalk. She slumped to her knees, put her hands to her face, and began to sob.

"Oh my God! This isn't what I wanted. This isn't what I'm looking for. Oh my God! Oh my God!"

"It's okay." I tried to comfort her, holding her, but she pulled away.

"No, not now," she said. "I can't do this. All I want is a good life. Some peace, some comfort. Not all this. I just can't do this."

"Maggie," I soothed. "We're okay now. We got away. You're not hurt, are you?"

In the distance the mob roared. Sirens were now in the mix.

"No, I'm not hurt. But I'm not like you. I can't deal with all this craziness. The war. The speeches and rallies. Why can't they just let us be?"

"It's no good," I said. "I know that. The police and the crowd. And that stupid kid with the brick. But we got away and we're okay. Let's go home."

She got up, still sniffling a bit, red-faced. I gave her my handkerchief and she mopped up as we walked together back to her car. Neither of us spoke.

"What now?" I asked when we got to the car.

"I don't know," she said, hanging her head. Her hair masked her face as we sat side by side in the car. Finally, she started the car, but she drove me back to my dorm. She stopped for a moment at the curb. Neither of us said anything. I waited. Then she reached in the back seat and took my duffle. "Here," she said. "Take this. You've got to go. I'll call you tomorrow. Or next week."

Stunned, I got out. She reached across and pulled the door closed. Then she drove away.

Maggie called the next morning and we agreed for her to pick me up at noon. I waited for her at the curb.

"We need to talk," she said as I got in. "Is there someplace quiet and peaceful we can go?"

I directed her out to Wellesley, to the Wellesley College campus. There is a path around the lake at the campus where I had run hundreds of miles when I was home during the summers. We went for a walk on the path, and finally stopped and sat on the shore of the lake. New, light green spring leaves on the trees shaded us and reflected on the water. It was quiet. For a few minutes we watched the water together, neither of us talking. Finally, Maggie started.

"You really care about ending the war, don't you?"

"Of course. You know that."

"And all these other injustices, too. I really like that about you, David. But it scares me sometimes. Not just back there at Harvard, with the tear gas and all. All the time. You're too passionate, maybe. You're a rebel with a thousand causes. And it gets you into some things where you might get hurt. And I could get hurt just being with you."

"But Maggie," I pleaded. "You don't want me to give up on everything, do you?"

"Of course not. It's a lot of what I like about you, that passion for things. Even in your running. I see it in your eyes when you talk about it. And I see it when I watch you race. It really matters to you. That's probably why you're good at it."

"So what should I do then? You don't want me to give up, but if not, what else can I do?"

Maggie looked down, not making eye contact. It made it easier for both of us.

"You need to go to grad school, and you need to become a teacher. And you need to keep running. Maybe you'll run in the Olympics or something one day."

"Okay," I answered. "That was pretty much the plan, anyway. So we're fine?"

"I don't know," she said. "Maybe I love you, but I don't think this can work. It's too much for me. I can't do this anymore."

"Is there another guy, Maggie?"

"No, of course not. I wouldn't do that. I don't think I can handle all the things you care so intensely about."

"What do you want, Maggie? What are you looking for?"

"I don't know. But I can't do this."

"So what happens now?" I was desperate not to lose her. "Can't we at least see each other?"

"Yes. Of course. I don't think I can handle dating you anymore. Can you deal with us as just friends?"

"If that's what you want. I guess I'll have to. But no. If we love each other, why can't we keep on the way we have been?"

"I simply can't do it. All I want is to go to law school, get a job, and settle into a nice life. A nice life, with enough money so I don't have to worry about anything. A nice home. You want so much more and so much less. Sooner or later, you and I wouldn't be able to work these things out. We might as well end it sooner before we both really hurt each other."

We were walking back to the car when I asked, "When can I see you again?"

"Let's take a little time to sort this all out," she replied. "I'll call you when I'm comfortable. I promise, I will call you."

I suffered through the summer without Maggie. I dated a couple of girls, but after Maggie they seemed dull. Nothing mattered to me anymore, and none of the girls lasted.

Early in September Maggie called. She had started law school in Boston, and I was in grad school north of Boston at Tufts. We met for lunch and she told me about her law studies. She worked as an intern at a law firm in Boston and studied international trade law. I described Tufts to her and told her about my student teaching. We agreed to see each other from time to time and keep in touch.

A couple of weeks later I called her and asked if we could meet for lunch again. She was busy.

She called me at Thanksgiving, and we met for lunch before Christmas. I asked her if she was dating anyone, hopeful that she would say no.

"Yes," she answered. "I've been seeing one of the lawyers where I work. He's older, and pretty serious about international trade law. He's not as much fun as you, and you could probably outrun him, if that matters. But he's nice. And he treats me well. How about you? You must have a bunch of girlfriends by now."

"I've dated a few girls. There might be one special one, I guess. But I do miss you, Maggie." I still held on to hope.

"I know. I miss you, too. But this is the best thing for both of us."

In April, she called again. "David, I'm engaged! Oh, it's just amazing. It's Jean Paul, the lawyer from the firm who I've been seeing. He's from Montreal, and he has an apartment there and another one here in Boston. We're getting married in June!"

Numb, I congratulated her. "That's wonderful, Maggie. Where will you live?"

"We'll probably go back and forth between Montreal and Boston. You'll have to come see us when I'm settled. And you're invited to the wedding!"

"Great. I'll be there."

"So how about you? Do you have a teaching job? "

"Yeah, I start teaching next September, outside of Boston. One short step ahead of the draft. I'll keep on working with my same old summer job until then just to bring in a bit of money. Then I'll start my real job, teaching history and coaching, too."

Maggie continued. "And a girlfriend? You must have a girlfriend, right?"

"Yes, there's a girl from grad school. Actually, she's got a job in Montreal starting in the fall. Maybe if I visit her, we could get together up there sometime."

"Maybe. A double date. I'd like to meet her," Maggie added.

I was scheduled to work on the Saturday of Maggie's wedding. I could have taken the day off, but I couldn't imagine sitting in the church and watching Maggie marry someone else. I went to work and spent all day checking my watch and picturing where Maggie was at that moment, and what she looked like, and what she was doing. I sent her pewter candlesticks as a wedding gift, the best thing I could afford with the income from my summer job.

Maggie sent me a short thank you note.

My dear David,

Jean Paul and I thank you for the candlesticks. I've put them on my mantle and will be sure to always keep them somewhere special so I can look at them and remember you. I'm so sorry you were unable to be at the wedding. I really wanted to see you there. Please, please stay in touch. And I mean this. Please come in and see us in our apartment in Boston.

Love, Maggie

One evening in October, I found my way in to Boston. I looked up Maggie's new address, the address from her thank you note. It was a high-rise apartment building near the Prudential Tower. A doorman was stationed in the mahogany paneled lobby. He stopped me, noting my shoulder length hair, my blue jeans, my athletic jacket, and my running shoes. I didn't fit the décor of his building, and he was ready to put me back out on the street. I gave him Maggie and Jean Paul's name, and he called a number from his desk. Maggie had him send me up.

Their apartment covered an entire floor near the top of the tower. My whole studio apartment in Framingham was smaller than their living room. From the living room, French doors opened onto a balcony. Beyond the balcony their view looked across Back Bay rooftops to the Charles River and the lights of Cambridge beyond.

Maggie introduced me to Jean Paul, a lean, dark, French-Canadian with slightly accented English. He appeared to be at least ten years older than Maggie and me. Maggie sat next to me on a sofa that might have cost more than my new Volkswagen. Jean Paul sat in a large chair across from us.

"So, you used to date Maggie?" he asked.

"Yes. A couple of years ago. I've got a new girlfriend now."

"Maggie's really something, isn't she?"

Cautiously, I answered, "She sure is. She's an amazing woman."

Maggie laughed a bit and told me to stop flattering her. Jean Paul asked if I had had dinner. I replied truthfully, that I hadn't, and he offered to go make some soup for me.

With Jean Paul in the kitchen, Maggie pointed to the mantle above their fireplace. "There are your candlesticks," she said.

My pewter candlesticks were beneath what must have certainly been an original oil painting. They looked small and very out of place with all the crystal and silver objects scattered around the room on tables. "You were so sweet to send them. Why didn't you come to the wedding, though?"

"I had to work. Are you working Maggie? You'll finish law school, won't you? When will you take the bar exam?"

"I still have a few courses to go, but I don't think I'll be able to finish law school. And no, I'm not working. Running back and forth between here and Montreal with Jean Paul, I really couldn't have a job."

Jean Paul came back with a bowl of soup. The three of us sat at a dining room table large enough to seat ten people while I ate. We made small talk. I told them about my teaching and my running, and my plans to run the Boston Marathon the next spring. I didn't mention that my girlfriend lived and worked in Montreal and that I visited her at least once a month.

I stayed less than an hour, feeling irrelevant and out-of-place. When I left, Maggie walked out to the elevator with me.

"Are you happy?" I asked.

"Of course. Look at the life he's given me. Why wouldn't I be happy?"

"Is this really what you want?"

"Of course," she repeated. She kissed me lightly on the lips and then traced her fingers down to my chest. "He's a good man. And he loves me and treats me well. This is what I want." But she leaned her head forward onto my chest and hugged me tightly. After a few moments, my elevator came. I kissed her on the top of her head, the only place I could. She turned suddenly back to her door, her face hidden from me by her hair. She called out as she went in, "Let's keep in touch." Then she was gone.

We never spoke again, but I think I saw her two more times, both during races. That spring I ran the Boston Marathon. New maturity and a hard winter of training had me ready, and I found myself running among the top two-dozen runners. Approaching the finish, I turned the corner onto Boylston Street within a block of Maggie's new apartment. Nearly delirious with concentration and fatigue, I almost missed her. Through my fog I heard her call to me.

"David! You're doing great! I love you!"

It almost stopped me. I looked over and saw her clap her hands once, ending with them folded in front of her smile in an almost prayer-like pose. But I turned back toward the finish, lifted by the sight of her. The road was wide and nearly empty, cordoned off to contain the spectators on the sides. A very few other runners were strung out ahead of me single file. I raced after them toward the looming finish line straight ahead, leaving the vision of Maggie behind.

Two years later I ran in a road relay race on loops inside a large park in Toronto. With a mile to the finish of my ten-kilometer leg I saw Maggie again. Cresting a rise, I noted a small figure beside the course, her hair an unmistakable beacon. I looked more closely to be sure it was her as I approached. She saw me, smiled, and waved. I grinned back at her and waved, still racing. In front of her was a baby stroller with the small bundle of a child in it. She said nothing but just waved and waved as I stormed past.

I finished my race, passed off to a teammate, and circled back on the course, still running nearly at race speed. Gasping to regain my breath, I trotted back out the road to where I had seen Maggie, but she was gone. A boulevard, lined with stone-front townhouse apartments, touched the edge of the park near the spot and I ran out to the street to look for her, but there was no trace of her. I checked for her name in the phone book before I left Toronto, but she wasn't listed. I never saw her again.

Did Maggie find what she was looking for? I believe that Jean Paul loved her. Certainly he gave her the homes and the lifestyle she might have wanted. I couldn't. Perhaps she loved him too, for the safety and the security she sought.

Maybe I was naïve. Maybe I was in love. Maybe I was blind to what Maggie wanted from me. Time passes and we gain a new perspective. People and things change. Yes, I am still an idealist. I believe we should all have audacious goals and dreams and never settle, though we may never find everything we want. I came to realize that beauty can be blinding but much more is needed to sustain a relationship.

I dated other girls and was fortunate to fall in love again, a textured, many-layered love. We got married, bought a house, and filled it with furniture and children.

Years later, with our children grown and off finding their own lives, my wife and I went to Italy for a vacation. We landed in Pisa and rented a small Fiat to drive the narrow roads to the Tuscan hill towns, to Siena and Assisi. When we got to Florence, we went to the Uffizi museum. In a gallery filled with Botticelli's work I found the Birth of Venus. I stood, stunned, in front of it, with a three-deep crowd of other awe-struck art lovers. Venus was luminous and windblown, her eyes staring straight into mine. Perhaps more than Maggie she knew me. My wife understood and waited patiently beside me. When I was ready, she led me away to other masterpieces.

Some of the things that mattered from my college years became different and less important as I grew older. Other things stayed the same. Injustices and other wars still disturb me. Maybe history does repeat itself. But back then I couldn't know where my life would take me. All I needed then was a good day to run and the peace I found when I saw Maggie.

The Deer Slayer

"HONEY, COME GET US MEN some beers!" Chris called from the kitchen, teasing as he usually did when he wanted something from Terry.

"Coming dear," Terry called, playing along with his game. With a resigned smile she finished folding a T-shirt, set it on the stack of clothes on the sofa, and stood up. She stepped over the laundry basket and walked into the kitchen followed by Sheila. Terry pushed past the two men at the kitchen table to the refrigerator.

Sheila stopped behind Tom, her boyfriend, and draped her arms over his shoulders, trailing them down his chest, pressing her body into the back of his head. "So tell me, Tom," she said. "What are you boys cooking up in here?"

Tom answered, his voice excited. "Oh Sheila, this is going to be the year. I've been scouting around the last few weekends up north. About ten miles up, near the lake. I've found some woods that are full of deer. I've been telling Chris about it. The deer are thick as squirrels this year. The two of us are sure to bag some good ones when the season opens in a couple of weeks. There's this one big buck," Tom's voice trailed off, unable to find the words, but his hands pantomimed a massive rack of antlers.

Terry turned from the refrigerator with two bottles of Bud. She twisted off the caps and handed them to the two men, Chris first, then Tom. "When are you going hunting," she asked.

Chris answered, speaking for both men. "Weekend after next. The season opens. Two weeks. That's all the time we've got to get our deer. Pack us a lunch, sweetheart, and we'll be off. You'll have the house to yourself for most of the day."

"Great," Terry answered flatly. "I'll find things to do while you're gone. I've got plenty to do here at home."

Terry went back to the living room sofa and resumed folding the laundry. Sheila kissed Tom on the top of his head. "I'll leave you boys to your planning," she said, trailing her fingers back across his shoulders. "Bring me home a big one, Tom. Shoot that big buck for me, okay? I'm counting on you for lots of venison this winter."

"You've got it," Tom called after her as she returned to the living room.

Sheila sat next to Terry, watching her fold, pitching in now and again. "Men!" she laughed. "Always out doing something. Hunting in the fall. Ice fishing in winter. Driving their trucks in the mud come spring. Always something going on."

"Well, it's fine with me," Terry added. "I get a lot more done around the house when Chris is gone. It's the best time for me to do the work for my college classes. No distractions. No problems. No interruptions."

"How's that going at the college?" asked Sheila.

"Good, I guess. I enjoy the classes."

"You know, Terry, I never figured you for a college girl. I never thought any of us would spend a day in a classroom after we got out of high school. But here you are taking one class after the other. How do you do it? And why?"

"I don't know. I like it." Terry paused, thinking about her answer. Sheila was right. High school had been boring, one irrelevant class after the other. But now, at the junior college, her classes made sense to her.

She tried to explain, seeking an answer as much for herself as to settle it for Sheila. "Down at work I helped out in accounting. And my boss, Rick? He liked my work and sent me to the college for just one class. I did okay, and I liked it, so I took another. The company pays my tuition. And Rick keeps telling me how well I'm doing. I've only got three more classes to go to get my Associate degree in Business. And I got a promotion at work. It's funny. I never thought I'd be doing this. But I keep taking the classes. I like what I'm doing. At work and at college."

Terry shook her head for a moment and thought more about her college classes. It puzzled her. In high school, and for the time right afterwards, everything had been about Chris. They went everywhere together. They did everything together. They began planning to get married before they had even finished high school. Later, they lived together for two years, sharing a small apartment in town, and saving money to buy a house.

As soon as they got married, just a year ago, things had changed. Life had been so simple before the wedding, and the promotion, and college. Just Chris and the small home they made in their apartment. It seemed more complicated now. She was always running to this place or that. To work, or college, or home to fix dinner for Chris.

Sheila interrupted Terry's thoughts. "Doesn't it take a lot of your time, working the new job and going to school?"

"Well, yeah," Terry answered quietly, almost whispering so Chris wouldn't overhear. "It does take up a lot of my time. And Chris hassles me about it sometimes. He keeps asking me why I'm doing it, too. Just like you. But he sure likes that I got a raise at work because of it. At least I think he likes that part. Sometimes I think he's upset that I make more money than he does. But the extra money's good. It helped us buy this house. And that pickup he's got out there in the driveway? With all the chrome and everything? That's from the money I'm making now. He does okay with his job down at the garage. But it's my job that's making it for us."

"I still don't get it," said Sheila. "You've got it all. Married to a great guy. Living in a nice house. I can't see you as a college girl. I can't imagine you graduating from college. Where do you think you'll end up? In some big time job? Running the company someday?"

"I don't know, Sheila." Terry stopped again, looking for answers. She had spent so much time trying to sort it out recently.

"I don't know," she repeated. "Maybe it's the money. Maybe it's the opportunity to really do something, to become somebody. All my life I always did what people wanted me to do. What I was expected to do. I've always tried to do the right thing. That's why Chris and I got married. That's the way it's supposed to be, right? You grow up, you get out of school, and you get married. So that's what I did. But I don't know if it's what I really want."

Terry paused for a moment, picking her words carefully, trying to seem sensible. "Lately, I keep thinking there's more. I don't know what it is. I don't know what I really want to be. Some days I feel like I'm faking it, getting through each day, and I hope nobody catches on. I'm doing the best I can. But each day takes me some place better. I guess I'll figure it out someday."

Sheila folded the last shirt and sat back. "Well, then," she said. "If you're making good money, and it's because of your new job and the stuff you're doing at the college, I say, go for it, Terry! I think it's great what you're doing. I kind of wish I could do it. Tom and me, we're happy. But we don't have a nice house like you and Chris. We probably don't have half the things you do. We're doing okay, but not like you and Chris."

"You're doing fine, Sheila. You and Tom are doing just fine. You don't know how good you have it."

The two men appeared in the doorway from the kitchen. Chris began, "Ladies, Tom and I have a proposition for the two of you."

Sheila shifted to the front of her seat, eager. "Ooh, a proposition! I like it, whatever it is you want. Just ask me! I'm game for anything."

"We want you two to come hunting with us."

"What?" Sheila exclaimed, puzzled and a bit frustrated, settling back in her seat, folding her arms.

Terry paused, a pair of socks folded in her hands, watching the men carefully. Thinking.

Sheila continued, "I don't want to go hunting. I don't want to spend all day sitting out in the woods with you, waiting to kill a deer. Just shoot the deer for me, Tom, and bring it home. Cut it up for me and I'll cook it."

"Well, here's the thing," Tom said. "We each get a deer hunting license and we can only shoot one deer apiece. That means Chris and I can only get two deer between both of us. But up where we're going, the place is just crawling with deer. We could easily get two apiece. So here's the plan. You girls get licenses along with us. That will be four licenses for the four of us. So we can get four deer. And then you come out into the woods with us with rifles. And you both wait around for Chris and me to shoot our four deer. Then we drag them out of the woods, toss them into Chris's truck, and away we go. You don't have to kill the deer. Just hang around and wait for us to do it. What do you say?"

"I think it's a stupid idea," said Sheila. "I don't want to waste a day out in the woods. You guys don't usually shoot any deer anyway. What's to say this year will be any different than last year? You didn't get a single one last year. I'm not going."

"Aw, come on Sheila, it'll be fun," Tom begged.

"No. You boys go out and have your fun in the woods, but I'll stay here with Terry and wait for you to come home."

"I'll do it." Terry spoke cautiously. Then more confidently. "Yes, I'll do it. You want me to come hunting. Well, I'll do it."

Chris, Tom, and Sheila looked at her for a moment. Chris spoke first. "You'll hunt with us? You'll get a license, dress in camouflage, and carry a gun out into the woods? It'll be cold, you know. Maybe wet. And there's no bathrooms out there."

"That's okay. It sounds like fun. Like an adventure. I've never gone hunting before. I think I'd like to try it."

"Have you ever handled a gun before?" Tom asked.

"No, but I can learn how to shoot. Will one of you teach me?"

Chris leaned down, confronting his wife as she sat on the sofa. "You don't need to learn how to shoot," he explained, talking to her like she was a simple child. "All you really have to do is buy the license, carry a gun into the woods, and wait for Tom and me to bring back the deer. You don't have to know anything. All you have to do is sit and wait." He stood back up, certain he had put a stop to Terry's misguided fantasy. It was Tom's dumb idea anyway.

"I'll lend you one of my old guns, Terry," Tom said. "I'll load it for you in case you see a deer or something. And I'll show you how to shoot. I think it's great that you're coming with us. We'll have a good time out there. You sure you're not up for this, Sheila?"

"No, not me! If Terry wants to go hunting, she can. But not me. I'll wait back at the house to see what you bring home. If anything."

Two weekends later the three of them were off at dawn riding north in Chris's truck. Terry squeezed in between the two men. She wore one of Chris's old camouflage jackets, oversized and bulky on her tiny body. The sleeves were rolled up once at the cuff to expose her hands, in wool gloves. She had a blaze orange vest on over the jacket with her new hunting license in a pocket. Her hair was in a ponytail, pulled through the strap in the back of a baseball cap. She wore no perfume, not even makeup. Chris had told her that the scent would scare away the deer. She felt small, out-of-place, and a little frightened. She said nothing.

They pulled off the road and parked the truck on the dirt behind a guard rail next to a gully. Terry could see a path leading out of the gully into the forest.

"This is the place," said Tom. "The trail goes through about a mile of woods and out into a meadow at the base of those hills." He pointed over the treetops to the mountains further to the north. "The deer are all over the meadow and up in the woods beyond it, up toward the mountains. So we head in here, and begin tracking them when we get to the meadow."

They took the guns off the rack in the back of the truck, and walked single file down the trail into the forest. Chris and Tom moved quickly, without talking. Terry hurried to keep up, clumsy, carrying the unaccustomed weight of the rifle she had borrowed from Tom. After a while they stopped. They were in a small clearing, a wide spot on the trail.

Tom pointed ahead to a low rise on the trail and whispered, "We're almost to the meadow. It's not far beyond that little hill. Terry, why don't you stay here and wait for us. Sit down and make yourself comfortable. You've got a bottle of water, and you've got my old rifle. Remember, it's loaded, just in case. I showed you how to aim and shoot. But you shouldn't have any need for that. Just settle in and wait. Chris and I will start moving more slowly now, stalking the deer. We need to be perfectly quiet, no talking when we're hunting. No distractions. So you wait here. We'll be back when we get our deer."

"Have fun, Terry, honey," Chris said quietly, smiling, amused that she had actually gone through with her threat to follow them when they went hunting. "And you be careful with that gun, sweetheart. I want you here, safe and sound when we get back." He moved up to her, kissed her quickly on the cheek and then headed up the trail, over the rise toward the meadow. Tom followed right behind him.

Terry sat on a fallen tree next to the trail. She propped the rifle next to her against the log and took a sip from her water bottle. And she waited.

The woods were not silent, she realized. Birds sang and insects buzzed. She could hear, but not see, small animals pushing around under the leaves in the underbrush nearby. Far away an airplane hummed.

What am I doing? thought Terry. *Why did I come out here? I don't belong in the woods with a gun. I always open my mouth and get myself into these situations. They always seem to work out for me, but maybe I should have just stayed home with Sheila.*

Yellow leaves fell from the trees whenever a breeze blew. The sunlight caught them as they fell. *They're almost like shooting stars*, Terry thought. *If I wish upon a shooting star, the wish will come true. How do you wish on a falling leaf? And what would I wish for? What do I want?*

Time passed. She sensed that the angle of the sun had changed. It was warmer than it had been at dawn. Still the birds sang, the leaves fell, the breeze blew. She unzipped the camouflage jacket part way, took off her gloves and tucked them into the jacket pockets and continued sitting, attentive to the woods living around her.

Suddenly, she was alert. The woods went silent. Terry sensed somehow that something moved on the trail just out of sight over the rise. A person? Chris and Tom coming back from the hunt with their deer, maybe? What if it was someone else? A stranger. Terry's heart raced. She was a vulnerable woman, alone in the woods.

Quietly, she stood and reached for the rifle. She brought it to her shoulder, released the safety, and cocked it, just as Tom had shown her. She aimed it above the rise, where a person would appear if they came along the trail. Tense, she waited. A breeze blew into her face.

The buck stepped to the top of the rise and paused, antlers held high, sniffing the air. The clearing in front of him was still, and at first, he didn't see the small woman at the side of the trail. When he saw her, he sprang forward, hooves flailing as he prepared to dash off the trail into the forest.

Terry saw the animal and froze. He seemed huge, the horns menacing, sharp and dangerous. Suddenly he snorted and leaped. *He's coming after me!*

she thought. *He's attacking me!*

She squeezed the gun, pulling the trigger. The gun exploded next to her ear, the stock slamming into her shoulder. One shot. A small spot appeared on the white chest of the deer, just below the thick throat.

The buck stumbled for a moment trying to turn into the woods. Then it took a staggering step forward, still on the trail, still coming at Terry. Panicky, she held her aim on the animal. *He's still after me,* she thought. *If he takes another step, I'll shoot him again. Tom said I've got two shots in the gun. One more step, and I'll shoot him again. Then the gun will be empty and I'll have to hit him with the gun. Or drop it and try to run from him.*

The buck tried to take another step, but his front legs buckled. He sank to his knees as though he were praying to Terry, begging for his life. His eyes looked into hers. His mouth opened, gasping, the tongue thick, sticking out. His hind legs caved in and he fell twisting to the ground, thudding as he landed. Still looking at Terry he made a faint bleating sound, like a sheep.

Terry sat back against her log and watched the animal. She kept the rifle aimed at him, afraid he would suddenly leap up and thrash her with his antlers and hooves. The deer was no more than two paces away from her, lying on the trail. His side moved up and down, up and down as he panted, gasping out his life. Then, with a sigh, he stopped. The barrel-ribbed thickness of his body sagged slightly and was still.

Terry sat edgy, tense, jumpy, both excited and afraid at the same time by what she had done. Around her the birds resumed their singing, the yellow leaves continued to fall, and the sun still shone.

Time passed. Shadows moved across the forest floor. Terry was aware of the smells of the trees, of the crumbled leaves and dirt on the forest floor. Of animals. Of blood.

She looked at the massive form of the deer lying in front of her. She looked at the gun and at her hands. Part of her felt like shouting, like laughing, jubilant that she had killed the deer. But a part of her felt like crying when she thought of the life she had ended. Terry waited next to the deer. She had no sense of how long she sat, but she became aware that the air was cooling, and the sunlight was less direct.

Far away she heard men's voices, talking and laughing. Tom and Chris were coming back along the trail. They cleared the rise and stopped.

"Holy shit," Tom shouted. "Oh my God, Chris, look at the deer!"

"Hey, Terry," said Chris, walking up to where she sat. "Where'd the deer come from?"

"I shot it."

"Yeah, right. You wouldn't know the first thing about shooting deer. Did some guys, some other hunters come and drop it off here for you to watch for them?"

"No, Chris, I shot it."

"How? How could you?" Chris asked. "You don't even know how to aim a rifle. How could you? I don't believe this."

"Tom showed me how to shoot the gun. The deer just walked down the trail, over the rise, right where you guys just came back. And I shot it."

"No way! I don't believe this. You want us to believe you shot this big buck? No way. No freaking way!"

Tom spoke next. "Look at the size of this animal, Chris! This is the one I told you about. We get back to town we'll take this right in to Ed's. He'll dress it for you. You guys will have tons of venison. You'll be eating well for weeks from this one big buck. And look at his antlers, Chris. Ed does taxidermy too. He'll do a great job on that head for you. Put it up on the wall in your house!"

Terry sat silently, watching the men. She felt suddenly defiant, proud of the buck she had shot.

Chris spoke, sarcastic. "Sure. Great antlers. Nice rack. A man gets his hands on a rack like that he's got to mount it. It'll make a nice trophy in our living room. We'll have everyone in to take a look at it."

Tom took charge. "Let's pick this baby up and get it back to your truck. We've got to get going if we're going to get out of the woods before dark."

Terry finally moved. She stood and reached for the deer. She picked up one of its front hooves. The thin leg, all tendon and bone beneath the cold hair and skin, lifted in her hand as though it wasn't connected to the deer. The thick body barely moved on the dust of the forest floor.

Chris stepped forward. "So you say you shot the deer, but you're not even strong enough to pick it up? Here. Let me do it."

He squatted, grabbed the deer by the shoulders and haunches, and hoisted it, grunting, to his shoulders. He staggered beneath the dead weight.

"You need some help with that?" asked Tom.

"No. I've got it. Terry, the least you can do is pick up my rifle and carry that for me. But be careful. It's loaded."

They proceeded back along the trail out of the woods. Chris led, with the wide mass of the carcass straddling his shoulders. Tom was next. Then Terry at the back with the two rifles slung one across each shoulder, Chris's and Tom's, the one she had borrowed. Tom's seemed lighter to her and she wondered if that was because it had one shot missing from the chamber.

At the truck, Chris slung the deer into the bed in back. Bits of leaves fell off the deer into the truck. A smudge of dirt, or maybe blood showed on the tailgate, and Chris wiped it away with his sleeve. Then the three of them climbed in and drove back to town without a word.

Tom leaned against the door, watching Chris drive. He felt out of place and sensed that something bad was going on between Terry and Chris. It baffled him but he knew enough to keep quiet.

Terry felt it, too. It wasn't new. Chris had gotten into his moods before. She knew he would give her a hard time for a few days, the way he did when she went to her first class at the college. And the way he had when she got the promotion and the raise. She sat fretfully, trying not to think of what she knew was coming for her.

Chris drove steady and fast, eyes straight ahead following the road. *How does Terry get off killing a deer?* he thought. *Isn't it enough that she makes more money than me? And going to college like she's somebody special? I'm a good man. A good husband. I work hard. I pull my weight making our home together. Why does she keep doing these things? Why can't she just work a simple job like Sheila? Or like me and Tom? Why can't she stay home? And now she's killed that big buck. I never got an animal like that.*

Weeks later, with the leaves off the trees, and a thin dusting of new snow on the ground, Sheila stopped by to visit Terry. The men were away, working on something in town. Terry brought in mugs of coffee from the kitchen and the two women sat together on the sofa in the living room. Across from them the deer head was mounted on the wall, turned slightly, the antlers nearly scraping the ceiling. Its blank, plastic eyes stared up and off, down the hall past the bedrooms, past the walls of the house, to the forests, and the mountains beyond.

Sheila shifted on the sofa, turning from the deer to Terry. "So, that's the deer you shot?"

Terry sat side-saddle, her knees sideways on the sofa, her bare feet tucked under her. She wrapped her hands around the warmth of the coffee mug. "Yes, that's him."

"You know, Terry, Chris is telling everyone that he shot it."

"Yeah, I know. He started that as soon as we got to Ed's and he took it in for Ed to work on. What makes you think I shot it?"

"Tom told me. Tom doesn't get why Chris is telling people he did it. The two of them, they didn't get a single one this year. Just like every other year. But Chris is out there bragging about this deer. And then Tom tells me you shot it."

"Who do you believe, Sheila? Chris or Tom? Who do you think really shot the deer?"

"I know you did, Terry. You do these things. I know you could do it. I believe Tom."

"Yeah. I shot it. And I know what Chris has been saying. Back at Ed's, that's when it started. Tom took Chris on about it. He said, 'Chris, Terry shot the deer, not you. Don't go telling Ed you shot it.'"

Terry paused for a moment, considering whether to go on. "Tom's a good man. Honest. He's a straight up guy. You're really lucky to have a guy like him. You and he should get married."

"We will some day, I guess," said Sheila. "I hope we're as good together as you and Chris."

"I hope you're better," answered Terry, shaking her head.

Sheila let the statement pass. "Yeah, anyway," she said. "So tell me what happened down at Ed's?"

"Chris was bragging that he shot my deer. And Tom said that he hadn't. Ed stood there listening the way he does and not saying a word. He was getting ready to dress it out when Chris said, 'Ed, don't you listen to Tom with his crazy talk. He's just angry that he didn't get the deer, and I did. Can you imagine a little woman like Terry shooting a deer like this? I mean really.

Seriously. It's mine. You fix it up and do a nice job on the head for me.'"

"Didn't you speak up? You should have said something."

"Why? What would have been the point? Tom knows I shot it. And he told you. So you know, too. And if Chris feels better telling people he did, when he knows it was really me, well…" Terry's voice trailed off and she looked away from Sheila, up to the deer first then down into her coffee.

"You should have told Ed that you shot it," insisted Sheila again.

"Maybe I should have." Terry's voice rose, an edge of anger moving into it. "Maybe. I might have still been a little confused back then. About a lot of things. But it doesn't matter. I know I shot it. For me, that's enough. It wasn't worth fighting about. Not right there with Ed watching and everything. But sometimes he makes me so angry!" Terry slammed her hand, palm down, on the sofa in frustration but then she stopped, embarrassed by her outburst. She looked at Sheila again, seeking support.

"Yeah, Terry," Sheila soothed her friend. "I believe you shot the deer. That's really something! Sometimes I wish I was you. I mean, none of the men get a deer, but you do. And you've got the great job too. And even going to college. What will you do next? How can you ever top this?"

"I don't know," replied Terry. "I need time. I need to sort out a lot of things. I need to decide who I really am, who I really want to be. For me."

A late winter day with a sky like iron and air that hurt to breathe greeted Terry when she opened the door for Tom and Sheila. The snow had started mid-morning, a flake now and again, then more, and by noon it was steady, blowing sideways, shifting around on the pavement, beginning to drift against the fence. Sheila came in, passing by Chris as he left to join Tom for an afternoon of plowing.

Sheila hung her coat on the rack by the door and sat on the sofa. Terry brought them both coffee. From across the room the deer on the wall watched them.

"Off they go," said Sheila. "Off for an afternoon of adventure, pushing the snow off of parking lots and driveways."

Terry nodded. "Yep. Off they go. Finally, we have some time for just you and me and some girl talk."

At first their conversation covered the usual topics. They talked about old friends from high school. They talked about television reality shows and the upcoming wedding of a girl they both knew. But Sheila noticed a new tension about Terry. She seemed distracted, reluctant to talk about herself or Chris.

Sheila had to open it up. "What's up, Terry?" she asked. "How are you doing? Things still good at work? You still in college?"

"Yep. Things are good. All good. Everything's fine."

Terry paused for a moment, thinking, choosing her words deliberately. Sheila waited.

"I've got other news. There is something else."

Sheila shifted forward on the sofa, sensing that Terry had something big to say. Bigger than her job, or college, or the buck she had shot. "What is it? What else?"

"I'm pregnant."

"Oh my God! Oh Terry! That's marvelous! When's the baby due?" Sheila hugged her.

"June. Right after my last class at the college."

"Right after graduation? That's wonderful!"

"No. I'm not graduating. Not right away, anyway. I'm only planning to take two classes this spring so I'll still be one class short of my diploma. There's not enough time to take more. And not enough money. Work only pays for so many classes each year. What with my job, and being home to have dinner ready for Chris and all, I don't have time to take three classes anyway. Not right now, and not right after the baby's born."

"Well, you'll have to go back and get that last class later on, after the baby's born."

"It's not that easy. There's so much going on right now. And now the baby's coming. I have to give up something."

"Don't give up school," Sheila begged. "You're too close to drop out. Here I'm wishing I had everything you have, and you want to give up? Don't give it all up just because Chris got you pregnant. You've got to go back."

"I will. But money'll be tight for a little while. I'm thinking of taking a leave from my job when the baby comes. I'll have to stay home this summer to take care of the baby."

"Let Chris do it. You make almost twice what he does. Have him stay home with the baby."

"I'm not letting him take care of my baby! He wouldn't know what to do. He'd be helpless."

Sheila fought back. "Chris is a jerk, Terry. I always thought he was pretty nice. But after all this? I see the way he treats you. And now the way he's bragging that he shot your deer. Don't give up everything for him."

"I'm not giving it up for him. I'm doing it for my baby. I know what I've done. And I know what I can do. What I will do. So does Chris." Terry looked up at the deer again, hoping that somehow the dead animal could give her the affirmation she couldn't get from Chris.

"Have your mom help out with the baby. You just can't quit work and college and everything. I can't imagine Chris really wants that, either."

"I think he does, Sheila. He's never really been happy with me working the way I do. He thinks I spend too much time there. And at college, too. Sometimes he yells at me about it. Says I think my job's more important than him. And he gets upset when I'm not home for him, waiting on him all the time."

Sheila started to say something, but Terry continued. "So here's my plan. I'll stay home for a while after the baby comes. Just the summer. That way I can take care of the baby and have the house clean and dinner set. It's the way it's supposed to be, isn't it?" Terry pleaded weakly with Sheila for her acceptance, for agreement that her plan made sense.

Then, before Sheila could answer, Terry continued, speaking with more confidence and a little anger. She had kept her planning to herself and her mom. Now, she felt, was the time to disclose her new direction to her best friend.

"Listen, Sheila, I'm thinking there's more to my plan. I'm going to go back to school in the fall. I'll pick up that last class and graduate. And I'll go back to work, too. They'll hold my job for me. And I'm thinking I'll move back in with my mom in the fall. You're right about my mom. Mom can help out with the baby. There's no reason I can't raise my baby, finish college, and go to work too. But I'll need some support, some backing. I'll get it from my mom. But not from Chris. I don't need Chris telling me what I should do, what I can do. Or what I can't. How to live my life. Putting me down for what I'm doing, what I've done. I don't want anyone doing that to me."

"What about Chris?"

"What about him?"

"You're going to leave him? What will happen to Chris? You'll be with your mom and your baby, and he'll be trying to live on his own again?"

"Chris will have to get used to that. I'll have the summer with me and the baby here at home. But when fall comes, I'm leaving Chris. Hunting season again. Chris will go off looking for another deer. He'll figure things out. He'll be okay."

Sheila gave a nervous laugh and reached for Terry's hand. "It's always been the four of us. Tom and me. You and Chris. But now it'll be different. But that's okay. You've changed," she said. "You seem to have it all together. How did you do it?"

"Maybe shooting the deer helped. Nobody expected me to do it. Nobody thought I could. Not you or Tom. Certainly not Chris. But there it is on my wall. I did it. I know now that it's okay to take a chance. It's okay not to do what I'm expected to do. If I can go out there into the woods and kill a deer, if I can shoot that big, beautiful animal, I know I can do anything. I was scared, Sheila. But look what I did! I don't care what Chris says. I guess I love him. I guess I always have. But I don't need him running my life, putting me down for every good thing I do. I still don't know exactly where I'm going or what I'm doing. Not at work, or at the college, or with my baby. But I know it could turn out to be good. I'm a little scared all the time, but I know I'm getting somewhere. I don't know where I'm headed, but I know it will turn out fine."

Terry leaned back into the sofa, confident, sipping her mug of coffee. Waiting. Ready for whatever might come to her next.

The enormity of what she had just learned finally took hold of Sheila. She leaned over and gave Terry a hug. "A baby!" she crowed. "Oh my God, that's so wonderful! Amazing Terry!"

The snow had stopped. The women heard noise outside the house, the sound of tires on gravel and ice. Chris and Tom were coming home. Instinctively Terry hurried to straighten the magazines on the coffee table and rearrange the throw pillows on the sofa. Making the house right for Chris. The men came in the door, stamping the snow off their boots. They pulled off their parkas and hung them on the coat rack by the door. Then they clumped into the living room, shoulder to shoulder.

"Geez, its cold out there," stated Chris. "Great, Terry. I see you've got coffee. Go get Tom and me a cup. You know how I take it, how I like it."

Terry remained on the sofa. She felt newly brave, flushed with confidence after her talk with Sheila. "Go right on in and get yourself a cup, Chris. You know how to make it, don't you?"

"Of course I can make a cup of coffee. It's easy, right? Boil some water and put it in the coffee maker. But that's your job, Terry. Now let's go. Tom and me are cold and tired." He walked toward his chair, under the deer, and began to sit down.

"No," answered Terry speaking firmly. "You go get it yourself."

Chris stopped, still standing in front of his chair. He turned and looked at Terry, an eyebrow raised.

Tom looked uneasily at Chris and Terry. Then he checked in with a glance at Sheila. He had begun to see Chris differently since he heard him lie about the deer. He too had noticed the way Chris treated Terry. But they had always been his friends. It was disturbing to see them fight this way. Now he just wanted to get away from what was turning into an ugly moment. "I've really got to run, Chris," he said. "Sheila, come on, we'd better be going."

"In a moment, Tom," Sheila replied, grinning, looking with fascination from Chris to Terry and back again. She needed to stay. For Terry.

"Terry and I were just talking," Sheila continued. "I'm not ready."

Tom fidgeted, shifting foot to foot, wanting to find a comfortable spot. He found himself unable to get settled in the tension of the living room.

Chris still stood, red-faced now, looking down at his wife on the sofa. "Well?" he asked again. "Coffee, Terry? You going to get us some coffee?"

"No."

"No?"

"No. No! You need to learn how to do that, Chris. That and more. You'd better start learning now how to take care of yourself. You'll need to know what to do after the baby comes."

"Baby? What baby?" Tom asked. He was following the conversation, but a lot was happening at once and he had to pause to absorb this, the most important news.

Sheila eagerly jumped in to explain. "Terry's pregnant! She's having a baby in June. Right after she gets out of school. And she'll take the summer off to be with the baby. And her mom is going to help out with the baby, too. It's amazing, isn't it?"

Tom grinned and rushed to Terry, hugging her as she sat on the sofa. "Oh Terry! That's fantastic! A baby! That's wonderful news! Congratulations!" He kissed her, then pulled back quickly, embarrassed by what he had said and done. He looked at Chris cautiously.

"Yeah, it's fantastic news," stated Chris sarcastically. "She's pregnant. So she'll have to quit her job and stay home with the baby."

Terry, still sitting, legs folded on the sofa, continued. "That's right. But I'm thinking 'home' will be with my mom. Back with her, not here. I'm going to go live with my mom when the baby's born. Then or sooner if I have to. And I'll go back to work in the fall, too. And back to college."

Her plan was now laid out for all of them to consider. Terry surveyed the room. Sheila beamed, supportive and eager, right by her side. Tom grinned too, overwhelmed by the news of the baby. But then his face shifted, first puzzled, then aware, and finally settling into a frown of concern as he digested the news of her leaving Chris. They had always been his best friends and now they were splitting up.

Chris, too, tried to sort it all out. He knew about the baby of course, and that she was taking leave from her job and the college classes. But this was the first time she had talked of leaving him. She couldn't leave him. Never. She couldn't!

"Why?" he pleaded. "You've got the baby. And you're my wife. You belong here with me. That's all you need. That's all there is to it."

"You don't know what I need," Terry answered. "I'm just now starting to figure out what I need for myself. But what do I need that's here? With you?"

"You need me, Terry. How could you make it on your own? Without me?"

"How can I ever make it here with you, Chris? I don't know what's going to happen if I leave. But I know I can't handle what happens if I stay. So I'm leaving."

Chris tried one last time. One last desperate ploy. "Your car's old. It's a wreck. It won't last much longer. My truck's the only sure way for you to get around. Sure, Terry. Run off to your mom, but you'll need a better car. You need me and my truck."

"I'll find a way," said Terry. "I know I'll find a way."

Terry swung her feet to the floor and pulled on her socks and boots quickly. Then she stood and walked to the center of the room. "I think I'll go now. I'm ready," she declared.

Her friends watched her, astonished. Chris backed away from her, stunned, and sat suddenly in his chair beneath the deer.

Tom turned back to the front door and took his parka off the rack. "You need a ride, Terry?" he offered quietly.

"Sure. Thank you."

Excited, Sheila grabbed her own coat off the rack and the old camouflage jacket Terry had worn on the hunt as well. She pitched Terry the oversized hunting jacket.

"Let's go!" Sheila said.

The three of them walked out into the cold; Terry leading, followed by Tom and Sheila together.

Outside the three of them walked through the darkness and the stunning cold. Tom unlocked his car and they got in; Tom in the driver's seat, Terry riding shotgun, Sheila's usual spot. Sheila got in the unaccustomed space of the back seat.

As they turned from the driveway into the road Terry paused for a moment and looked back at her house. Back there was her life, her love, her man and husband, the father of her child. All of it was now gone. She began to shake and turned back to stare out the windshield at the road ahead. For a moment tears silently started from her eyes.

Then she steadied herself, took a deep breath, and slowly let it out. "Well, I did it. I finally left him."

Sheila leaned forward and reached around the headrest to give Terry's shoulders a squeeze. "Yes, you did. You really did. You go, girl!"

Terry continued to breathe deeply and to blow back out through pursed lips. "I'll be fine," she said. "It's all going to be okay."

Tom looked over at Terry across the console as he drove. His thoughts were unsettled. Finally, he spoke. "Chris has always been my best friend. I guess he always will be. But I'm with you on this one, Terry. Leaving him is the best thing you could do."

"Thanks." The tears had stopped but it was all Terry could say.

Tom picked up again. "Sheila and I have your back, Terry. Stay with your mom or stay with us. You're going to be fine."

"Yes, I will," Terry affirmed. "I absolutely will."

Chris heard the sound of tires on gravel as Tom's car pulled out. He sat, suddenly alone, confused, and lost in the silent house. Above him, the dead buck continued to stare away into the distance. Slowly, Chris stood and started for the kitchen, dazed. He wanted a cup of coffee. He would have to figure out how to work the coffee maker. How hard could it be? He had no idea where to start, but he thought he should be able to do it. *After all,* he guessed, *if Terry can do it, I'm sure I can. I'm a grown man. I can handle whatever comes next.*

Sky City

Summer, 2006

SHE DROVE WEST FROM ALBUQUERQUE on the interstate, taking Henry to Acoma Pueblo. It was time. She had married an American and settled in Albuquerque where she and her husband had raised Henry like any other American kid. He went to public schools; she checked his homework each night. She watched him play in his Youth Soccer and Little League games. Every weekend she took him to Catholic mass. But she was a Native and a member of the Keres tribe, and that meant that Henry was as well. He had turned twelve in the spring. It was time for him to go to his grandfather. Her husband understood and agreed.

"Mom," Henry asked anxiously. "What will grandfather do with me all summer?"

"I don't know. I'm a woman so I can't know. It's something only the men do. You will learn about your heritage. Grandfather will teach you."

"You said it will be hard. Do I have to go?"

"Yes Henry, it will be hard. But yes, you have to learn about who you are, where you come from. Trust your grandfather. He will take care of you."

She turned off the highway and drove the final miles on a narrow road paved through the red dirt, the harsh grasses, and the sage brush. Lines of barbed wire marked the edge of range country, but even the wire stopped after a few miles.

The pavement changed to a dirt road at the crossroads. The mesa rose to the left, Acoma Pueblo. Sky City. She turned in front of the Visitors Center, pulled onto the gravel shoulder and stopped. Her father, Ben, waited for them, sitting on a black rock back from the road. They got out of the car; Ben stood and walked toward them.

She hugged her father quickly and whispered to him, "Take care of Henry, father. He's a little bit scared."

"I will take good care of him. He will be fine," Ben whispered back.

"Hi, grandfather. Ready to get started?" Henry dropped his duffle of clothes for the summer and hugged his grandfather. His words showed courage but his voice cracked.

"Ready."

Ben took the duffle in one hand and the boy's hand in his other. Henry looked back at his mother then turned back to his grandfather. The transfer of the boy from the mother to her father took only seconds. The old man and the boy turned without a word and walked down the ancient trail toward the mesa.

She watched them silently for a moment. Then she called after them, "See you in a few weeks."

There was nothing more to say or do. She got back in her car and turned onto the road to head back to Albuquerque. As she sped along the interstate, she was afraid for her son. She held back tears. But she reassured herself, "Mothers have probably felt like this for countless centuries when they turned their sons over to their grandfathers. It's always worked out. Henry will be fine. He'll be different when I see him again. He'll be a man. It will all be okay."

Her husband had supported her in the decision to give their boy over to his grandfather for the summer. He would be waiting in Albuquerque for her. She would need to draw on his strength this summer.

The old man and the boy sat together on the red rock. Grandfather and grandson. Ben and Henry. Ben wore an old plaid work shirt and a University of New Mexico baseball cap tipped back, his gray hair in a pony tail hanging from the back. Henry had his red Albuquerque Little League T-shirt, a connection with the fast, modern other world he lived in the rest of the year. Both wore blue jeans, wrinkled and softened with age. On both their feet were handmade leather moccasins. Henry's were new; his sneakers were stored away for the summer.

To their left dawn began to color the horizon. Light gray at first, then white, pale yellow, finally golds and reds mixing with the clear blue of the desert sky. The massive bluff of Acoma stood to the right, the pueblos, and the church on top, all still shrouded in darkness.

A stream passed in front of them filled by last evening's thunderstorms, bubbling over the pebbles. Beyond the stream were short corn stalks, low leaves dusted with the gritty desert dust. Later in the morning women would come down from Acoma carrying pots to fill with water from the stream. They would pour the water around each corn plant, one by one. Red puddles would remain when the women left, slowly sinking back into the desert dirt.

A rabbit hopped carefully on the other side of the stream. It began to nibble at the plants and flowers the rain had brought. Slowly Ben reached down and touched a blue flower that grew next to the rock they sat on. Yellow pollen dusted his flat fingertips.

"Do I have to go?" asked Henry. He had asked this question often over the past few days, first of his mother and now of his grandfather.

"Yes. It is what we do. It is what you should do," answered old Ben.

"You said that I will get tired. It's a long way to walk."

"Yes. You will be very tired. And hungry. Very hungry and thirsty. But you will do good. You know what to do. You know the way now. You will be okay."

"You did this, grandfather? You walked all the way to the mountains? And walked all the way back?"

"Yes. I did this, Henry. So did my grandfather before me. And his grandfather. It is what we do. Every Keres man does this."

"But my father never did this."

Your father is a good man, Henry. But he's an American. He's not Keres Indian. So he didn't do this. You're Keres because your mother is Keres. This is what you will do."

"You were tired?"

Ben remembered his journey. He sat and thought about the weariness. The endless passage through the desert. The heat and the hunger.

"Yes. Of course I was tired. It is a long way to go."

"What did you see when you got to the mountains?"

"I can't tell you what I saw. What I saw is mine. What you see will be yours. You will come home to Acoma and tell me about your journey. I can tell you the way to go, but what I saw when I was there is mine."

"But you were changed by your journey grandfather? You still remember it?"

"Yes. I remember it," Ben said. "It is part of me. It is part of who I am. I will always remember."

To their left the sun rose. First a white line of light, then a hot, bright ball popping above the distant mountains. The old man leaned forward so that his body cast a shadow, shielding the smaller boy. He squinted against the glare and looked back toward Acoma.

"Come with me, young Henry. Let's go back to my house. I'll fix Corn Flakes for breakfast."

They stood and followed the path back to the butte. The old man led the way; the boy followed. As they walked, the boy imagined the ordeal he would face in the days ahead. Ben let his mind wander back to how it had been for him when he was a boy. It had been so hard. And what he had seen had been so terrifying. But it was best to remember; never to forget. He remembered that dawn so long ago that had been the start of his journey.

SUMMER, 1945

A young Ben climbed the ladder, emerging onto the roof of the kiva. His short legs climbed quickly, bony knees poking out to both sides of the pine log ladder. It was symbolic; a ritual that reenacted the emergence long ago of the Keres people from the middle of the earth through the sipapu into this world. He had followed his grandfather up the ladder just as he had followed him in preparation for his journey every day during the past weeks.

They stood together, man and boy, on the edge of the roof facing the approach of dawn. Beneath them lay the dusty streets and the pueblos. On the far edge of the mesa, past the last house, was the expansive church to Saint Stephen. Beyond the church was nothing but the emptiness and open space of the desert. The sun edged over the far-off mountains, sending long shadows across the desert toward Acoma.

"Today. Tomorrow. This week. They will change you, young Ben," said Henry. Ben was his American name. Only Henry and Ben's mother knew his real name, the one that connected him to his ancestors. Ben was the name to be used outside, in front of other people from other families and other clans. It was the name to be used with the Americans. Like Ben, Henry's real name also was kept secret, a part of his soul.

Ben looked up at Henry and spoke, trying to make his voice deep like that of a man. He wanted Henry to understand that he understood the importance of the day. For a moment, though, a small bit of a child's anxiety showed in his tone. "I am ready, grandfather. I know the way. I will find what I need to find. Learn what I need to learn. I am sure I am ready to start on my new way."

"Be careful, Ben. We have prepared together tonight and these past weeks. The feast and the dancing. And then Saint Ann's Day. They are behind us. You showed that you knew the traditions when you danced with the men on those days.

"But out there. In the world. There are dangers I cannot describe for you. There is the desert and the heat, the animals and the snakes. Those you know and understand. You know how to protect yourself from those dangers.

"But there are the people, too. The Americans and the Spanish. Be watchful, grandson. We are not like the Apache. Or the Navajo. When we have been attacked, generations ago, we have defended Acoma against the Apaches and the Spanish. But we are the Keres people. We are peaceful people. The Americans have their war. It is far away across the ocean against people from Japan. The Navajo go to fight with the Americans against these Japanese. We are a people of peace, but we live in a world surrounded by the dangers of these people. Be careful.

"Follow the path and you will be safe. Your journey is like that of our ancestors. You have emerged out of our clan's Kiva the way our ancestors did at the beginning of time when they came to this world. You will go now, as they went. Out from the center, here at Sky City till you know you are there. Two days. Follow the path I have told you to follow. Into the mountains. Stay there until you find what you will find. Then you will return. Two days again. You will tell me what you have found. What you have learned."

Impatiently, eager to start, Ben spoke again, repeating himself. "I am ready grandfather. I will be careful. I will stay away from danger. I will stay to myself, away from other people. I will go now."

Ben climbed down a second ladder on the outside of the kiva into the street. His mother met him at the base of the ladder. "You have everything you need," she stated, checking her son. He wore only a traditional leather loin cloth and moccasins. A woven strap hung across his chest holding a leather pouch on his hip. A second strap with a water-filled gourd crossed his chest from the other shoulder. "Henry has prepared you. Go now. You will be changed when you return. Your world will be different. You will come back to us a man."

She put her hands on his shoulders for a moment and looked quietly at her son. Then she moved aside to let him start his journey. Ben said nothing, looking back solemnly at his mother. He started on his way, walking slowly down the middle of the street, heading west, away from the sun. Silhouetted against the early light on the roofs of the pueblos he could see people from his clan and his family. Some stood silently in the street, watching as he walked past.

When he came to the edge of the mesa he began to climb down the trail through the cleft in the rocks, using the ancient handholds and stairs that had been cut into the rock by his ancestors. Though it was steep, and the stairs were slick with dust and the slight dampness of dawn, he felt safe. He had been down this trail many times, and the climb was easy for him. Step by step, hand after hand, he climbed down through the rock, following the well-worn path.

The trail brought Ben out of the tumble of rocks at the base of the mesa onto the floor of the desert. He turned to his right and began to trot, moving past the columns of red rock that rimmed the edge of Acoma. He circled past the north end of the mesa and looked across the desert to Katzimo, the Enchanted Mesa, where his people had first settled generations ago. Katzimo was forbidden, a bad place where many people had died, according to the legends. Ben turned away from Katzimo and continued to run around the base of Acoma. He took one last look up at the rim of his mesa, seeing his people lined up on the edge watching his progress. Then he turned east, squinting into the sunlight, and jogged away from Acoma into the desert, toward the distant mountains and canyons.

Ben was alone. He moved smoothly and steadily. Even without a horse, he was accustomed to traveling across the desert on foot. Running was a natural, easy way to go. He was not a fast runner, though, having the thick body common to the Keres people. His progress across the desert was slow, taking most of the morning. He followed a faint trail, first passing the familiar corn fields and low rows of beans planted by his tribe. After the fields the trail moved through the cactus and scrub, the sand and the rock of the desert. It was a path used for centuries by other Indians, and by antelope and rabbits. The heat of the sun wore down on him. The gourd and the pouch hanging across his shoulders bounced against his hips as he ran. His shoes, made of antelope leather, protected his feet from the hot sand and rocks. But there was no escape from the heat or the sun.

By early afternoon, Ben was in the canyons and slopes of the hills east of Acoma. This was new country for him, but looking back he could still see his mesa in the desert haze. He was too far away now to see the small rock-colored houses that lined the rim. He had never been so far from home. But he was not concerned. The path was exactly as Henry had described it to him. He found the stream where Henry had told him to look, and he paused, kneeling to wash the dust and the salt off his face and his young torso. Then he took a long drink of the cold water and refilled the gourd. When he was full, he stood and began to move again toward the east. He reached into the pouch and found a strip of dried meat, kept separate from the pollen and other spiritual tokens. He took the meat out, bit off a piece and chewed, walking now.

Ben had followed the trail out of the canyons onto the eastern side of the hills by nightfall. He found a small rock shelter, abandoned for years by those who had built it. Henry had told him about it. When he was a boy, Henry had told him, he had stayed here on his own journey to become a man. It was special and would be a safe place to spend the night, free of snakes and sheltered from mountain bears and other predators. Ben crawled in, ate some more of the dried meat, and fell asleep, exhausted.

Sunlight woke him at dawn. He found pinon nuts by a stream in a canyon near the shelter and paused long enough to eat and drink before he started on his way again.

Late in the morning Ben came to a shallow river. As he had done at the stream on the first day, Ben stopped, bathed, drank the water, and filled the gourd. But unlike the cold mountain water he had found in the stream, this water was warm and sour. Hot as he was the water still refreshed him. He splashed across the river, waist high at the deepest point. Then he continued on his way relentlessly moving east, as his people had done for so many generations. Following the way that Henry had told him to follow.

He was alone in the wide space of the desert. Around Ben were the rocks and sand, red, yellow, tan, sometimes black. Whenever he saw white rock or clay he thought of Acoma, of the white rocks there, and the white clay the women used for their pots. The desert was dotted with sage. Washed out gullies sheltered trees, waiting for rain. Canyons opened from time to time to his north, cool with shade, but Ben continued to follow the trail, passing the mouths of the canyons. Above was a vast expanse of blue sky. Now the sky began to fill slowly with billows of pure white clouds. If he were fortunate, Ben thought, there would be rain in the afternoon, cooling him and giving him fresh water to drink.

Ben came to a paved road. He climbed the slight grade up to the black, lava-like surface and looked first to the south, then to the north. Far away in the north, toward Albuquerque, he saw the shimmer of a car. Ben had never been to Albuquerque or to any American town. And he had only seen a few cars, driven by the scientists and tourists who came to visit Acoma. Those people had seemed kind and good, mostly just curious about the mesa, the pueblos, and the Keres people. But he remembered Henry's warning. *We are the Keres people. We are peaceful. The Americans have their war and the Navajo go to fight with them. We are a people of peace, but we live in a world surrounded by the dangers of these people. Be careful.*

Quickly, Ben slid back down the bank and hid in the brush near the road. The car came closer, its tires humming on the road, its engine growling like a strange, mythical animal. It roared past, above Ben on the road, hurrying south to towns Ben had never heard of. San Antonio, Carrizozo, and Alamogordo. He watched through the bushes. The black fenders were humped like the haunches of a big cat waiting to pounce on its prey.

When the car was gone and out of sight, Ben climbed back to the road, ran across, and hurried on his way toward the Manzano Mountains. The peaks were clear for him to see now. And they were shrouded with thunderclouds. Beneath the clouds, as he watched, a veil of rain fell, darkening the distant slope of the mountain. He could see lightning flash inside the cloud, but also a double rainbow in the rain beneath the thunderhead. A cool breeze blew past Ben. He moved on, trotting toward the mountain range.

By late afternoon, when he reached the first low slopes of the mountain, the storm had moved on to the south. The ground was still wet, and pools that had gathered in low spots gave him fresh water to drink. Thunder rumbled on the slopes above him as he climbed, following Henry's directions toward the southern-most peak.

At dusk, he was on a rock ledge near the top of the mountain. Beneath him to the south was the spread of a new desert. This desert was sandy and barren, nearly devoid of the vegetation and life found in the desert around Acoma. As empty as the space beneath him was, the black rock ledge above where Ben rested was covered with clusters of petroglyphs. The peak had been visited for centuries by his ancestors on their journeys. Each had left a testimony on the rock to the experience that had come to them at this special place. There were pictures of animals and of spirits; designs that he understood and some old ones that he had never seen before. He wondered what Henry had drawn when he was here; what he had seen that he felt compelled to record.

A new thunderstorm blew up around him. In moments, he was soaked by the rain. He shook for a moment, chilled by the wind, but it left him refreshed after his two-day trip across the hot desert. Hunger and fatigue remained. He had finished the last of the meat shortly after crossing the road and was weary from the miles he had traveled. He drank some of the cold rainwater that gathered in the rocks and sat back to wait for night to fall. Tonight, he would not sleep. Tonight, he would learn what he had come to find.

For hours he sat alone in the dark on the ledge, watching thunderstorms pass across the desert in front of him. Lightning flashed, illuminating the clouds and the desert and mountains. Breezes blew through the pinon trees near him, shaking their branches, dropping nuts on the ground around him. Hungry as he was, he couldn't eat them. Not yet. The nuts would still be there later, for sustenance on his trip homeward.

Late at night, dizzy from hunger and lack of sleep, as dawn began to streak the horizon to his left, Ben became aware of a squirrel. The squirrel hopped cautiously across the rock and sat next to Ben's foot. Then it turned and looked with Ben out across the sand desert to their south.

"Be aware," the squirrel said. Ben heard it speak, even though he knew it was only in his mind. "Tonight, you will see something you have never seen before, Ben." The squirrel did not call him Ben, but used his spiritual name; the name known only to Henry and to Ben's mother.

What is it? Ben thought. *What will I see?*

"Wait. Watch. You will see it. It will change you, and it will change the world. Nothing will ever be the same for any of us."

What should I do when I see it? thought Ben.

"Be wary," answered the squirrel. "There is nothing you can do about it."

"Will it be good? Will it be evil? Will it hurt me?"

"Beware. It is about to happen. Be careful, Ben. And then go away from here. Quickly. Start as soon as it's over. Go back to Acoma. You will be safe there at Acoma."

The squirrel sat quietly now, watching the desert with Ben. Waiting.

Out on the horizon, across the desert to the south a brilliant white light flashed, illuminating the crags of the rocks around Ben and the squirrel. Moments later they heard a deep, sustained howling roar. The ground beneath them shook. A pressure wave of hot air rushed past them, turning the pinons, swaying them more than any thunderstorm could have. Then it was gone, and for a few moments everything was still again. Ben saw a cloud growing on the horizon. Unlike the thunderheads he had watched throughout the night, this cloud rose rapidly upward, swelling, tumbling within itself. Flashes like lightning were within the cloud, but these were brightly colored, golden, purple, violet, grey and blue. The freak cloud remained for several minutes, rising still. Then it began to dissipate, dispersed in four directions by winds.

"Now you know," said the squirrel. "Now go. Back to Acoma where you are safe. This is a bad place now. This place is evil worse than Katzimo. Only a few people died at Katzimo. Trapped by a storm and starved on the rock. This is very bad. Many people will die because of this. Go back to Acoma where you are safe."

Ben stood slowly, stiff after the long night of sitting. He looked down and then around for the squirrel, but it was gone. It was time. He knew the ritual. Henry had told him what he should do now. He reached into his pouch and found a sharp obsidian blade, sheathed in leather. He exposed the blade and began to scratch in an empty space on the face of the black rock behind him. First, he drew the squirrel, in the traditional way his people had drawn animals for generations. Then he added a second drawing. He was supposed to only create one drawing, but he felt compelled to show what he had seen. He drew a flat line representing the desert. Above the line he scratched a circle. And more circles within the first circle, each smaller than the last, till there was just a dot at the center. That was the hot, multi-colored cloud he had seen.

Finished, he sheathed his blade, scooped some nuts from the ground for the trip back to Acoma, and began his descent from the mountain. Early light showed the way but he moved slowly, picking his footing carefully on the unfamiliar trail. He stayed away from low brush and rocks where snakes might be. The squirrel could be right that this was a dangerous place for him now. He must hurry away and get back to the safety of Acoma.

By daylight, he was into the desert again and running west. From time to time he slowed to a walk and ate some nuts. But he kept moving, always hurrying back to Acoma.

Before noon he arrived back at the paved road. Yesterday, there had been only the one car rushing by, going from Albuquerque toward Alamogordo. Now the road was busy with car after car, some going north, others south. He waited, hidden in the brush, for a long time. But every time he ventured up the bank to the road, he saw a car somewhere, coming toward him, and he would slip back into the gully to hide. Finally, there came a time when Ben got up to the road and saw no cars near him. He rushed across the road and kept running, following the trail into the safety of the desert.

Ben crossed the warm river again and continued moving west. The trail was hard to follow in spots, but looking carefully he could see his own footprints from the day before, sometimes washed out by rain, but still visible to him. Late in the afternoon Ben found the shelter where he had spent the first night. He thought for a moment of passing the shelter, running through the night to get home by dawn. He was desperate to see Henry and his family again. But his journey was supposed to last four days. He had to stop and wait for tomorrow.

He ate more nuts and drank the last of the water he had carried from the river in the gourd. Then Ben lay back in the shelter and slept; the first sleep he had had since the last time he had been in the shelter. Tired as he was, he slept badly, disturbed by visions from the night before. He heard the squirrel warning him. *"Be aware! Be wary! Beware!"* He saw again the bright flash, heard the roar, felt the ground shake and the hot wind rushing past. He saw the strange-colored cloud swelling and rising in front of him. And the squirrel again, advising him. *"There is nothing you can do about it. Go back to Acoma. You will be safe at Acoma."*

Ben woke finally before dawn and left the shelter for the final part of his trip. He moved quickly now, pulled by a need to get home, to see Henry and his mother. He paused only briefly at the stream for water and pressed on to the west. He was out of the hills by mid-afternoon and able to see the mesa with his home in the distance. He tried to keep running but was too tired and slowed to a walk, sustained by the thought that his family and clan would be waiting, watching for him from the eastern edge of the mesa rim.

They were. But small as Ben was, and with his body being the color of the rocks and the desert itself, he was nearly home before they noticed his movement along the trail. When they were sure he was coming, they spread the word throughout Acoma. People gathered in the streets and on the roof tops to see him arrive. His mother sat at the top of the climb through the rock cleft to meet him there. Henry went to the roof of the kiva to wait.

Ben turned left at the base of Acoma and circled the mesa on the southern side, completing his journey by finishing the circuit around Acoma. Then he began the climb up the steep trail through the rocks. He knew every step, every handhold, but it was hard for him now, fatigued, hungry, and thirsty.

Ben heard his mother before he saw her. "Welcome home! My son is now a man." She touched him briefly on the top of the head, the shoulders, the body and the hips as he emerged from the crest of the trail onto the top of the mesa. Then she followed behind Ben as he walked down the street to his kiva. Without looking back or saying a word to his mother Ben climbed the ladder to the roof and followed Henry down the second ladder into the kiva.

They sat together facing each other in the darkness. Only a small, smoky fire lit the curved rock walls. Henry gave Ben a bowl of water, some bread and a stew with meat mixed together with beans and corn. Ben drank and began to eat, gobbling the food after so long with nothing but nuts and dried meat.

"Slowly, Ben," Henry cautioned. "There is time. Your body will take back to the food and water slowly." Ben began to eat more slowly. He still had not spoken. The two men sat in silence while Ben ate.

Finally, when the food was finished, Henry began. "Tell me of your journey. What did you see? What happened?"

Ben started at the mountain. The travel to get there was less important. "There was a squirrel. He came and sat with me, and we talked."

Henry sat quietly, contemplating Ben's statement. Ben waited for Henry's guidance.

"Yes," Henry answered. "What did the squirrel say to you?"

"He warned me of what was to come. And then it happened."

"What did he warn you about? What happened?"

"There was noise. Louder than anything I've ever heard. And wind and heat. The ground shook. And there was a beautiful cloud. A round cloud of many colors appeared. It frightened me, but it was very beautiful."

Henry sat again in silence. He thought about what Ben had seen before he spoke again. "Then what happened? What did you do?"

"When it was over, I took my knife and I drew the squirrel on the rock."

"That is good."

"And then I drew the beautiful cloud."

"You drew the squirrel. And then you drew the cloud? You are to draw only the one vision. Not two. You know that." Henry's tone showed his concern. Maybe even anger.

"Yes, grandfather. I should have drawn the squirrel. But the cloud. It was special. I had to draw that, too. I am sorry. Was it wrong to draw the cloud?"

Henry sat quietly again, looking into the darkness of the room. Ben waited. When he had made some sense of it, Henry replied, "It is not what we have done. It is not what we are to do. But now it is done. It cannot be undone. We will see what it means."

The two men sat in silence, thinking about it. After some time, Henry spoke again, probing, questioning. "You were safe on the journey home?"

"Yes. Many cars were on the road, but I was safe. They didn't see me."

"That is good."

"I was so tired at the end. I kept thinking about the cars. If I had a car, like the Americans, I could make a journey like what I did and not be so tired."

"It is not what we do. The Keres people have always traveled the way you have done. We can ride horses, too. But not for this. For your journey there is only one way. Traveling alone. No horse. No car."

"But grandfather. I could go so much farther if I had a car."

"It is not done. Our ways are what we do. They keep us the way we are. They keep us safe. Our ways are good. You were to go to the mountain. You did that. You were to spend your night there. You did that too. You came back. A car was not needed for that."

The two men sat together in silence in the darkness of the kiva. At last Henry spoke. "You are not the child who left us four days ago. Your world is now not the same. You are a man. You are one of the Keres people. You will do what you must in your new life as a Keres man. You will follow our way."

SUMMER, 2006

Ben sat waiting on a plastic chair at the table in the truck stop off Interstate 40 west of Albuquerque. Country music played. Across the fresh-paved parking lot was the tented roof of the casino. In front of Ben, on the table, sat a red plastic tumbler, molded with a rough texture so that it looked frosted. The plastic glass was half-full of Coca-Cola and hollow cubes of ice. Ben's hair was gray and long, held in a ponytail with a piece of leather. His dark face was creased and pocked. A faded and dirty University of New Mexico baseball cap sat on the table next to his elbow. He wore a long-sleeved plaid cotton shirt and old blue jeans. A wide leather belt, cinched with a silver buckle the size of a saucer, sat below the paunch of his belly. On his wrist he had a silver bracelet with turquoise. No watch. No rings on his calloused fingers. On his feet he wore, as he always had, homemade leather moccasins.

A younger man, lean and dark haired, dressed in black pants and a black, short-sleeved shirt, banged through the door of the truck stop. A blanket of heat followed him into the air-conditioned chill. He slid onto the chair across the table from Ben. "How are you doing today, Benny?" asked the man in black.

Ben sat back in his chair and smiled wryly. *Why does he always call me Benny*, he thought. *I'm not a boy anymore. I'm an old man. Twice his age. Benny, he calls me, like I'm a child.* He paused, picking his words before he replied.

"I'm doing all right, Father. How are you doing?"

"I'm fine, thank you. What are you up to these days, Benny?"

"Working."

"That's good. A man your age, though. You've spent most of your life working. You don't really need to work anymore, do you? What are you working at?"

"A little of this. A little of that. Odd jobs. Construction. That sort of thing. Gotta keep busy you know."

"Yes, yes. Got to keep busy. Construction's hard work, though, for a man your age. Did you ever work in the nuclear business? They've got some jobs open over at Los Alamos. Basic work, not the technical engineering things. Basic maintenance work. Have you ever worked in the nuclear business, Benny? I could put a word in for you."

Ben looked out the picture window across the heat of the parking lot. Two heavy semi-trucks were pulling out, preparing to move onto the Interstate. *Nuclear business*, he thought. *I've got no need for that. I was there when it started. At the test. I saw it happen. It's bad business. I don't want anything to do with it.*

"No, I don't have much need to work right now," Ben answered, careful to keep his face placid so the priest wouldn't know too much of his thoughts. "I'm spending most of my time at Sky City these days. Acoma. It's home for me now."

A young waitress, Spanish, brought Ben's lunch, a cheeseburger and fries to go with his Coke. "Do you want anything?" she asked the priest.

"Sure. I'll have the same as my friend, Benny. Cheeseburger and Coke."

The waitress left and the priest turned his attention back to Ben. "You're still staying sober, Benny?" he asked.

"Yes. It's been years. Not a drop. I'm staying good."

Ben remembered for a moment the dark days when he was young in Albuquerque. Scavenging for food in the alleys. Fighting. Stealing. A time lost. It was another time he wanted to leave behind. He had struggled for years with the nightmares. The test he remembered as a moment of awesome beauty. But when he learned that two more bombs, just like the one he had seen, had eliminated two entire cities in Japan, he realized the true horror of what he had witnessed. He still thought of the thousands of lives that had vanished in the moments of those two bombs.

Nothing had mattered to him then when he remembered the test. He had left Acoma and gone to Albuquerque. He had found poverty and alcohol. Some mornings he woke up on the street bloody from the fights. Twice he had woken in jail. Then he remembered Henry's words to him. And what the squirrel had told him. *Go back to Acoma. You will be safe at Acoma. Follow the Keres path and you will be good.* He had returned to Acoma, and everything was good.

"How's your family?" asked the priest.

"They're good."

"What are they doing? Where are they?"

Ben thought again for a moment before he replied. *Why does he ask me so many questions? Always the questions. It's not his business. He worries about me I suppose. And my family.*

"My daughter's still in Albuquerque with her husband," Ben answered. "He's an American, but they're doing okay. Her son. My grandson. His name's Henry but people call him Hank. He's with me at Acoma this summer."

"School vacation? What's the boy doing up there all summer? Not an awful lot for a kid to do up there for a vacation."

"School's out. But it's not really a vacation. He's working with me. He's learning things."

"You're working him? Benny, he's just a kid. How old is he? Twelve? Thirteen? What's he doing? What sort of work?"

"Traditional stuff. You know. I have him with the women to see how they make the pots. I show him some things we do up there. How we make our bread. We go for walks in the desert. We hunt a little. I show him where the fields used to be and talk to him about things. Our stories. He's learning our stories."

The priest leaned forward, his elbows on the table, getting closer to Ben, making contact he hoped. "Don't go too hard on him, Benny. He's not going to live up there forever, is he?"

Ben laughed and took another bite of his cheeseburger. He daubed at his mouth with a paper napkin before he answered. "Oh, no. He'll go back with my daughter and her husband in a few weeks. He'll go back to school then. But he'll learn things this summer. Things he'll come to know that he needs to know. Things they can't teach him in a school."

"Like what?" The priest was puzzled.

"Indian things. You know. Some things I don't even know, he'll find this summer."

"Well, you take care of that boy. Henry, you say he's called? You bring him to church on Sunday, okay?"

"Sure. I go to church. He goes with me. And we have our ceremonies in a few weeks and the Festival of Saint Ann. He'll do all that with me, too. And then some other Indian things. I'm getting him ready for all of that. So don't worry, Father. I'll bring him to church on Sunday. He needs to learn about that, too."

Church is important, Ben thought. *It's a different way, a different God, maybe. But a connection with the spiritual is always a good thing to have, however you make that connection.*

The waitress brought the priest his cheeseburger and his Coke. She placed two checks on the table, one beside each of the two men. The priest reached across and pulled Ben's check over with his own. "Let me get this, Benny," he said. Ben leaned back in his chair and let it go.

"Where's your pickup, Benny? I didn't see it parked out front."

"I walked down."

"That must be ten, twelve miles. It's hot out there in the desert. Isn't your truck running?"

"I wanted a cheeseburger. So I came. Yes, my truck's okay. I just like walking. I've always walked."

"You want a ride back up? I'm heading over to McCartys when I finish lunch. It's not much out of my way."

"That would be nice. I'm getting old and the walking isn't so easy for me anymore. I've got the arthritis."

The priest ate his lunch, chatting with Ben about ordinary things. Sports. The Arizona Diamondbacks. The fall elections. He finished, paid their bills, and led the way outside into the heat. Ben followed, putting on his University of New Mexico baseball cap as he went.

They drove south, the Enchanted Mesa of Katzimo looming ahead. They passed Katzimo and stopped at the new Visitors Center at the crossroads at the base of Acoma. On the top of the mesa the houses were hardly visible, blending into the terrain and the rocks. It looked exactly the same as it had for centuries. Ben got out but paused for a moment, leaning on the open door of the priest's truck.

"Thanks for the lift, Father," he said.

"Not a problem, Benny. You've got everything you need up there? Food? Water?"

"We're all good. Plenty of food. Water we bring up now. The cisterns on top are getting dry, and they're dirty now. But we have what we need to have."

"You take care of yourself. Be careful. I'll see you in Saint Stephen's on Sunday. With your grandson, Henry."

"We'll be there, Father."

Ben closed the door of the priest's truck. The priest turned the corner at the crossroads in front of the Visitors Center and drove into the desert, west toward hills, toward McCartys. Ben walked the other way, returning to Acoma. As he got close to the mesa, he turned off the pavement, following the ancient trail. At last, he was at the base of the mesa. He began up the cleft in the rock, climbing, using the old steps and handholds that had been cut there by his ancestors. It was a path he had used his whole life. A path he was teaching his grandson. Henry would be waiting at the top.

LAWRENCE

I SAT ON MY FRONT porch with Leonardo waiting for Lawrence. It's what I did late each afternoon. There wasn't much else to do. I was little, not yet having started school. It was 1952 in a small town in Virginia. Life was simple. I didn't know much then. I had a lot to learn.

I did know that Lawrence was cool. I had learned the word "cool" listening to Rod's Record Rack on the radio. Rod played Rock and Roll and said "cool" to describe any music or singer who was different or special. Cool was good. It was clear to me that Lawrence was cool.

Lawrence had a cool job, too. Two jobs, actually. He worked downtown during the day. I don't know what that downtown job was, but his cool job was stoking furnaces at dawn in houses in my neighborhood and again in all those houses in the late afternoon. He did it on his way to and from his other job each day. Sometimes in the morning I could hear him through the floor beneath my bedroom. I would wake up at sunrise, and hear the basement door open. Then the furnace door clanked and Lawrence shook down the grate to sift out the pieces of burnt coal. "Clinkers," he called them. Next, the crunch of his shovel digging fresh coal sounded and there was a rattle as he threw it into the furnace. Finally, I would hear and feel a thump when he closed and latched the basement door as he left.

I got to help when he did our furnace in the afternoon.

Now I sat, waiting on the porch with Leonardo so I could help Lawrence with the furnace on his way home. The bus stopped. When a bus came from downtown, he off and started to walk slowly toward our house. He came up our front walk and sat on the step next to Leonardo like he did every afternoon. He scratched Leonardo on the head. The cat purred and arched his back. Lawrence stretched for a moment as well and ran his hands over his gray hair. His long legs reached down two steps to the sidewalk. He wore heavy work boots, rough black rawhide leather polished smooth with wear over the hard-capped toes. White dust from his other job lined the creases.

"How are you, Young Man?" Lawrence asked. He always called me "Young Man," and it made me feel very grown up.

"I'm fine, Lawrence," I answered politely. Manners mattered, I had been told. "How are you?"

"I'm tired. Work gets hard when it's hot in the summertime. What were you up to today, Young Man?"

"Dale and I built a fort out back in the woods. We piled branches up to make walls. It's huge, Lawrence. We got the walls so high we can hardly see over the top!"

"A fort, huh? Well, that's fine. If we get attacked by the Russians, or the Chinese, or maybe Koreans, I know I'll be safe with you and Dale down there in your fort protecting the city."

"What are Rush Ins?" I asked. I only knew my small town and the people who lived nearby. I hadn't yet learned to be afraid of anyone.

"They're bad people who live far away," Lawrence answered.

"Are they going to attack us?" Suddenly I was a little scared.

"Only if there's a war, and I don't think we're going to have another war. At least not here."

"Were you ever in a war, Lawrence?"

"Yes. Years ago. But that's all over now."

"Wow! That's cool Lawrence. You were a soldier!"

"War's not cool. It's bad stuff. But don't you worry about that, Young Man. You've got no reason to worry about a war. At least not now. Hey, we're wasting time here. What do you say you and Leonardo come and help me take care of that furnace?"

We got up and walked around back to the basement door. Lawrence opened it and stooped to enter the dark basement. The basement was cold and the dirt floor filled the low space with a damp smell. Against the far wall was the furnace, hot, with fire glowing around its door. The coal was piled nearby. Lawrence walked over to it, ducking his head under each of the rafters. Leonardo and I followed but stopped a few feet back and sat on the floor.

"You stay right there while I work," cautioned Lawrence. Sometimes, after he finished, Lawrence would let me get closer and throw a chunk of coal into the open furnace. But most days Leonardo and I stayed away and watched.

Lawrence took a shovel and tipped the latch on the furnace door to pull it open. Heat rushed out. The furnace roared. Yellow flames and coals glowed white and red, the colors shifting as cool air rushed in. Lawrence took a metal poker, hooked it on the grate below the coals, and shook it. Clinkers fell out, and he shoveled them up and put them on a pile beside the furnace.

Some days Lawrence would save a nice clinker for me. They were glassy and dark, with rainbows of color on them. I had a collection of them in my room. Lawrence shoveled in a load of fresh coal to finish his job. Then he closed the furnace door and we were ready to go.

Outside, he straightened and groaned. "Man. This work is hard on my back. When you grow up, Young Man, you don't want a job like this."

"Yes, I do. It's a cool job."

"It's a hot job," he chuckled.

He put his hand on top of my crew-cut head and said, "Weekend's coming, Young Man. I'll see you on Monday. You be good, now." He walked off down the street to take care of other furnaces in other houses before he went home.

At supper that night my mother said to me, "School starts in a few days. We're going to have to buy you some new shoes. I talked to Dale's mom, and she and Dale will be coming with us tomorrow morning when we go downtown to shop for shoes."

We didn't go downtown often, but when we did, we rode the bus, just like Lawrence. It was an adventure to ride the bus downtown.

The next morning Dale and his mom stopped by, and we went out to the bus stop. When the bus came we got on and my mother and Dale's mom dropped coins into a big glass box that stood on a post next to the driver. There were two of the glass boxes. One was at the front with the driver. The other was halfway back by another door that opened in the middle of the bus. People got on at either door. They dropped their money into the boxes. I watched the coins sliding and rattling in the glass boxes as we rode along. They were like the jar of pennies my father kept on his dresser, only much bigger. And there were two of them. I thought they looked like pirate treasure, or maybe a king's. The bus driver was cool. He got to drive a bus and collect all that money. I was sure he was rich.

When we got downtown, we got off and walked along the sidewalk. My mother held my hand, squeezing it so I wouldn't get lost in the crowd. We went into Leggett's department store. Glass cases, higher than my head, lined the aisle on both sides. I smelled perfume and popcorn. We turned a corner and were in the shoe department. A man made me stand in my socks on a metal rule to measure my feet. He went away and came back with a pair of shiny leather shoes in a box. I put aside my summer shoes, dirty, soft canvas sneakers and put on the new school shoes. They were stiff and they cut my ankles. But they were cool. Black and shiny with hard new laces. I stomped around the wooden floor of the store while Dale tried on his new shoes. When my mother asked me if they fit, I told her, "Yes." I loved everything about them. I asked if I could wear them home.

"All right," my mother replied. "But don't scuff them or get them dirty. You want to look nice when you start school."

The salesman put my old sneakers in the shoebox and did the same for Dale's. Then we headed back to the bus stop for the ride home. Dale and I carried our shoeboxes and walked carefully in our new shoes to keep them nice. The new soles were slick on the concrete.

The bus came and we climbed on. *Lawrence gets to ride the bus every day*, I thought. I watched the people getting on at each stop through the two doors and dropping their money into the glass boxes. And then, there he was! Lawrence got on at the middle door, put his money in the box and went to sit down.

"Lawrence!" I called out. "Lawrence! Look at my new shoes!" I jumped down from my seat and ran back to show him the shoes. I sat down next to him and put my foot up in his lap. "Look how cool they are."

Things began to happen. Lawrence said nothing and looked away from me out the window. The bus driver pulled to the curb, stopped the bus and turned to stare at me. My mother came back and dragged me up to the seat next to her. At last, the bus driver started the bus again. Nobody said a word the rest of the way home. When we got home Dale's mom and my mother went in the house, leaving Dale and me out front on the lawn.

"What happened on the bus, Dale? Why did everyone get upset when I went to see my friend Lawrence?"

"He's not your friend," Dale answered. "He's a nigger."

"What's a nigger?"

"Niggers are bad people," said Dale. "You don't want to have anything to do with them."

It seemed like Dale and I had talked about everything at other times. But not this. I had never seen him like this. I needed to explain to him about Lawrence. I needed to make him understand.

"Lawrence isn't bad. He's good. He's cool. He's my friend."

"He's a nigger! He's bad! They all are! They want to marry your daughter!" Dale shouted at me.

"That's crazy. I don't have a daughter. I'm not even married. How can I have a daughter when I'm not even married?"

Dale was red now. A flush crossed his face and went up under his blond crew cut. A bit of spit foamed at the corner of his mouth.

"It's not crazy! You're crazy," he screamed. "He's a bad man and you better stay away from him if you know what's good for you. They're all bad! And dirty! And smelly! And they all carry knives. I know about this stuff. And you don't know anything if you like him. They're nothing but trouble. My dad told me all about them. Lawrence is a nigger, so he's bad. That's all there is to it."

I tried again to make him see that Lawrence was good, but Dale wasn't listening. He pushed me and started calling me names I'd never heard before. Then we were fighting, rolling on the lawn. Our mothers pulled us apart, and Dale's mom took him home.

"Look at your new shoes," my mother said. "Let's see if we can clean them up so you'll still look nice on your first day of school."

I took off the shoes and handed them to her. I stood in my socks on the cold linoleum floor in the kitchen and watched while she worked at the sink, sponging the dirt off my new shoes. "Why did everyone get upset when I went to see Lawrence, Mother? What's a nigger? Dale said that Lawrence is a nigger."

"It's pretty complicated," she answered. "And it's wrong. But it's the way things are. And please don't use that word again. It's a bad word."

"What word, Mother?"

"You know. The word Dale used for Lawrence."

"But Mother. Dale used it. And he told me all sorts of bad things about Lawrence. But he doesn't even know Lawrence. Lawrence isn't a bad man is he, Mother?" I started to cry again.

She carefully swabbed the shoes, her back turned to me, not wanting to look at me, concentrating on the shoes. "No, Lawrence isn't a bad man. But some people think he is. Maybe they're wrong, but you can't change that. It's just the way things are.

"What you need to do is think about getting ready for the start of school," she continued, brightening. She put my clean shoes on the counter beside the sink and turned, bent down, and hugged me. "This is such an exciting time for you! You'll learn a lot in school. You've got so much you can learn. And there's so much you will be able to do some day when you've been to school. Don't let things like this get in the way of all the wonderful things you can do when you grow up. It doesn't have to be so complicated. Just go to school. And read. Everything you need to know is in the books. You'll understand better when you've been to school."

It was Monday afternoon. Leonardo and I were on the porch again, waiting for Lawrence. And waiting for answers to questions I didn't even know. I needed to understand. Lawrence would have the answers for me.

The bus came, and Lawrence walked up to the porch. He sat down, patted Leonardo the way he always had, but said nothing. He hunched forward, his boots one step below us, his knees drawn up so he could rest his arms across them. He watched the traffic passing by on Rivermont Avenue. Leonardo purred and rubbed against his leg. For the cat, nothing was different.

"What happened on the bus, Lawrence?"

He sat quietly for a moment, still watching the cars on the street. "The world's a pretty mixed up place," he replied. "I can't explain it. Chile, there are some things I wish you don't need to ever know. And this is one of them."

"Child." He called me "Child." Not Young Man. Things weren't right anymore.

"I don't understand, Lawrence. What happened? Why can't you tell me?"

"There's a lot you don't understand. I hope some of it you never do understand. You and me, we're not alike. We're different. When you get older, you'll go off and get a good job. Not like this furnace thing. This is just what I do. This and a job downtown that's no better. I break my back every day to make a few bucks. You'll do much better. You're a good boy. A good kid. And we've had some fun working on that furnace down there together. But you have so much ahead of you. You'll do fine."

There was so much certainty in the way he said it. But I still didn't understand. Understanding would take time. We sat there a while longer without talking. Finally, we got up and went down to stoke the furnace. Neither of us said anything. When he finished, we came back up to the front of the house and Lawrence stopped. He put his big hand on top of my head. "Now you take good care of yourself, Young Man. And you take good care of Leonardo. And your mama and your daddy, too. You'll grow up to be a fine man some day."

I reached over and hugged him, squeezing his legs, thin inside his coveralls. He reached down and hugged me back for a moment. When I let go, he stepped back. Then he turned his head so I couldn't see his face and walked away.

"Goodbye, Young Man," he said.

"Goodbye, Lawrence."

I went back to the porch and sat on the steps. Leonardo came and rubbed up against me and purred. He was still there, still my friend. I could still count on Leonardo. I wasn't so sure about either Dale or Lawrence. And I still didn't know what a nigger was.

I began to learn all sorts of new things when Dale and I started school together a few days later. We still played together, but we never spoke about our fight. Still, it was always in my mind, and a new distance grew between us. Lawrence kept coming to our house each day and stoking our furnace. I talked with Lawrence whenever I saw him, but I never went down to work on the furnace with him again.

That part of my life was gone.

ANNA

EVENING SUMMER SUN SIFTED THROUGH maple foliage and slanted through the hospital windows casting shadows. Through the trees I could see the rooftops of the old tenements and mills in the city of Manchester down the hill. These days the work in the mills was mostly gone, and they were now filled with high-priced condos and offices of tech start-ups. People still lived in the tenements.

"Today will be a long day for you, John," Dr. Endicott stated. "You've been on since morning, and you're scheduled to be here till dawn." Around us nurses in pastel scrubs carried trays to their tables to rush through early dinners. Families of patients, some of them visibly anxious, ate together as well.

Dr. Endicott was my advisor, the legendary chief of OB-GYN at the hospital, and I was privileged to be able to work with him. W. Homer Endicott III, son of a doctor, the current heir in a long line of Endicott doctors. Endicotts had been practicing medicine in New England for more than a hundred years. Homer was in his sixties, nearing retirement. He had started at the hospital in the prime of his career, more than twenty years ago. I could not have found a better, more experienced doctor to be my mentor.

Dr. Endicott leaned forward over the table and paused, looking at me over half glasses with mild concern, assessing my fatigue and my ability to work through the night. "You should be all right," he added, nodding. "What do you plan to do tonight?"

"I'll check on our patients, and discuss their postpartum status with them. Then I'll catch up on my charts and notes and records when things get slow later. Are we expecting anyone else to deliver tonight?" We had three new mothers in the hospital. One had delivered by C-section a day ago while I observed. Together, Dr. Endicott and I had delivered the other two during the morning. Both were standard births with no complications. They were scheduled to be discharged tomorrow. I would see that they were ready.

"No, not that I'm aware of," Dr. Endicott replied. "You've been here a while now, John. You're ready. You can handle a delivery by yourself. But call me if anyone comes in. I'd like to know. And tell me to come right in if anything unusual starts to happen. I can observe you on the standard cases, and you can help me with anything tricky. I should still take care of the difficult cases while you observe and assist."

"Fine, Dr. Endicott. I'll call if anything should come up. But I should be all right. It's slow tonight."

"Please, call me Homer. Now make sure you get some rest. You look tired. You need to be on top of your game with a delivery. You can't let the fatigue get the better of you. It's okay to nap a bit if it's late and you become sleepy and nothing is happening. Just keep your phone and your beeper turned on so the nurses can call you. Find an empty room here in the hospital to rest, and you should plan on doing your charts and paperwork here in the hospital as well. That way you'll be close to our patients if they should need you."

"But my office is over across the hospital parking lot in Harrison House. I can probably work best over there. It'll be quiet and it's only a minute away."

"Too quiet, maybe, over there. Consider staying here in the main building. But remember it's okay to get your rest while you're here on third shift."

"I'll do it if I need to, Dr. Endicott. Homer. But I'm fine. And I have a lot of paperwork to dig through. I can do that in my sleep, but it's got to be done. Tonight will be a good time to get it out of the way."

He patted me on the arm, a touch of friendship, and left for the evening.

"Too quiet maybe," he had said. Words I would remember later that night.

I had been told that life is different at night. During the day, when most people are awake and working, night shift residents are home asleep. When the rest of the world is sleeping, the night shift is out, going about their business. It is living upside down and inside out. That was Anna. She was not like any patient I had ever worked with. I am relieved to say that I have never had a patient like her since that time, either.

That first night began according to schedule. Nothing seemed the least bit out of the ordinary as nightfall arrived. After Dr. Endicott left, I headed down to Maternity. It was still visiting hours, so husbands and families were in the rooms with my patients. I made a quick tour of the floor, more to talk with the families than to check on the mothers. Then I hung around the nurses' station to wait for the end of visiting hours.

The nurses loved to talk with me. They knew that I struggled to maintain my relationship with my girlfriend, Sara. Her job had taken her to New York and we only saw each other once or twice a month. The nurses all knew about it; it's hard to keep secrets working as closely together as we did. So the single nurses flirted with me, and the married ones tried to fix me up with their friends. I enjoyed the attention and looked forward to spending my time at the nurses' station. But I couldn't imagine leaving Sara. Our relationship was difficult, but I remained committed to her and none of the nurses seemed right for me.

Three hundred miles. That's how far away Sara was from me. I worked at the hospital in New Hampshire. She lived in New York. It's never easy being separated from loved ones, whether by distance or by time. How great that distance or the time might be, what it finally comes down to is that you can't be with the one that you love. It helps that there are the day-to-day distractions of a job or of life itself, but there is always loneliness. There is a sense of being apart and of needing to be together.

When visiting hours ended the families left, leaving the mothers and babies behind. I checked on the new mothers again, spending more time with each of them than on my earlier visits. Then, a little after eleven, I turned on my beeper, picked up a large coffee in a paper cup from the cafeteria, gathered my charts, and headed across the parking lot to my office in Harrison House.

Mary Harrison House was built before the turn of the century with money from the Harrison family. The Harrisons had become one of the wealthiest families in New Hampshire with the profits from their textile mills in Manchester. Harrison House was only one of many buildings they had built for the city. For years it served as a dormitory for students in the hospital's Nursing College. I didn't know if Mary Harrison was the wife of the benefactor, or a daughter, or one of the early nursing students. A new nurses' residence hall was built in the late fifties over at the college and Harrison House had become overflow office space for the hospital.

The building was a three-story brick structure with a slate roof. Seven brownstone stairs led to a columned porch at the front door. Through a modern aluminum storm door and the old, oak-paneled main door were three more steps up into a center lobby. Halls ran off to the left and right of the lobby with four offices at both ends of the building; two on each side of each hall. A center staircase went up from the lobby to a landing, turned and continued to the second floor. There were eight more offices on the second floor, again off of halls running to each side of the lobby. The stairway continued up to the third floor. There were only four offices on the third floor clustered under the eaves. My office was at the end of the hall on the first floor, on the corner. My windows looked out across the parking lot to the Emergency Room entrance and the Security station.

I locked myself in the building, walked in the dark to my office, unlocked my door, and turned on the lights. The house was dead silent. I turned on my radio for company, peeled the top open on my coffee, and settled in with my charts for the night. I was alone in the building. I missed Sara. I pushed the charts to the side of my desk top and called her.

Her sleepy voice answered. "Hello?"

"Hi Sara. It's John. Sorry to call you so late, but I'm on nights now, and I just got free." I usually called her earlier in the evening, and I guessed that I had woken her.

"I just got to bed, John. So how's it going?"

"Uneventful so far. I did my rounds and now I'm in my office with a stack of paperwork. Unless I get called, I'll be stuck here till dawn when Dr. Endicott comes back in."

"Sounds like fun," Sara said, a touch of sarcasm in her sleepy voice.

"Not much," I answered. I felt the emptiness of the building around me. I wondered if that was why I felt her absence as much as I did at that moment. "I wish you could be here to brighten it up for me. To talk with you just for a moment. Who knows what kinds of mischief we might get into all alone here in a dark, empty office building? How was your day?"

"Uneventful as well. Just another day at the office. Yes, I miss you too, John. Maybe some night I'll drive up there and surprise you in that office of yours."

"That would be nice. Do it. Just come on up to New Hampshire and join me here."

We talked for a few more minutes; just casual chatter about the events of the day. She was tired, and I had to get started on my charts.

"Well, you sound tired," I said, trying to keep my tone upbeat. "I'll let you get to sleep. Is it okay for me to call you this late? I'll be working this shift for a few weeks."

"Yes, call me anytime. Earlier if you can. It's almost midnight. Just talk to me. Let me know how you're doing. I miss you."

"Me too, Sara. Good night. I love you."

I hung up and looked at the stack of patient charts. Outside in the parking lot an ambulance pulled into the Emergency entrance. I used the diversion to procrastinate; anything to do before digging into the boredom of charting. I watched as nurses, men and women in scrubs, rushed to the ambulance. They pulled a stretcher from the ambulance, the hump of a body strapped to it. One of the nurses began CPR, pumping the chest of the body on the stretcher as they ran with it back into the hospital. When they were gone the ambulance drove slowly back through the parking lot toward the driveway. The distraction past, I began the tedious work of documenting my patients in the charts.

Sometime after midnight I heard the footsteps for the first time. At first, I thought they might just be the noise of old plumbing; there were bathrooms on each floor at the end of each hall. I stepped out of my office and listened at the open bathroom door, but it was silent. Then I heard the footsteps again. Regular. One step, then another step, then another echoing above me. There was no doubt that they were footsteps. The steps moved along the second-floor hall above my head, paused, and started down the stairs.

A chill of fear coursed through me and my ears roared as adrenaline rushed through my body. I was alone in the building late at night with an intruder. You never know what to expect. I thought of calling Security, but found the courage to check it out myself first. I switched on the hall lights and walked to the base of the stairs. The footsteps stopped, and when I got to the staircase, no one was there. So I returned to my office and started again with my work. But I left the lights on in the hall and the stairway.

"Mice," I said to myself. "Probably just mice. It's an old building. Old buildings make noises. Nobody was there."

A few minutes later, I heard them again. I listened carefully, sitting so still I could feel my heart beating. Definitely footsteps. And again, they were in the second-floor hall and coming down the stairs. Quietly, I tiptoed out my door and then ran to the stairs. I heard the footsteps hurrying back up the stairs, but the stairway was empty by the time I got there. I ran up the stairs and turned on the lights in the second-floor hall. Again, no one was there and it was deathly silent. I went up and down the halls, checking the office doors. All were locked. The bathrooms were unlocked but empty. Finally, I checked the third floor as well, but again I found nothing.

Puzzled, I returned to the first floor and my office. In my office, I dragged my chair at my desk as though I were sitting back down. Then I kicked off my shoes and slipped quietly back down the hall in my socks. I waited silently just around the corner from the stairs. I would trap the intruder.

I heard the footsteps again. They came again down the second-floor hall and started down the stairs. I waited. Then, when I heard them on the landing, only eight steps from the bottom, I leaned around the corner. My eyes met the startled, wide dark eyes of a young girl. She was perhaps twenty years old, maybe a little younger. Her hair was thick and black, and pulled back, clasped at the back of her head. She wore a stiff, starched gray dress and a white apron with a bib front, white stockings, solid white shoes and a small white cap on top of her head. She looked like a caricature of an old-fashioned nurse. Maybe, I thought, she was trying to impersonate a nurse. But nurses today dress in scrubs; light green, pink and blue, or pastel prints. They wear white Reeboks; white clogs if they work in the OR.

I started up the stairs and shouted, "What are you doing here? Who are you?"

She hitched up her skirt and ran back up the stairs. I heard her running back down the second-floor hallway. I chased after her up the stairs, but when I got to the top, the hall was empty and the doors were all still locked, the bathrooms empty.

I returned to my office and settled back into my paper work, trying to concentrate and stay awake. But my mind kept wandering back to the vision of the girl on the stairs. Why did she have the panicked look in her eyes? I wondered about her flight back up the stairs. Was she afraid of being caught by me? Why did she seem not to want to be seen? Where had she gone? I heard no more from the girl the rest of the night.

I stopped by the Security office at dawn on my way home. Armand LaBossiere, the head of Security, sat at his desk with the sports page open and a paper cup of coffee. Behind him television screens showed the hospital entrances, the main lobby, and the parking lots.

"How are you today, Armand?" I started.

"Fine, Dr. Sullivan. You're up early this morning."

"Late last night is more like it. I started my night shift rotation last night. I'm just now heading home."

"That's a tough shift. I don't know how third shift people do it," he said.

"I only have it for a few weeks. I'll adapt just in time to go back on days," I laughed.

"Better get used to it." Armand chuckled and shook his head. "Those mothers always seem to choose to come in late at night to deliver their babies. You'll spend the rest of your life here on nights dealing with babies being born."

"You're probably right." I paused, considering the wisdom of telling him about the girl. "Listen, Armand. Something happened last night over in my office in Harrison. I thought you should know."

Armand sat up a little straighter and turned toward me. Warily he asked, "Okay, what happened?" He took out a pad of paper and his pen, ready to take notes.

"I heard footsteps. And finally, I saw a girl. In a gray dress, like an old nurse's uniform."

Armand put the pen and paper away and sat back in his chair. "Do you know anything about this?" I asked, puzzled by his reaction.

"You saw a girl?" he answered skeptically. Then he turned his back on me and looked away, first checking the array of televisions then staring again at the newspaper.

"Sometimes vagrants sneak in the buildings," he explained casually, his face still averted. "All the old buildings are connected by tunnels for the steam pipes underground. Vagrants get in and move from building to building underground at night. That's probably what it was."

"No, it wasn't a vagrant. It was a clean, well-groomed young woman dressed like an old-fashioned nurse."

"You sure you saw her?" He turned away from the newspaper, swiveling in his chair to face me again.

"Yes, Armand I saw her. Now what's this all about?"

Again Armand dismissed my words. "Nothing. You probably just imagined it. You were tired. First night on third shift it happens a lot. People drift off and hallucinate or maybe fall asleep and dream. You're not used to it. It's just something you imagined."

"No. I was awake. I walked out to check on the footsteps several times, and finally I caught the girl. Surprised her. She ran off but she was real. I wasn't dreaming."

Armand put the sports page down, folded his thick arms, and sat back in his rolling chair. "Well, I guess I need to tell you then, Dr. Sullivan. You saw Mary Harrison. That's what we call the ghost who lives over there. I really wouldn't blame you if you chose not to work there at night. We used to have office cleaners go in there to work at night after everyone went home, but they all quit. That's why we clean it during the day now. And my own security guys don't want to go over there at night. People hear the footsteps, and see lights turning on and off. But you're one of the few to actually see old Mary Harrison. Let me know if you decide to stay over here in the hospital at night. It'll be safer for you."

"I don't know," I answered. I was skeptical. Armand was famous for his tall tales, and I thought he might be pulling my leg. "She may be a ghost, if you say so, but she didn't seem that dangerous last night. No blood or screams or anything. It makes me a little edgy, but that's where my office is. And she seemed more afraid of me than I was of her. I'll give it another night and see if I can survive."

"Suit yourself, doctor. But you might want to leave all the lights on and have an escape route planned just in case. And don't hesitate to call us if you get in trouble. I can't promise my men will go in that building at night, but they can at least be alerted. I'll leave a note for them. Give them the heads up."

I went home in the early sunlight and went to bed. My sleep was restless. My body wasn't used to the odd hours. No matter that I had drawn the shades; the room was still light. When I did sleep, I dreamed of Mary Harrison. I saw her pale face framed by the thick black hair. I dreamed of her frightened eyes meeting mine before she ran back up the stairs. A ghost? I couldn't accept that she was a ghost. She certainly looked real. She seemed to have as much substance as any other flesh and blood person.

That evening I met again with Dr. Endicott. We reviewed the patients, and then began a more informal chat. He talked about some of his experiences in med school and asked about Sara. I didn't mention to him my encounter with the girl in Harrison House. Time had passed and the whole experience seemed unreal, maybe a bit ridiculous. I didn't want to appear foolish with my mentor.

When Dr. Endicott went home, I set out on my rounds, following the same routine as the night before. Late at night I again picked up a coffee and went to my office in Harrison House. I called out loudly as I went down the hall to my office.

"Hello, Mary! I'm back. I'll be working here in my office again until dawn. Why don't you stop down for a visit?"

I turned all the lights on in the halls and left my office door open. But I didn't turn on the radio as I had done the night before. I didn't want its distraction, and I didn't want the music to obscure the sound of anyone moving about the house.

I heard the footsteps again only a short while after I settled in with my charts. As they had done the night before, they paced up and down the second-floor hallway. Twice they started down the stairs but stopped and went back to the second floor. I stayed at my desk with my medical records spread before me.

When I heard the footsteps on the stairs for the third time I called out, "I'm in my office. Why don't you come on down here so we can talk?"

It seemed like a bit of bravado on my part. What if it really was a desperate vagrant intruder looking for drugs or money? What if Armand was right and it was a ghost? He had told me to keep an escape route cleared, but if the ghost came to my office door I would be trapped. Only the windows would offer an escape. I was on the first floor and the windows were close to the ground. Still, what I had seen the night before looked not at all like a ghost. It was just a scared young girl. I knew I would be fine.

The footsteps ran back up the stairs after I shouted. For a time, I heard no more footsteps. I settled into the task of completing the records. One after another, I reviewed each chart, added my notes, set the chart aside, and moved on to the next.

There was movement at the corner of my eye. I looked up, and the girl stood in the doorway to my office. As the night before, she wore the archaic, starched uniform of a nurse. Her brown eyes looked into mine, and she gave a slight smile.

"Hello," she said. "I'm Anna. And you must be Dr. Sullivan."

I was startled that she already knew my name. How could she know who I was?

"Yes, I'm Dr. Sullivan, Anna. How are you this evening?"

"I'm fine."

"How did you know my name, Anna?"

"Oh, I came in one night a few weeks ago," she answered. "I saw your name on some papers on your desk. I like to know who's in the building."

She clung to the edge of my door, holding onto it as though the hall was a safe haven for her. She seemed reluctant to come into my office now that I was there. How, I wondered, had she been in my office earlier? Had I left my door unlocked?

I stood up and she pulled back slightly as though she might run off again. I dragged a second chair up to my desk and said, "Would you like to come in and have a seat? I'm almost finished with my work here, and I would enjoy your company. We can talk."

Anna smiled more warmly. "All right," she said. "I have some time, too. I would enjoy getting to know you. It's been a long time since I had someone to talk to."

I was shocked as she stepped through the door to see that, beneath the crisp nursing uniform, she was obviously very pregnant. In the eighth month at least, I guessed. She caught me looking at her thick body, blushed briefly with embarrassment, and explained.

"Yes, I'm pregnant. I guess my boyfriend and I made a mistake. Or maybe we were just careless. We're in love though, and we're going to be married. He's a medical student too, just like you. We haven't got enough money yet to get married. His family is well-to-do, but he's on his own till he finishes medical school. Unfortunately, the baby will come before we're able to get married. But he's promised me. He'll help take care of the baby, and we'll be married by this time next year."

"Well, okay," I replied, taken back by her sudden candor with me. "I'm glad to meet you. Tell me about the baby. And about the father. You say he's a med student? Do I know him?"

"No, I don't think you do. Let's just call him Bill. He's still trying to keep this a secret. Not that I'm pregnant, but that he's the father. He cares for me, but he's worried it would hurt his career if we were found out. It would be a scandal for his family and their reputation."

It occurred to me the girl might be insane. Here she was wandering a dark office building in the middle of the night, wearing an outdated nursing uniform. Maybe she really was a ghost. But a more plausible explanation would be that she was no more than some poor girl from Manchester who had gotten herself pregnant and was now sneaking away from home and hiding at the hospital trying to sort out her life and care for her unborn baby.

"So, Anna," I began. "Tell me a bit about yourself, then. Are you from Manchester?"

"Yes, my mother and father both work at the mill. They're both very proud of me for studying nursing. And they're both excited that my boyfriend is going to be a doctor."

"Do you live at home in Manchester? Where do you live, Anna?"

"My family has a house down near the mill. And my brother and sisters live there, too."

I started to think my hunch about her had been right. She was no ghost. She was just a scared teenage girl looking for some help with her pregnancy.

"Where is your house, Anna? And how do you find yourself here at night? Can I help you somehow?"

"Oh, I don't live at home now. I live here, Dr. Sullivan. In Harrison House.

It's where all of the nursing students live. It's easier for me this way. It's difficult for me to go home, being pregnant. People talk. My parents are so proud of me for studying up here at the hospital, but they're ashamed I've gotten pregnant. And the priest is always pointing his finger at me, and blaming me. It was all right when I wasn't showing, but now it's pretty obvious what's going on. It's a lot easier for me just to stay here at the Harrison House."

At that moment, we heard noise at the door to the building. Anna turned to look over her shoulder. Someone was unlocking the door and coming in. In a moment, they would be coming up the stairs from the entrance and into the hall. Before I could get out from behind my desk she had run into the hallway. When I got to my office door she was gone. The hallway was empty.

Two young security guards stomped down the hallway together, wearing their pseudo-police uniforms, toting long flashlights.

"Dr. Sullivan," one of them began. "We saw all the lights on over here. And Armand told us to look in on you tonight. Said you saw a ghost last night. I'm Sean and this is Keith."

The second guard, Keith, gave a small smile and a nervous laugh. "Yeah, he said you might have met old Mary Harrison. I don't believe in any of that shit. But when we saw all the lights on, we figured we'd stop over and see for ourselves that you're all set. So, what's happening? Any ghosts wailing, moaning, screaming, or anything?"

"Call me John," I told them. "And no, there's nothing to be scared of here. I'm fine. Why don't the two of you split up and each of you check one of the floors upstairs? If you're not afraid, that is. I'll call if I hear anything. But I'll leave the lights on just in case."

"We'll take your word that there's no need to go upstairs," Sean said. "We don't believe the old ghost story anyway. You know how Armand gets sometimes. Armand and his stories. We'll tell him we checked on you, and there's no problem."

"Thanks, guys," I said. They went back down the hall, their boots loud on the hardwood floor boards. Then they were out the door, banging it behind them.

Anna didn't return that night.

I stopped in with Armand again on my way home at dawn.

"Armand, your night guards checked on me last night. Thanks for looking out for me. But I think I was mistaken. It's just an old, creaky building. You know how they make noises. Old walls that settle and old plumbing. I don't think there's a ghost."

"Well, you're wrong on that, Dr. Sullivan. People have known about old Mary Harrison for years. As long as I've worked here, anyway. We'll keep an eye out for you. Keith and Sean are good kids. They'll watch out for you. Don't hesitate to call them if you ever need their help."

That evening I started my shift by meeting with Dr. Endicott again. He began, "How have things been for you the first two nights, John?"

"Routine so far, Dr. Endicott."

"Please, John. We're both doctors. We work together. Just call me Homer."

"Certainly, Homer. Everything has been fine these first two nights. No problems."

"Good, good. Again, let me assure you. If a patient comes in with anything unusual, anything at all that you are unfamiliar with, don't hesitate to call me in to work with you. Middle of the night, I don't care. That's what we do. Babies and women don't work a nine to five schedule, so neither do I. And neither will you. Get used to the odd hours, John. And get ready. The moon's almost full. It's not just an old wives tale that more babies are born during the full moon than during the rest of the month. C-sections we can schedule any day and any time. We take care of those during the day on our own schedule. But regular births have a time of their own. Babies decide to come whenever they want to. You can expect a bunch of mothers coming in to deliver in the next few days. They always seem to show up in the middle of the night when the moon is full."

"The hours are fine. I even slept during the day today. I'm getting used to the third shift."

"Good. I know I can depend on you for most deliveries. And I'll be here if you need to call me in."

I paused, deciding if I should tell him about Anna. "There was one thing a little unusual, maybe. Just a ghost. I think I met a ghost over at my office." I hoped Dr. Endicott wouldn't think I was crazy.

"Really!" He laughed. "You know I've heard people who've been around here for years talking about the ghost over there. Mary Harrison, right? "

"Yes, but she told me her name is Anna."

"You spoke with her? Most people just hear her moving around, or maybe see her far away through a window. You met her?"

"Yes, I guess so. Or maybe it's just some girl from town who snuck into the building for the night. It's no big deal. Have you seen her? Have you met her?"

"No, I never have. I guess I've just never been in the right place at the right time to encounter her. There was a nurse who worked with me for a while who thought she saw the ghost twice. My nurse would be getting out of the car in the parking lot first thing in the morning when she was just coming to work. She'd look up at Harrison House and see a girl in a window. She said she thought the ghost watched the doctors and nurses coming in to work, like she was looking for someone. I've just heard the stories from her and some of the old timers here. And I never knew whether or not to believe them. My father worked here briefly a long time ago, when he was just starting out as a doctor. So long ago that Harrison House was still a nursing dormitory. I asked him if he knew anything about it and he said he'd never heard about ghosts here at the hospital or over at Harrison."

I could see a look of skepticism in Dr. Endicott's eyes. Here I was trying to establish myself as a competent doctor but telling him I had seen a ghost. He seemed supportive, but what might he be thinking?

"Dr. Endicott, you've got to believe me on this. I saw the young girl over there in a nurse's uniform. I don't know for sure that she's not just some scared, pregnant teenage girl. But Armand LaBossiere told me the ghost story. Who knows? Maybe it's a ghost; maybe it's just a girl. But I did meet someone over there."

"You say your ghost is pregnant?" Homer laughed. "John, listen. I don't doubt that you met someone. But you've been working hard. Long hours. And I know you miss being with your girlfriend. And adjusting to working nights can be tough, too. It can get a little confusing at first. But if you think you saw the ghost, I believe you. I trust your judgment. You're all right alone over there at night, though?"

"Yes, Homer, I'm fine, thanks. If it's a ghost, it's harmless. Just entertaining. And like I said, it's probably just some local kid sneaking in at night. Nothing to worry about."

"I'm not worried about you or the girl or ghost or whatever it is. Just keep your eyes wide open. You're here to learn medicine, to learn all you can about delivering babies, no matter how difficult the birth may be. I'm here to help you with that, and it's going to get really busy in the next week. I need you fresh and alert, so don't let this ghost get in the way. Do your work and get your rest. Why don't you think about staying over here in the main building for the next few days? Closer to Maternity. Leave that old office building to the ghost."

Dr. Endicott left for the evening. I thought about his suggestion, but I was comfortable in my office in Harrison House. I settled into my nighttime routine. I made my rounds, picked up the charts, went to my office, and called Sara.

"Hi, John." She knew it would only be me calling that late. "How are you?"

"Hey Sara. Sorry to call so late again, but this is the first moment I've had."

"You didn't call at all last night. Is everything all right? It's not like you not to call."

"Yes, everything's fine. But I've got to tell you. I met someone last night here at my office. A girl and I've got to tell you about it."

"Oh, great! Here it comes." Sara gave a long, exasperated sigh. "I knew if I left you alone in Manchester, you'd meet someone. So, come on then. Out with it. Tell me about her."

"No, Sara. It's not like that. I think my office is haunted. I heard these footsteps the first night. And I caught a peek of someone running up the stairs, but she wasn't there when I went upstairs to check. I told Armand at Security about it the next morning. He told me that people have seen a ghost here for years. He sent two security kids over last night. They also knew about the ghost and checked on me, but they were too nervous to stick around. I actually met her last night. She's dressed like an old-fashioned nurse, and she's about eight months pregnant!"

"Oh, come on, John! That's crazy. What are you telling me? Your office is haunted? Are you scared?"

"No, she seems harmless. Just a young, pregnant nurse. I told Dr. Endicott about her, too."

"You didn't! Think how that can look. You're trying to get started as a doctor. People need to see you as a responsible, sensible professional. What did Dr. Endicott say? Did he think you were crazy?"

"No, Homer had heard of her, too. But he's never seen her. We just had a short talk about her and a laugh."

"So you're alone there now?"

"Yes, I'll start on my charts when we finish talking and I'll see if she comes back again tonight. Her name is Anna."

"Sure it is. Well, you say 'hi' to Anna for me. And take care of yourself, John. I miss you." Abruptly, she hung up.

I thought as I hung up that Sara almost sounded jealous of Anna. I considered that as I pulled up the stack of charts. It had been over a month since I had seen Sara, actually spending time with her, touching her, kissing her. I missed her, missed the feel of her body, her smile, but I was committed to making my relationship with her work. So I kept to myself and deflected the nurses who flirted with me. Sara certainly had no reason to worry about Anna being with me if I could resist the nurses I worked with every day. Anna was too young and too pregnant to attract me. Sara needed to know that. I would explain tomorrow night, I decided.

I pushed thoughts of Sara away and settled into the charts. I was nearly done when Anna came again to my office door.

"Dr. Sullivan, I'm sorry I ran off last night. I just don't feel comfortable meeting people in my condition. I trust you. But I don't like to run into other people who don't know me. I don't know what they might think of me."

"Not a problem, Anna. How are you feeling? How are you and the baby doing?"

"The baby seems fine. Kicking a lot, but good. And I'm doing all right, I guess. Lots of false labor. Bill examines me every day to make sure I'm doing well."

"Bill?" I asked.

"Bill," Anna repeated. "My boyfriend. The doctor. He's going to be an obstetrician too, just like you. He's such a good doctor, and such a good man. I still can't believe he loves me. It's like a fairy tale come true. He comes from a very wealthy family, and my family is just mill workers. We're getting by, but it's hard. And here I am going to marry a handsome, wealthy doctor.

Sometimes I have to pinch myself to make sure it's all real."

It does seem a little too good to be true, I thought. Maybe she lived in her fantasy world, imagining how perfect everything would be, to avoid the reality of being an unwed mother with all the complicated issues that carried. And I knew that the mills had been out of business for years. Some of our younger doctors had their homes in the condos in the mills. But Anna said her family worked in the mills.

Anna relaxed, and we continued to talk for nearly an hour. I started to tell her about Sara. How I had a girlfriend who was far away. That I loved her, missed her, and couldn't wait to get back together with her. At that, Anna smiled slightly and said, "Oh, I understand about that, John. I miss my family terribly. It seems like I've been up here on the hill at the hospital in Harrison House forever. It's so long since I've seen my parents. I know what it's like to be away from the people you love." Then suddenly she sighed and said, "I have to get back, Dr. Sullivan. It's almost time for me to go."

She stood stiffly, walked out my door, and disappeared.

I began looking forward to my nights at the hospital, as much because of meeting with Anna as because of my work. For a week I fell into my routine. Each night I met Dr. Endicott for dinner and reviewed our patients. He didn't ask again about Anna, and I didn't bring her back up for discussion with him. After dinner each evening, I made my rounds, visiting with all my patients and their families. Then I gathered my charts and took them to my office. When I got to my office, I called Sara and talked for few minutes. Then I went to work while I waited for Anna. One night led to another, each one very much the same as the one before. The moon became fuller each night, and the maternity unit began to fill up.

One night as I talked with Anna, she became restless in her chair, squirming and stroking her round belly.

"Are you feeling all right?" I asked.

"It's more and more difficult each day. Bill says I'm too small, and the birth could be difficult. I know it's going to be soon, and I'm a little scared. I'm having false labor all the time. I know it won't be long. Any day now."

Again I asked, "Would you like me to examine you? I could help with the birth if Bill's not here."

"No, Dr. Sullivan, Bill will come. He'll be here for me. I just want it to be over with. I just know it will be a baby boy. All I really want is to see him. To watch him grow up. I'll bet he'll be a doctor, too. Just like his father and his grandfather. Sometimes I imagine how wonderful it will be to see him all grown up. But right now, I just want it all to be over. All I want is for my baby to come."

"Well, Anna, count on me to be here if you need me. I'm happy to help."

"Thank you, Dr. Sullivan. But I've got Bill. He'll be sure to be here with me when our baby comes."

At the start of my second week of night shift coverage, I had an idea as I walked by the library of the Nursing School. I went in and found several yearbooks with lists of the nursing students for the first half of the twentieth century. If Anna was, in fact, a ghost, she might be listed in the books somewhere. I was no expert on the fashion trends of nursing uniforms, but what she wore appeared to be from sometime early in the century.

I took several of the books along with my other papers and went to my office. Medical Records and charts are boring. It would be a long night. I would have time for the charts later. It would be a diversion, but tedious, to go through the books looking for a student named Anna.

Before I started with the books, I called Sara. After the usual chat Sara brought the conversation back to Anna.

"Is that girl, Anna, still hanging out with you each night?" she asked.

"Yes. I'm keeping an eye on her. I don't know if she's a ghost or not. Let's say that she isn't. But I do know she's pregnant. If I can help her through that, it would be good. So we talk for a while each night."

"It just concerns me, John. I don't feel comfortable about you being there alone each night with a girl. She's trouble. Be careful."

"Sara, I'm fine. And I love you. Don't worry. It'll be okay."

"It's not natural, you there alone each night with this girl. If she's really a pregnant girl, get her over to the hospital and have the nurses look after her. And I just don't know what to do if she's a ghost. I don't believe in ghosts anyway."

"Listen, Sara, I tried to talk her into coming with me over to the hospital one time, but she won't go. She says she wants to stay here in Harrison House. She seems afraid to leave here. And I've tried to check her condition, but she won't let me examine her. She's definitely pregnant, and from the best I can see, it won't be long now till she delivers. It looks like the baby may have dropped. She'll give birth any day now."

"It's not right, John. I don't like being here without you. I think about you up there alone and this girl sneaking in to see you every night. It worries me. That's all. I can see it leading to all kinds of trouble for you. For both of us."

"Relax, Sara. I love you. That's all there is to it. Trust me. We'll be fine."

We ended the call but I felt a gap growing between us. I knew that she had no reason to be jealous. If Anna were an odd sort of a pro bono patient, an indigent teenager in trouble, there was no reason for Sara to worry. And if in fact she was a ghost, how could Sara be concerned about losing me to a girl who had probably passed away years ago? But it was clear that she was increasingly unhappy about my relationship with Anna.

I looked at the stack of charts and at the books from the Nursing School. The charts could wait. I set them aside and opened the first book from the Nursing School. The books appeared to be bound volumes combining annual yearbooks into thick decade-long compilations. I looked at the binding on the first book. Mary Harrison School of Nursing, 1901 – 1910. For each year there was a listing of the students, with a brief biography and an address. Most had addresses from southern New Hampshire, from the country towns and farms nearby and from the cities; Manchester, Nashua, Portsmouth and Concord. Each year there also featured a group picture with all the nurses in rows. The front row sat primly in straight-backed chairs, their hands folded, right over left in their laps. The second row stood. The nurses' names were listed beneath the picture.

I studied the names, looking for "Anna". And I looked carefully at the nurses' uniforms and the faces. The uniforms were similar to the one I had seen on Anna, but not the same; longer and more pleated. She wasn't in the 1901 – 1910 book. I moved on to 1911 – 1920. Classes were smaller during the war years and my search moved more quickly. But still no Anna.

My mind wandered as I looked at all of the faces. All of these nurses had once had lives. You could look at the sparkle in the eyes in a photograph and imagine the nurse laughing with her friends, falling in love, maybe with a doctor, like Anna had. You could imagine a story for each of them, caring for the ill and the dying people in Manchester, helping young mothers give birth. If any of these nurses were still alive today, I realized, they would be about a hundred years old. They would possibly be living in nursing homes, themselves being tended to by young nurses. Most would already have died.

I set aside the second volume and moved on to 1921 – 1930. The Roaring Twenties, I thought. Now the book had individual portraits of each nurse as well as the group picture. Still no Anna. I was just beginning with the 1931 – 1940 edition when Anna appeared at my door. She stood politely, waiting to be invited in, and smiled.

"Good evening, Dr. Sullivan."

"Call me John, Anna. How are you doing tonight?"

"Oh, I've had better days. The baby kicks a lot. Cramps. I'm not comfortable. You know I'm due any day now."

I wondered suddenly what it would be like if a ghost gave birth. Would the baby also be a ghost?

Anna continued. "I'm all right, I think. Bill examined me this morning. He says, 'I got you into this mess. The least I can do is to make sure you and our baby are fine.' He takes very good care of me, and I know he'll take good care of the baby when the baby comes."

Then she noticed the stack of books on my desk and the one volume open in front of me.

"Oh, I see you've got my yearbook. Or at least a book with all of our yearbooks together. I'm in there. 1938."

I flipped through the book and found the class of 1938. Anna pointed to a face in the second row of the group photo. "There I am."

I looked at the picture of the face of the young girl who stood before me. The photograph was decades old. The girl in my office was young. She had to be a ghost. I looked at the list of names in the caption, counting the faces and the names till I came to hers. "A. Marchand"

"So, you're Anna Marchand," I said. "I didn't know your last name."

She nodded. I flipped into the biographical section and found her again. The portrait was unmistakably her. Beside it was her address in downtown Manchester.

I closed the book and looked at her, amazed that she was undeniably a ghost, sitting right here in my office. I couldn't think of a thing to say.

She changed the subject. "Tell me about yourself, John. You've hardly told me anything about yourself. Tell me about your family. Tell me more about your girlfriend. You said her name is Sara?"

"Yes, Sara. She's working in New York. I haven't seen her in weeks."

"That must be hard," Anna said. "You must miss her. I certainly know what it's like being separated from the people you love. Does she miss you?"

"Yes, we miss each other. It means we really have to pack the relationship into our phone calls and into the short times when we are together. We're getting by, though."

Anna looked pensive. "Bill had a girlfriend back in Maine. They were engaged to get married. But being away from her, they couldn't keep their relationship alive. Bill and I were always together. Maybe that was the problem. He worked late one night, and he snuck over here to see me when he was done with his patients. This was my room, the room that's now your office. Bill knocked on my window and begged me to let him in. He worked long hours, just like you're doing now. He said he was too tired to go home and just needed a place to rest. Men weren't allowed in the building back in those days. But it was late, and the housemother was asleep. So I opened the window, and he climbed in."

"We talked quietly, and he climbed into bed with me. I didn't think anything would happen, but it did, and now I'm pregnant. It was a stupid mistake. But we love each other, and when we're married, we'll have a ready-made family."

"You're doing okay, aren't you, Anna?" Her story seemed so innocent, but I knew the social stigma she must have faced being unwed and pregnant in that era.

"Yes, I'm fine. Once the baby comes and we're married, it will be easier. My parents will forgive me, and Bill will be a good father. We'll get married and everything will be right. Everything will be perfect then. Me and Bill and our baby."

"How does his family feel about all this?"

"I haven't met them yet. But he tells me they'll be fine with my condition. The hard part is the girlfriend back home in Portland. I know it was difficult for him to break off the engagement. But she was back there, and Bill and I were here. We fell in love. And even if I didn't get pregnant, he would have left her."

"I can understand about you and Bill and his girl back in Maine," I said. "But I'm not going to fool around with anyone here just because Sara's in New York."

Hurt, Anna scolded me. "Bill and I aren't fooling around. We love each other and we're going to get married in the fall."

"No, Anna, I didn't mean that you and Bill weren't serious about each other. It's just that I won't see anyone while Sara's away. I'm sure that your relationship with Bill is different."

"It is. We're in love. And we conceived our baby right here in this room."

"Is that why you come here every night, Anna? Because this is where it all happened for you and Bill?"

"Yes, I guess. And because I know that if Bill can't get here on time to help me when our baby comes, I know that you can help. I may need you to help bring me my baby. You're the first person I've met in a long time who I know can do that for me."

My beeper went off. I checked it. A mother was on her way in to the hospital to deliver. Another of the many babies we could expect during the full moon.

"Anna, I'm sure you can understand this. I just got a call. I've got to go deliver a baby. Please understand that I meant nothing bad when I said that I wouldn't fool around with Sara out of town. That's just me, just the way I am. Now I've got to go. I'll see you tomorrow?"

"Of course. I'll come see you when you get in tomorrow."

Anna walked down the hall with me, holding onto my arm tightly for support as I started to head back over to the hospital. She let go of my arm when we got to the stairs. But I paused for a moment before going out the door. I watched her walking away down the hall. I noticed now how slowly she walked, swaying slightly from side to side, her hands folded beneath her belly. She was almost ready to deliver.

I ran across the parking lot and met the expectant mother as she arrived. But Anna and her baby consumed my thoughts. I couldn't imagine how a ghost could possibly go through a delivery

The next night I met with Dr. Endicott again.

He began, "Nice work last night with that delivery. Mother and baby looked fine when I checked them today. It went smoothly?"

"Yes, no problem. It went pretty easily. It was her third child, so she pretty much knew what to do. I just helped her along."

"Good, good. Anything else I should know about?"

"No. Nothing out of the ordinary."

"No sign of your ghost?" He chuckled for a moment.

"Oh yes, she is back. And I found her in an old nursing school yearbook. Anna Marchand. Class of '38."

"Really. That's about when my father was here. I wonder if she knew him."

"Why don't you ask him, Dr. Endicott?"

"He passed away a few years back. But I could check with my mother. They were married right after he worked here. Just before I was born. I expect she would have come here to visit him while he was here. Maybe she would remember. 1938. That's a long time ago. Mother is old. It would be interesting if she did remember, though. I'll ask her. You say the ghost's name is Anna Marchand?"

Dr. Endicott left for the evening. It seemed to me that he might actually be starting to believe in the ghost. I hoped so. It made me feel a bit less crazy and I hoped he thought so as well.

I made my rounds and started heading over to my office when Sean, one of the security guards, caught me.

"Everything go okay last night, Dr. Sullivan?" he asked. He smiled slightly and winked at Keith, the other guard.

"No problems. Thanks for asking. I delivered a baby over here, and it was quiet while I was in my office." I didn't want him or the other guard coming over and scaring off Anna.

"Call me if you see a ghost, okay?" He laughed and started back to his security station. He waved his hands above his head, laughing and made what I guessed was supposed to be a spooky noise. "Woo! Woo!"

"Of course I will, Sean. And if I do, you'll come right over to help me with my ghost?"

"Yeah, sure. Right away. Me and Keith will be right there for you." He laughed again and turned in to the security office lit with the glow of all the television monitors.

The kid thinks I'm making it all up, I thought. Maybe I should show him Anna's picture in the book. But I realized that seeing the picture of a nursing student from decades ago wouldn't prove a thing unless he actually met Anna and matched her to the picture.

Anna appeared in my office door in the early hours of the morning. She looked more pale than usual and she sagged onto her chair with her legs splayed wide in front of her.

"Mother Mary help me," she said. "I can't wait for the baby to come so I can be done with this."

"How are you feeling? You look tired."

"I know the baby's coming very soon," Anna said. "I'm so tired. And I don't feel good at all."

My phone rang. It had to be Sara. I answered, "Hello, Dr. Sullivan here."

"Hi, it's Sara. I couldn't sleep and figured you'd be there working alone and want some company."

"I'm not here alone, Sara. Guess who just came to my office? Anna's here."

"Let me speak to her." Sara replied, coldly.

I handed the telephone to Anna. "It's Sara, Anna. She wants to speak with you."

"Hello, Sara. This is Anna. I've heard so much about you. You're fortunate to have such a great guy for a boyfriend. He's a lot like my boyfriend. They're both going to be doctors, you know."

I could hear Sara's reply. "Yes, of course. How old are you, Anna?"

"Nineteen. Why do you ask?"

"And what year were you born?"

"1919."

"I see. And you're pregnant?"

Anna paused before she replied. Her answer was curt. "Yes, I am. But I'll be married soon. Just as soon as Bill finishes medical school."

"Anna. Listen to me," Sara said. "1919 was a long time ago. There is no med student named Bill there. What kind of a bullshit story is this?"

"You're wrong. Bill's my boyfriend and he's a medical student. He's going to be a regular doctor soon, an obstetrician, delivering babies. He's going to deliver mine. And he loves me. I'm pregnant, and I'm going to have his baby any day now. And we're going to be married next year. Why are you saying this to me?"

"I don't know what sort of a game you're playing up there in Manchester, but you stay away from John. You leave him alone."

"Oh, please understand, Sara. I'm not interested in John. I'm in love with Bill. John's just a friend."

Anna started to cry and handed the phone back to me. "She thinks I'm after you," she said. "Tell her we're just friends. I love Bill."

"Sara," I said. "What did you say to her?"

"I told her to stay away from you. I don't believe in ghosts. So she must be insane. The last thing I need is for you to have some crazy pregnant girl chasing after you while I'm stuck down here in New York. Watch out for her, John. She's not normal. And I don't like her hanging out in your office alone with you in the middle of the night."

"Don't worry. I love you. Anna will be okay. Trust me on this."

Sara hung up just as Anna rushed from my office in tears. I walked through the building calling for her, but she didn't come back the rest of the night.

Dr. Endicott met me the next night. The moon was full, he had delivered four babies during the day, and he was tired. There were a lot of cases to review but he just tossed the records of the mothers and babies in front of me and began talking, his voice loud with excitement.

"I called my mother this morning. I asked her if she remembered anything about a student nurse named Anna Marchand. She seemed puzzled and wanted to know why I was asking. I told her about your ghost, and it seemed as though she might have known her. From the way she talked she seemed to recognize the name. But she wouldn't say anything about Anna. She didn't seem to want to talk about her."

"Those were different times. Anna herself has talked with me about how embarrassing it was for her, for her family, and for the father's family that she was pregnant. Things are different now, it's more accepted. Less of a disgrace."

"You're right, John. I'm not sure that's such a good thing. But it is less of a scandal today for a girl to get pregnant before she's married. At any rate, mother said she wants to talk with me more about this Anna of yours, and maybe with you too. She'll call later, she said. Maybe tonight. But she wouldn't tell me anything last night when we talked. This is certainly odd.

It's not like her to keep things from me."

"Not a problem. Let me know if I should talk with her," I answered.

I called Sara when I got to my office. We were talking when Anna appeared in my doorway. Anna looked pale but said nothing as she stood waiting for me to finish my call with Sara.

"Listen Sara," I said. "I've got to go. I just got beeped that I've got a patient I've got to check on. I'll call you in a bit."

As I hung up the phone Anna began to moan. "Oh God, my water just broke a few minutes ago. The baby's starting to come. I've been cramping all afternoon. I think it's time. Could you call Bill for me please?"

How, I wondered, could I call a doctor who had been a med student at the hospital in 1938? "Do you have his number?" I asked.

Anna handed me a business card. On it was printed, "Dr. William H. Endicott, Jr., telephone 5-4338"

Stunned, I stared at the name and at the out-of-date telephone number. I picked up the phone and dialed the number of my mentor, Dr. W. Homer Endicott III.

"Dr. Endicott? This is John up at the hospital. You know how you asked me to call you if anything unusual came up? Anything I might need your help with? Well, I think you need to be here."

"What is it, John?"

"It's Anna. She's in labor. And I think you might need to be involved."

"Anna? Your ghost? You want me to come up there to deliver a ghost's baby?"

"Believe me. Dear God, please! Believe me when I tell you. I need you here. I'll explain when you get here. Meet us in my office. And hurry. She's not looking good."

"I believe you. I'm on my way."

I hung up the phone and looked at Anna. In pain, she lay down on the office floor, moaning.

"He'll be right here, Anna. He's on his way."

She moaned, "Tell him to hurry. Oh, it's hurting! He can't be late. Not again."

I realized that her distress was more than the usual labor pain. Dr. Endicott lived close to the hospital. Still, it would take him a few minutes to arrive. I might need help sooner. I called the security desk.

Sean answered. "Security. How may I help you?"

"Sean, this is Dr. Sullivan over in Harrison. I may need your help."

"The ghost is back?" He laughed.

"Something like that. Can you come over?"

"Keith and I will be right there."

From my window I saw them leave the security office and start running across the parking lot. Moments later I heard them bang through the front door of Harrison House. As they were coming down the hall Anna, gave out a shriek. "Oh God! It hurts!"

Beneath her on the floor I saw a spreading pool of blood. Sean and Keith stopped in the hall when they heard Anna. I ran to my door and called them. "Don't just stand there. Come on. I need your help here. We've got to get her over to the ER!"

Sean, the braver of the two, reluctantly looked into my office.

"Shit. What happened to her?"

"She's in labor and it's not going well. Come on. Help me get her over to the hospital."

"No way, man. If she's a ghost I'm out of here. And if she's not, you better handle it here. You're the doctor."

Sean ran back down the hall, shaking. Keith followed him at a trot, laughing. Out my window I saw them running back through the parking lot to the hospital. Keith continued laughing. "It's just a prank," I heard him say.

"No way, man," shouted Sean. "You didn't see it. Blood everywhere. That ghost had blood all over his office."

"Then we ought to help him."

"Not me. Let the doctor do it!"

I turned back to examine Anna. Through the blood I could see that the baby's head had crowned.

"You've got to push, Anna. The baby's ready to come. The next time you feel a contraction, you push. I'll help the baby along."

I didn't tell her how badly she was bleeding, that she was losing too much blood. That she could bleed out and die if the baby wasn't delivered quickly so that I could begin working to stop the bleeding. Moments later she screamed again, but she pushed and the baby's head was out.

I heard the front door of Harrison House open. Homer called out to me. "Dr. Sullivan, I'm coming."

I turned the baby so that the shoulders would come more easily. I heard Homer's footsteps in the hall.

With a thick rush of blood, the baby was born. I held a baby boy cupped in my hands.

Dr. Endicott strode into my office. "John, what is it? Why are you kneeling on the floor of your office? And where's this ghost of yours?"

I looked from Anna, to the baby I held, to Dr. Endicott.

"You don't see her?"

Anna, pale and sweating, looked at Dr. Endicott and gasped. "There you are. I knew you would come. You're beautiful. I knew you would be beautiful. Oh thank you, John for bringing me my baby."

"Dr. Endicott, she sees you. You don't see her?"

"All I see is you here on the floor of your office. What's this all about?"

I looked back at Anna. She was growing faint, transparent. Even the wide pool of blood was vanishing. I looked at my hands, still cupped, holding a baby who was gone. My hands were clean and dry. No blood was left.

"Thank you, John. You're a good doctor," she said. Then she too, was gone.

"Dr. Endicott, I swear to you. She was here. And she gave birth. I gather you couldn't see her, but she was here."

"Either you've been working too many long hours and you imagined the whole thing, or you really saw her, John. But there was nothing here for me."

"I saw her. She was here, and she had a very tough time with the birth. A lot of bleeding. She had a healthy baby boy. But she seems to be gone now."

"I have to say I'm having a hard time believing you, John. But I trust your judgment even on something as bizarre as this. Something must have happened for you to bring me out. Are you all right? Is there anything I can do for you?"

"I'm fine. I'm fine." I told him. He shook his head, put a hand on my shoulder for a moment and started to go.

I saw the business card on my desk. "Wait, Dr. Endicott. Just a moment. There's this card. Can you see this?"

"Yes."

"She wanted me to call her boyfriend, the med student. This is the number she gave me to call." I handed him the card.

"This is my father. What are you trying to say?"

"I think we need to ask your mother," I answered. "But your mother's not here."

All people grieve. The living feel the emptiness left by the ones who have died and they mourn the loss. Perhaps the dead also grieve, mourning for those they miss most; those they love and have left behind.

Sara came to visit a week later. Dr. Endicott took both of us out to dinner. After I introduced Sara to Homer, he began, "John is a fine young doctor, Sara. He does excellent work even with some of the most difficult deliveries. You've got yourself a good one here for your boyfriend."

Cautiously Sara answered, probing but avoiding the subject of Anna. "Yes, I know he's a good man. And I'm glad you believe he'll be a good doctor. He's doing all right? How is he doing with the tougher cases? What sorts of difficult deliveries has he had?"

Homer laughed as he started to answer. "The usual hard cases. Breach births. Other complications. He performed his first C-section yesterday."

"I understand he told you about his pregnant ghost. How did that go?"

"That would have been his most unusual case. And mine too, it would seem. He handled it magnificently."

Puzzled, Sara thought about his answer for a moment. "So where's the ghost's baby, and where is the ghost now?" she asked.

"Oh, the child is here," Homer said with a smile. "But Anna's gone. It seems that she died in childbirth. My mother is very old, but she knew about the whole thing because my father worked here when it all happened. Mother filled me in on the details."

Homer gave me a small wink and Sara caught it, too.

"What?" asked Sara, looking from Homer to me and back at Homer. "What's the story with you two? What am I missing?"

"Nothing," I answered. "Just accept that Anna is gone. She delivered her baby and now she's gone. I haven't seen her since."

"Good. Whatever she was, I'm glad she's gone. If she was a ghost, she belongs someplace else, not here. Not spending every night with you, John. The last thing we need is a pregnant nursing student coming between you and me. Ghost or no ghost, they shouldn't be interfering with doctors and their girlfriends. They should leave us alone and let us get on with our lives."

"I couldn't agree more," said Homer. Then, lifting his wine glass he stated, "I would like to propose a toast. Here's to young doctors and their far-away girlfriends. May they get married and raise babies together. And may they all live happy lives, and never, ever be separated from the ones they love."

Moebius Trip

MELISSA OPENED THE APARTMENT DOOR and faced her husband. "Jeffrey!" she cried, hugging him. "Thank God you're back!"

Then she remembered the weeks that had gone by without an explanation. The nights she had lain awake wondering where he had gone. All the time she had spent worrying about him. Had he been hurt? Had he simply run off? Why would he have left her?

"Come in right now," she began, her relief fading into anger. She dragged him into the living room, slamming the door behind them. "Where have you been?" she scolded. "Why did you leave me?"

"Oh Melissa, it's amazing! You're never going to believe this! You know that research I've been working on with the Moebius strips? How they're somehow connected to the time and space continuum? Well, it works! I don't quite know how, but it really works. Sit down and let me tell you all about it."

Reluctantly Melissa slumped onto the futon sofa and waited, arms crossed. She had fallen in love with him because of his mind. The way he thought about things and talked about his work. But she rarely understood Jeffrey when he talked about his mathematical research. No one understood his work but a small group of mathematicians; professors and grad students at a few colleges scattered around the world. Even so, she knew she needed to hear his story to understand what had happened.

"All right then, Jeffrey. Tell me. Something happened with your Moebius paper chains. And you went away. Somewhere. And you stayed for six months. So go on, then. Tell me. Where have you been for all this time?"

Melissa waited for him to respond. Time passed. Through an open window she smelled the fresh air and the damp earth of early springtime. She could hear the traffic on Massachusetts Avenue and the small voices of children playing on the Cambridge Common. The sounds seemed so natural, the everyday sounds of a normal world, not at all like the bizarre world where Jeffrey seemed to live with his Moebius strips and his mathematics.

Jeffrey ran his hands through his hair, excitedly pacing around the living room. He searched for the words. Finally, he started the way he always did; the way most scientists would, by asking questions, seeking answers rather than explaining what he already knew. "I've been gone six months? I had no idea. I've honestly lost track of the time. So what month is it anyway?"

"April," Melissa replied. "Don't dodge the question. Where have you been for all this time?"

"I'm not sure. I really don't know. I was at Cal Tech yesterday. And they chipped in to buy me an airline ticket to come back home. But I'm not really sure how I got there or where I was in between. And I really had no idea it was six months. It felt like just a few minutes. It's April? My God! I had no idea, but that too, is huge!"

"You're talking nonsense, Jeffrey. Now what really happened?"

"Well, let me back up and explain it as best I can. I know you don't think much of my research, Melissa. You don't think it amounts to much. But that's because you don't really understand it. So let me explain to you again what a Moebius strip does."

He pulled Melissa up off the sofa, pushed open the door to his study and led her in. The room was small, with a single closed window looking out to a fire escape landing. On one side of the room was a fireplace with a box of kindling and small logs next to it. In the middle of the bare floor was a head-high ball made of loops and rings of paper. The only furniture in the room was a single, straight-backed wooden chair next to a desk stacked with a shamble of papers. Smaller garlands of paper chains lay about in the corners of the room and on the desk and the chair.

Jeffrey pushed through the stuffy, cluttered room to the window and opened it. A fresh breeze blew in, shifting the stacks and loops of papers on his desk. Jeffrey weighted them with books, to hold them in place. The breeze stirred the tangles of paper on the floor as though they were dust bunnies, pushing them towards the draft of the fireplace.

Finally, Jeffrey began his explanation. "This is it," he exclaimed, his eyes wide. He scooped one of the twisted paper loops off the floor and waved it in the air to demonstrate.

"This is the future! This is the past. This is the present. It's here in this room. It's everywhere else, too! All we have to do is find the opening, and we're in. We can go anywhere. We can go everywhere. Through time. Through space. Anywhere we want!"

"Watch," he said as he began to fiddle with the single large twisted loop. "It's only got one side. If you trace along one side of the paper, you find yourself on the other side without ever crossing over an edge to the other side. It's only got one edge too. Follow the edge and you find yourself on the opposite edge. And then you're right back where you started. So it's only got one dimension, or maybe two."

Melissa was unimpressed. She'd seen it all too many times before. "I know, I know," she said. "And if you cut along the length of the paper strip, when you're finished it's become a two-sided piece of paper again, but with two loops."

"That's right," Jeffrey continued, the excitement building in his voice. "That's right! And if you cut the strip again it turns into two interlocking loops, neither of them a Moebius strip. It's amazing! You hold a one or two-dimensional object in your hands. But it keeps shifting back into the three-dimensional world each time you manipulate it."

"It's a waste of time, Jeffrey. A stupid trick. A mathematical game. That's all it is. But you spend hours every day down at your office at MIT playing with those strips of paper. And when you're not there, you're here at home doing the same thing. Why couldn't you just be a professor? Teach some classes, present some papers at a mathematics conference, maybe write a book?"

"Well, then. Is that what you would have me do? This is my work. It's research. It's how I make my living. They gave me a grant to do this work. I've sensed for a long time that it was somehow connected with matter and time and space, and if I could only figure it out, there would be a breakthrough that would show mankind a way to move easily through time and space. Elizabeth understood it. She was right there with me when I fell into the solution."

"Elizabeth. Well, there it is!" Melissa folded her arms tighter, pulling her cardigan closer around her.

"What about Elizabeth?" Jeffrey asked, sounding truly puzzled.

Melissa turned and walked angrily back out of the study into the living room. "That's all you do. You spend all day with her doing whatever it is you two do. You call it research. But when you left last fall, I went down there looking for you, and she was gone, too. It doesn't take a genius to figure out where she went. She was with you."

Jeffrey paused, leaning on the doorjamb of his study, comforted by the haven within the papers that lay about him. "No, actually she's down at Harvard. She started working with me when she was a grad student. But she got a teaching job and started up at Harvard in September. She came back to MIT when I called her and told her I thought I was getting close to a solution."

"Whatever you say. All I know is she vanished from MIT about the same time you did."

"Come on, Melissa, let's get back to the real story of what happened. Elizabeth was there to see it, but she didn't go along. She didn't know how. I'm the only one who knows how to make it work. Let me tell you. It's incredible!"

A fresh breeze came in the window. It carried the damp, wet smell of the Charles River's stagnant water a few blocks away. The breeze rustled the paper coils in the office again, pushing them across the wooden floor, still closer to the fireplace.

"Be careful," shouted Jeffrey, gathering the paper mass into a corner by his desk. "We can't let it be disturbed. Someone might get hurt. Or lost."

"Nonsense," answered Melissa. "It's only scrap paper. It's nothing."

"On the contrary. Let me tell you what happened."

Melissa gave in and returned to the study. She pushed the papers off the chair, dragging it to a spot by the door so she could sit down. He would have his say, she knew. She might as well hear what he had to tell her.

"Here's what happened. I went down to my office at MIT. I knew I was close to figuring it out because I had done so much work on the Moebius project there and here at home. So many calculations. So many failed attempts. I had a ball of Moebius strips strung together there, identical to this one here. I knew that there was a spot, a key, if you will, within the ball. Somewhere within the chains of Moebius strips was a way to connect to the time-space continuum. I had made Moebius loops out of the strips and intertwined them, one with the others. And I twisted the chains into Moebius loops as well. Hundreds of them. Sometimes when I worked with them, I could feel a sort of energy, an electric tingle. The hair would stand up on my arms and the back of my neck. I was close with this ball here in our apartment. And I was even closer, one Moebius chain closer, to finding the key with the ball I worked on at my office over at MIT."

"Don't be ridiculous," interrupted Melissa, perturbed. "They're nothing more than paper chains. Plain, white paper strips. They look like the paper chains I used to make when I was a child to decorate Christmas trees. They're a waste of paper and a waste of your time."

"No, Melissa, no! Listen to what happened back at MIT in my office. I had a small chain of Moebius strips. Just like this one here." Jeffrey held up a short garland of eight twisted loops of paper.

"So?" asked a puzzled Melissa. "You made one more chain. What happened?"

"I began to feed it into the ball of Moebius chains, twisting it into a Moebius loop as I did it. And I felt a jolt of energy, like I'd hit an electric power line. That's when I knew I was on to something. And that's why I called Elizabeth and had her come over from Harvard to my office to see what I was doing. I knew I was about to make the break through."

"And Elizabeth came?" Melissa was not happy about this. She had met Elizabeth only a few times, but she had noticed that she was young and slim and attractive. It worried her that Jeffrey spent so much of his time alone in his office working with her. There had never been any reason to believe that Jeffrey had a romantic interest in the girl. It appeared that the only attraction he found in her was the exchange of ideas that is the fabric of a scientific community. But when Jeffrey had vanished, and Melissa had discovered that Elizabeth was no longer at MIT, she had been certain of the fact that the two of them had run off together.

Jeffrey answered carefully, sensing the hostility his wife felt toward his research assistant. "Eventually she came. The T ran slow that day, I guess. It took her forever to come over to MIT. It's only a few miles, but it must have taken an hour. I sat around waiting for the longest time."

"Time is relative," answered Melissa. "You waited an hour for your Elizabeth to come. I've waited six months for you to come back home to me."

"Yes! Yes! Time is relative." He laughed at the play on words. "That's exactly right. And so is space. And mass. And energy. And I tapped into it as soon as Elizabeth got there!"

"Okay. Go ahead, Jeffrey. Tell me. What did you do?" Melissa waited, anticipating the worst.

"I twisted that last chain of eight Moebius strips, making it into a new Moebius loop as well. And I fed each end of it into the big ball of Moebius strips I had in my office. As I connected the ends together deep inside the ball, I felt that electric tingling again, and then I felt an incredible pressure all along both of my arms where they were reaching inside the ball. It pulled me closer, sucking me into the loops of paper. The last thing I saw was Elizabeth, watching me as I slipped into the ball as though it were quicksand. Then I was completely inside.

"For a moment or two just after I went in, I could still see through the paper. I could see my office and Elizabeth, but faintly, like looking through fine gauze or cheese cloth. I heard her calling for me. 'Jeffrey, Jeffrey,' she called, 'where have you gone?' But then I fell further into the paper. It felt like floating, drifting on a soft bed of feathers, or in a flowing stream. There was a slight rushing noise like distant traffic. Sometimes I thought I heard voices, but far away, and often speaking languages I didn't understand. Maybe Chinese, I don't know. Mostly it was a foggy, white misty place, but sometimes I was aware of faint colors, pastels and beige or gray."

Melissa sat stiffly on the straight-backed desk chair. Jeffrey's story was too far-fetched for her to accept, but she had to give him the time to explain further. "How long were you in there?" she asked.

"It seemed like only a few minutes. Then a hand touched my arm. I thought it was Elizabeth so I grabbed on and held tight. And another hand reached in. And then they pulled me out. And that was yesterday. At Cal Tech. Two grad students were there with a ball of Moebius strips not unlike mine. And they were working on it just as I had been. When they found out who I was they were thrilled, because they had read some of my papers. Apparently, they were basing their research on some of my earlier work. I was flattered."

"And where was Elizabeth through all of this?"

"I don't really know." Jeffrey paused, contemplative for a moment. "Back at Harvard, I expect. I haven't had time to call her since I got back. I came right here to see you when I got to the airport. I couldn't wait to tell you all about it. And there it is. Isn't it great? Isn't it amazing?"

Melissa got up and walked back to the window in the living room. Two floors below her she could see the street, and the Cambridge Common beyond it. Children were playing tag, chasing each other on the grass. Their mothers sat on benches and watched. *That's all I really want*, thought Melissa. *Children with Jeffrey. That's why we got married, so we could have children. But he spends all his time working with that Elizabeth. And now he comes home after six months and acts like nothing at all has happened while he's been away. Going on and on about these stupid Moebius strips, and not even asking what I've been doing all this time. What I've been thinking, what I've been feeling.*

Jeffrey couldn't help noticing Melissa's reactions as she stood looking out the window. He went to her and put his hands carefully on her shoulders. "What's the matter, sweetheart?" he asked. "You seem upset about something."

"Upset? You ask if I'm upset? You go away for six months. And when you come home you have nothing to say but to tell me all about this big scientific break-through?"

"Well, yes. It is great. It's huge. What do you expect me to say?"

"You're the genius. You figure it out."

"Come on, Melissa. Sweetheart. You're pretty smart, too. There's nothing wrong with being an English Lit major. Your degree got you the job at the publishing company, and it's important, too. Is that what the problem is?"

"No, Jeffrey. That's not the problem. You just don't get it, do you? Come on, smart guy. Don't you see it?"

"I guess I don't. Explain it to me."

"You're gone all this time. And then, when you come home, you're all worked up, and all you can do is talk about how you and your Elizabeth made this great discovery together. You don't ask how I've been all this time. It's just you, and the Moebius strips, and Elizabeth."

"Is that it?" Jeffrey answered, starting to figure it out. "You think I'm seeing Elizabeth and that she and I…" He paused, at a loss for the words to describe what he hypothesized might be disturbing his wife.

Melissa completed the thought for him. "You come home, and all you can talk about is the big break through you made with her. And I haven't seen either of you for months. Two plus two, Jeffrey. Isn't it obvious?"

"Oh please! This is ridiculous! I come home after this major discovery, and all you can think is that I ran off with my grad student? Please!" Jeffrey turned from his wife and stormed back into his study, slamming the door.

Melissa remained standing at the window, watching the children in the park. She cried for a moment then pulled herself together and tried to sort it out. Jeffrey had always been a good husband. He had always been enthralled by her. She knew that for sure. He said that together they had balance. Her love for the humanities; his sense for mathematics. He had never given her any reason to doubt that he loved her. Not until last autumn when he had vanished, and Elizabeth, too. But maybe his story was real, and Elizabeth really wasn't a problem.

Melissa knew that she loved Jeffrey. For his mind, of course, but for his awkward but gentle manner with her as well. Maybe she was making too much of this. Maybe he really had gotten somehow lost in the paper chains. He had said to her the first thing he did when he flew home was rush back to see her. Maybe they could work through this.

Melissa turned from the window and went to the closed study door. "Jeffrey," she called, knocking. "Can I come in? Can we talk? Can we work this out?"

There was no answer.

"Come on, Jeffrey, honey. I'm sorry for the things I said. I am really excited about your big discovery with the paper strips. I really am. Can I come in so we can talk?"

There was still no answer. Melissa opened the door and looked into the study. The room was cluttered as it always was, dominated by the huge ball of Moebius strips next to the fireplace. But Jeffrey was nowhere to be seen.

Melissa went into the room. She looked at the open window and the fire escape outside. Then she called one last time, angrily. "Jeffrey! Where are you! Don't tell me you've run off again. Just because we had a little fight. You can't leave me again!"

But there was no sign of Jeffrey. "Damn him," she said. "And damn these stupid strips of paper. He gets all wrapped up in them. His work is all that matters to him. That and Elizabeth. Damn it all."

She kicked the ball of paper and stamped on it, crushing it. Then she jammed it into the fireplace and held a match to it. It burst into flames in an instant. Melissa stood back flushed, watching it burn.

Far away, as though it came from deep under water she thought she heard a voice. Jeffrey's voice. "Melissa, no! I'm not far enough in yet. Don't light the match. No! No! Not fire! No!" Then the voice faded.

Puzzled, Melissa went to the window to see if Jeffrey was on the street below, calling to her. The fire escape went down toward the street level. But the ladder to reach the street was still raised. Jeffrey had not left by the fire escape as she had thought.

In the fireplace behind her, the last of the paper strips flickered out. The breeze blew the ashes out onto the floor.

SEASONS

PROLOGUE – THE VERNAL EQUINOX

THEY WALKED ALONG THE EDGE of Potter's orchard, the trees budding but still leafless. It had become one of their favorite retreats; a place to come to recharge themselves. Today was their first visit after the end of winter. Soon there would be clouds of white blossoms on all the trees. Later, if the bees did their work, there would be apples.

None of that mattered right now. He had brought Amy to the orchard with a special purpose. He had something much more important than apples on his mind today. Plans mattered to him in his well-organized world. If things went according to his plan, as he hoped they would, as he expected they would, today would be a day they would always remember.

He directed Amy to a well-worn path that climbed a ridge out of the orchard into the woods. Amy led the way. He pointed directions to her whenever they came to a fork. They worked their way upwards together, stepping carefully around spots that were still muddy from the recently melted winter's snow. Finally, breathless and sweating slightly, they came to a clearing at the top of the trail. They were alone. He took Amy by the hand and brought her to the granite edge of a cliff.

For a moment Amy felt dizzy, frightened of falling from the sheer drop off the precipice. Beneath them, beyond the forest, lay their town. Further out, they could catch the sparkle of sunlight on the ocean. At the horizon the sea and the sky blended perfectly; water and air, both the same color.

"Look at the view!" he said. It was the start of the speech he had written. He had planned how he would deliver the speech and rehearsed it many times alone in front of his mirror.

Amy had an idea what might be coming. He had hinted at it so many times. "Mmmm. It's beautiful. What a day," she replied.

"Yes. What a day. It makes me think, being up here with you, Amy. You see our little town down there. And the whole world spread out there around it. There's so much we can do in the world, you and me together. There are so many people out there. But there's no one else I'd want to be with than you. No one else I'd want to share my world and my life with than you."

His speech had seemed to make sense when he had first written it down several weeks ago. Now, hearing his voice actually saying the words to Amy, it sounded foolish, too romantic. He stopped, flushed and embarrassed, and said no more.

Amy saved him. "Why, that's a lovely thing to say. Thank you." She leaned up and kissed him lightly on his sweating cheek.

He forgot the rest of his speech. All but the closing line. "Let's get married, Amy."

"Are you asking me or telling what we should do?"

"Asking. Yes, asking, not telling. Of course I'm asking you. Will you marry me?"

"Of course I will. I'll marry you and follow you anywhere on this earth." Laughing in the exhilaration of the moment, she made a sweeping gesture encompassing the valley below, the town, the forest, the sea, the world. She pirouetted away from the edge of the ledge, laughed and hugged him

He was stunned. When he had planned the day and the hike and the speech, he had assumed she would say yes, but he hadn't planned what to do or say next. He kissed her.

Amy leaned back in his arms and looked at him. "You seem surprised. Didn't you know I'd say yes?"

"I guess. I'm thrilled. Overwhelmed! I love you, Amy."

"I love you too. And I'll marry you. We'll live happily ever after."

"Till death do us part," he added.

Amy finished it. "And even longer."

DAWN - THE SUMMER SOLSTICE

He woke in the gray, pre-dawn light. Outside the bedroom window he could see the green of the trees that guarded the yard silhouetted against a brightening sky. A breeze pushed through the haze, swaying the trees, turning green leaves white sides out. He caught a flash of lightning and a moment later heard a low growl of thunder. Wind swung through the open window next to the bed, swirling through the room, flapping the curtains. Chilled, he pulled the sheet closer, huddled on his back, shivering.

She rolled toward him beneath the sheet, resting on her side, snug in the curl of his left arm. Her legs tucked up together, fetal, her knees pressing into his left thigh. Out of habit he lifted his leg over hers, his foot fitting into the space behind her knees. They were locked together like two pieces of an intricate jigsaw puzzle. He felt goose bumps on her arm. With his free right arm he gathered the sheet again, wrapping it around her, feeling the heat of her skin against his.

Rain began suddenly, driving down straight, silver, beating on the porch roof outside the window. She pulled closer still, and he felt sheltered, comforted by her presence, like a child with its mother. She slept on. Her breath was warm. It tickled the hair on his chest. *How strange it is*, he thought. *How many times I've done this. How many hours must I have lain here at dawn, in just this position with Amy, watching her sleep?*

But Amy was gone. The cancer had come so quickly. Day after day, night after night, in the dark of winter he had cared for her, neglecting his job. Turning from his friends and from his family. If he loved Amy enough, he hoped, perhaps he could save her. Each day as he watched, it was as though pieces of Amy fell away from her. It felt like his body was breaking away as well, and that he, too, was dying. The doctors held out little hope, passing Amy over finally to hospice. Still, he held onto her. She was all he had ever wanted. After so many years, Amy was all he could remember, all he had ever had. She was his life.

In the end, the doctors were right. It seemed like the horror of her dying had lasted months. It had only taken weeks and she was gone.

He thought of the endless time that had passed since then. Winter ended and spring stumbled in. A cold, wet, typically New England spring. Day after day, he threw himself into his work; if he stayed busy, he had no time to think. To remember. But each day he had to come home after work. To the silent, empty house. To eat dinner alone. He sealed himself off from people. They didn't understand his pain. He had to get through this alone. Without Amy now.

The television didn't keep him company. Music didn't cheer him. The loneliness slowly drained the life from him. But he couldn't bring himself to go out at night or on the weekends. Being alone among crowds of happy people, couples that were still together, hurt too much. Everyone had someone. The weekends without Amy were the worst. He lived by counting the hours till Monday morning when he could return to work and immerse himself in the chaos there.

He found that he couldn't push Amy out of his mind. Not that he wanted to. He wallowed in his grief. Thoughts of her were all that he had left. He clung to his memories of Amy, even though the memories made him miss her more. He dreamed about her at night. During the day, something would happen that amused him or worried him, and all he wanted to do was rush home and tell her about it, to laugh about it with her when it was fun, or to draw on her strength for support at the other times. That's how it used to be with Amy when she was alive. But now she was gone, and he had no one to talk to.

The worst part was that the devastation, emptiness, anger, and guilt he felt were the sorts of things he would have talked through with Amy before all this. Amy could have helped him.

Last night. She had always been there. Even in the years when he was with Amy she had been there. A friend of Amy's and of his since they were all in college together. Several months after Amy died, he had bumped into her while grocery shopping. She had asked how he was doing, and he had answered, "Fine." As he always did when people asked, hiding his hurt.

He had been surprised to see her eyes brim with tears for a moment. "I miss her terribly," she had said. Then she smiled, a hard, forced smile, and looked away from him, intent on the racks of vegetables for a moment.

"Amy was my best friend," she continued, still not looking at him. "But I expect you must feel it even more than I do. I can't imagine what it is for you to have lost your wife."

He nodded. He could say nothing.

"But we have to move on, don't we?" she stated boldly. "I guess we just don't have a choice." Her eyes still glistened, but the tears never quite overflowed. He nodded again.

He had asked her to join him for a cup of coffee after they finished shopping. For the first time since Amy died he had someone to talk to. She shared her stories about Amy with him, and he found himself talking, too. They laughed together that first night, telling some silly story about Amy. It was the first time, he realized later, that he had laughed since Amy died. Then they had gone to dinner together. That one dinner led to another. After that, they were together every weekend, and then, several nights after work during the week.

As the days passed, he felt himself growing closer to her, bonded by their common love for Amy. He looked forward to talking about Amy with her. He felt odd at times to be with her, but it was so good to unburden himself of the pain of the past few months. To talk so openly and intimately about watching Amy fade and die, and about the emptiness afterwards, was a relief. He needed to get it out of his mind and finally speak about it. It allowed him to purge himself of a little grief. He looked forward to seeing her each day. But always he worried. He felt guilty, as though he were cheating on Amy by seeing another woman. "Is it too soon? Is it right? Should I be doing this? Is it disrespectful of Amy? Would Amy want me to do this?"

Last night had seemed so natural. It had started like the other nights, but, being a weekend, their dinner together was more elaborate, moving at a more leisurely pace. They had more time. They prepared a seafood dinner together. There was wine. Music. They had kissed, as they had many times before. Suddenly they made love. Now she slept beside him. It felt perfectly right to have done it. And all wrong.

The rain pounded down outside on the porch roof next to the window. Thunder rumbled again, but it was farther away now, beyond the trees. Final words from the beast as it slunk off across the valley. As suddenly as it had started, the downpour slowed and stopped. The sky brightened. Birds began to sing in the early light. Water rattled in the downspout and dripped from the eaves.

His arm had grown numb beneath the weight of her body. Slowly, careful not to wake her, he lifted his leg back over the width of her hips and slid his arm out from beneath her head. She stirred for a moment and almost spoke but then she settled her head back onto the pillow, snuggled deeper beneath the sheet, and went back to sleep.

He slipped from the bed, smoothed the sheet back over her bare body, and moved to the closet. He picked out a change of clothes, shorts, a long-sleeve T-shirt and sandals, and headed downstairs. He turned on the shower in the bathroom then went to the kitchen to give the shower water time to heat. He started the coffee maker in the kitchen and returned to the shower. It was the way he had taken to starting every day. A shower, so hot it was barely tolerable, cleansing and washing away the aches. And a big cup of coffee, strong, to kick-start him into another day.

The thunder woke her. Storms had always scared her. While she was married, Dan had teased her, mocking her fear. "It's only a storm. No big thing. Don't be such a big baby."

Dan hadn't put up with much about her, though they were married for nearly ten years. She still wondered why she had ever married him. He was her college boyfriend. After college it just seemed like the next step, the next thing to do, the logical progression of a person's life. They had both known almost immediately that it was a mistake. Finally, he left her, running off with a younger girl from work. "Trading in the old one for the newer model," she heard him joke with their friends.

She thought about how Amy sustained her then. Amy had carried her through that time. Amy's husband, too, but mostly Amy. Amy had spent hours, days, over coffee helping her sort out her life after the divorce. Amy listened when she talked about the lies, the betrayal, the hurt, and the loss she felt when Dan went to the woman from work. Sometimes, Amy had offered advice; mostly she had just listened. When Amy died last winter, it left her feeling like she was walking a tightrope with no net beneath her.

When she lost Dan, she had turned to Amy for support. But when she lost Amy, she was left with no one.

She shifted her thoughts from Amy to him. Seeing him in the store that day had been one of the best things that had happened to her in the years since Dan. He picked right up where Amy had always been. He listened to her and seemed to feel what she felt. Once, after an evening of talking about Amy, he said, "We're good for each other, you and me. We seem to keep pulling each other out of these rough spots. Whenever I have a bad day, you're there for me, and I'd like to think I've done a bit for you as well."

Last night had been an accident. They had an unusual bond because of Amy. That had led to a unique closeness. And after weeks of being together practically every night, sharing their grief, their loneliness, having kissed many times before, everything felt natural. They made love and slept together through the night. She was thrilled by it, but overcome with guilt. Maybe she loved him, but he was Amy's husband. Amy might be gone, but he was still her husband.

The rain poured down hard on the roof next to the bedroom window. She rolled closer to him. He wrapped himself around her, an arm and a leg folding her in, and he pulled the sheet up to her shoulder. His bed and his body were a sanctuary. *How could this be wrong?* she thought. *I think I might love him. I need him. And I think he needs me too. But he's Amy's husband. He's my best friend's husband.*

She slept again, comforted by his nearness. She woke when he slid from the bed. The rain had stopped. She heard him rummage in the closet and go down the stairs. Water started in the downstairs bathroom. She dozed.

She awoke finally, smelling coffee. A trace of sunshine lit a patch on the wall and floor. The shower downstairs wasn't running; the house was quiet. She got up, dressed, and went down the stairs.

"How much has changed since last night when I first went up these stairs to his bedroom," she mused. "We're adults. We knew what we were doing. We'll be fine with this."

She found him sitting on the top step of the porch, feet on the next step down, hunched, his elbows resting on his knees. His hands wrapped around the warmth of a large mug of coffee.

"Coffee's out on the counter. Fix yourself a cup. Then come on out and sit with me. If you'd like."

She got her coffee and came back to him, sitting close, but not too close, beside him on the top step. Neither spoke.

They watched the mist rising from the soaked ground as the sun warmed it. Birds foraged for breakfast, hopping on the wet grass. Across the road in the orchard a family of deer gathered. Two does picked at last year's dropped apples beneath the trees. A single buck stood still, its head turned to watch the people on the porch, keeping guard.

At last he began to speak, leaning back to rest on his elbows. "It wasn't supposed to be like this. Amy wasn't supposed to die."

She nodded and moved closer, shifting the coffee mug to one hand and resting the other lightly on the top of his knee.

"I know that death is supposed to be a part of life," he continued. "But it's not. It's just death. The human body is such a ridiculous, poorly designed thing. All those specialized organs and glands all connected by little tubes. There are so many ways it can fail. And if any single thing goes wrong, the whole deal comes down like a house of cards."

He stopped, shaking his head, looking away from her, first to the ground then out at the deer in the orchard.

"There was nothing you could do," she consoled him. Familiar words would come, she knew, phrases they had already repeated so many times before. The same words again and again, trying to make some sense of it all. "You did everything you could. So did the doctors. You know that."

"Yes, I know. But it's just not right. It still it hurts for her to be gone."

"Are you okay about last night?" she asked him. It was new ground, a new conversation. One they couldn't have had before last night.

"Yes. You?"

"Yes."

He continued, thinking out loud. "It's been a long time since Amy died. Maybe too long. Maybe not long enough."

"Do you think we made a mistake?" she asked.

"No." He answered quickly, but then he thought for a moment more. "No.

I wanted you. We wanted to do it. And maybe I love you. It's just very confusing. There has never been anyone but Amy."

"I know," she answered, though they both knew she couldn't really understand the complexity of his feelings. "If you could do last night again, would you change anything? Would you do it again?"

"Yes, I'd do it again." he replied without hesitation. "You're the best thing that's happened to me since Amy. But it scares the hell out of me."

"Why?"

"To get so close to you, to love you, makes me so vulnerable. There's a lot of risk involved here. When Amy died, I promised myself I'd never get involved with anyone ever again. It hurt too much with Amy. I don't want to go through that again. But to love you is to risk all that. I don't know if I can do that again."

"Would it be better if I left?"

"No! Don't go!" He pulled her to him and held her tightly, a frantic grasp. "I need you. Don't you see that?"

"Okay. I'll stay. I don't want to leave you. Of course I'll stay. As long as you want me, I'll be here."

"There will be a price," he said.

"What? What price?"

"We're not young, you and I. We're not like these young couples you see. The young ones can't see where they're heading with their relationships. They've got stars in their eyes and don't see what lies ahead. Because of Amy, we do. Someday, one or the other of us will have to bury the other. That's how it will end with us."

"Is that a reason for us not to be together?"

"I don't know. No. But you have to know that if we stay together, we have that out there for us. Maybe years from now. But it's out there. Can you deal with that?"

"Yes. But I'd rather not dwell on that side of our relationship. I'd rather think of all the good days we can have before that day comes. Which would be better? To be together and risk having to go through another time like we had with Amy, or to face each day alone? Would it be worth the risk for us to have this time together?"

He thought about what she had said, and after a moment he nodded again. "To be with you, even knowing you'll die someday, is better than being alone. We need each other. We need to be together."

They sat in silence, watching the sun dry the grass. Awareness of the day came to her. "Do you know what today is?' she asked suddenly.

"Saturday?"

"More than that. It's the summer solstice. It's a cusp day. The change from spring to summer. Today is the longest day of the year. And the shortest night. More sunlight today than any other day."

The deer finished their old apples and vanished into the trees of the forest. Sunlight began to creep up the porch steps toward their feet.

"It looks like it might be a beautiful day," he said. "Can we enjoy it together?"

"Yes," she answered. "I believe we can." Confident, she stood and reached down to him. He took her hands and allowed her to pull him up.

AFTERNOON – THE AUTUMNAL EQUINOX

It was high tide, but turning. After each wave crashed in, water rushed out of tidal pools, pulled away by the gravity of the moon. Shoals of flat granite surrounded the pools, streaked with kelp and seaweed, laden with periwinkles and mussels. They walked down a washed-out path from the bluff and found a wide slab of level rock next to one of the pools. Together they set out folding chairs and a small camp table. They settled into the chairs on either side of the table and took off their sandals to feel the late summer sun's warmth on the smooth rock.

She opened the picnic basket, spread a white cloth on the table, and began to put out their food. A baguette, brie, shrimp, and a dessert salad of strawberries mixed with blueberries. He opened a bottle of pinot grigio, her favorite, and poured it into two glasses. Then they sat back quietly, sipping the wine, picking at the food, and watching the shifting ocean in front of them.

After several minutes she spoke. "It's been a good summer. It's sad to see it end."

"It has been a good summer," he agreed. "We've come a long way together. I was in such a dark place last winter. It's good to be here now. With you."

"This is the perfect way for us to end the summer," she said. "And I love this spot. It's very calming, even with the water churning all around us. How did you ever find this place?"

"Amy found it. She brought me here on one of our first dates. We used to come here several times a year to picnic or just to sit on the rocks and watch the water."

"Amy! Does it always have to be about Amy? Can't we have a day without Amy being a part of it? Just the two of us on a date or a picnic?"

She stopped, worried that she had said too much. But the thoughts had been nagging at her for weeks. It had to be said. She needed to get it out there between them. There had to be more bonding them together than their shared love for Amy. Fretful, she picked up a shrimp, bit off a piece and threw the tail towards a flock of waiting seagulls. The birds swarmed, fighting over the bit of food. When it was gone, several of them settled on the rocks near the picnic, brazenly close, but casually pretending to ignore the people. She took another shrimp and tossed it whole in the air near the gulls. The birds flew to it, snatching it from the air.

He sat sullen and silent, not looking at her, hardly watching the birds. He tore a piece of bread off the baguette and hacked a chunk of brie off the wedge. He stacked the cheese on the bread and began to chew.

She had to turn the conversation in a better direction. She softened her voice and tried a new tack. "You still miss her, don't you?"

"Yes. Don't you?" he answered quietly.

"Yes," she answered. Then she busied herself by slicing the brie and the baguette, making a cluster of little sandwiches on a plate.

"Of course I still miss her," he said, carefully bringing gentleness to his tone. "And I still think about her. I guess I always will. But it's more tolerable."

"I'm doing okay, too. It's been good for me to have you to talk to about her." She paused for a moment, then added critical words. "About her dying."

"Me too. You've been great to me with all this."

"Let me ask you this," she said. "Do we have anything other than Amy? I mean, we can't live a life where the only thing we have is her. There has to be more."

He thought for a moment. She waited. His reply was essential. Finally, he answered, sorting it all out. Picking his words carefully to be sure she understood him. "Amy's what brought us together. Maybe it was meant to be that we would come together this way. I don't know. What else do we have except for Amy? I'm not sure. What do we have in common?"

"We care for each other," she answered. "I've really needed you this summer. We have that."

"Is that enough?"

"I don't know. But it's what we've got. So what happens now?"

"There's no reason why we shouldn't stay together beyond the summer," he said.

"And about Amy?" she asked.

"She was the catalyst for us. But we can be together, live together without her. I simply mean that right now we belong with each other. When we met a long time ago, I was dating Amy and you were with Dan. The timing wasn't right. But maybe it is now. To be with each other now feels right. We'll always share Amy, but we are what we are just as ourselves. I think we're okay."

"Yes. This is a good place for us to be," she answered. "Still, there's the risk you talked about a few months ago. Are you okay with that now?"

"I think so. I probably won't know until the time comes for one or the other of us. How about you? There's risk for you, too. And I expect I'm a handful with all the baggage I'm carrying."

"We both carry baggage," she stated. "We share that load. We just have to move forward a step or two each day. Better days must lie ahead."

They sat then without talking, watching the water and the birds, finishing the cheese and the shrimp and the berries. He reached over carefully and found her reaching for him as well. Their hands touched and held.

The water continued to recede from the pools, carrying bits of sea life out to the bay. When the wine was gone, they packed up the scraps, folded the chairs and the table, and climbed back up the trail, up the bluff, leaving the ocean behind.

Summer was ending. They could already feel a coolness at sunset in the evenings. Wood was stacked in their yard. There would be fires at night soon. They would be warmed together.

Epilogue – The Winter Solstice

Fire burned in the fireplace casting shadows. They sat together with the blanket covering their knees. Outside, hard snow rattled on the side of the house. Inside, with each other, they were warm.

"So many years," he said. "We're still together."

Her body nestled against his, familiar, knowing how to fit. She didn't speak for several minutes, watching the fire. Beneath them in front of the sofa the dog slept, content with their company. His needs were simple: food in his bowl, a warm house, and their companionship on his walks and in the house. Their needs were more complicated.

"We know what's coming," she said. "We'll both be all right when it's over?"

"I hope so," he replied. "We learned years ago with Amy's death. It will be very hard for both of us, but we'll both get through this. You'll be there for me till the end. That I know."

"Yes. And you for me."

The fire continued to burn down. Logs shifted and a shower of sparks went up the chimney into the cold night.

There is friendship. There is companionship. There is love. They found themselves drawn to each other, burning together, like twin stars in a complex galaxy. Relationships defy reason and logic. For the time they had with each other they were more than two people together. They were a single being, deeply connected first by a shared affinity for Amy, but later by a common need for each other. People die. The world goes on. People come together and sustain each other.

That need is infinite.

Running Home

JACOB PAYNE WAS ALL RUNNER, nothing but legs and lungs. If God designed a bird's body and wings for flight, Jacob's was made to run. Jacob was blessed not just with natural speed, but with a body that, for the most part, tolerated the fatigue of long training miles. The weary work of running a hundred miles or more each week never broke him. The miles carved his body, shaving away any flesh that didn't make him faster. He was small, his torso flat and lean, his arms and legs as thin as the branches of a sapling.

Running defined his life. Jacob built his daily routine around his scheduled training times. He ran for a half hour at dawn when he woke up and for an hour more every afternoon. The afternoon runs became personal battles, intimate struggles within himself. He pressed the limits of the pace and often added an extra mile or two at the end of each run, taking a longer route home, or circling an extra mile of streets when he was the most tired. He wanted to stretch the pace a little farther, a little faster each day. It left no breath or energy for talking, so he usually ran alone.

Jacob's obsessive pursuit of fast times carried over to every part of his life. He thought of the food he ate as "fuel". He stretched his legs on the floor each evening while he watched television alone in his Boston apartment.

He slept ten hours each night. For a time, he lived a monkish life with little interaction with anyone. But he suffered with the loneliness and began to approach a social life with the same intensity that he brought to his training. Friends, he realized, gave him the balance he needed to be happy. And Jacob knew that he raced best when he was happy. So he made it a point to make friends. To Jacob, friendship was as much a part of his race preparation as the miles he ran or his diet.

Jacob believed that girls made the best friends, because with them, there was always the possibility of sex. He liked sex. It relaxed him and left him ready to run fast. Girls liked him as well, he discovered. Jacob could be charming and witty, and he learned that there were always girls who were willing to spend time with him for a week or two. Usually, though, Jacob drove the girls away after a few dates. They found him attractive at first, but they were put off by his arrogance, by his compulsion to run, and by the locker room look and smell of his apartment. It was a nuisance to Jacob to lose the girls, one after the other. Nothing more. There were always more college girls in a city the size of Boston. He worked his way through one woman after another the same way he worked through the miles of training.

Heather and Jacob met at a Saturday night party in a Back Bay college apartment. Jacob had heard about the party from some of his college teammates and had gone there prowling for new women. He was tired from the day's miles, and he worked on a bottle of Sam Adams as he sprawled on the floor next to a couch. He knew the girls would find him. They always did.

Heather's roommate, Emily, had dragged her to the party, telling her, "You need to get out. Come to the party with me. Forget about that old boyfriend of yours. He was a bum, running around all summer while you were back home. You did the right thing getting rid of him. But it's been three weeks since you dumped him. You've got to get out and meet someone new. It's time to move on."

Heather was into her third beer and starting to feel lonely and sorry for herself when she saw Jacob. She was attracted by his lean body, his face, tanned from the sun and wind, the shag of hair. She was intrigued by his unorthodox position, reclining in a room full of standing people. She sat down cross-legged on the floor next to him.

"What are you doing down here?" she asked.

"Resting. My legs hurt."

"Why? What happened to them?"

"I ran a mile or two too far this afternoon. It was a good day, and I just kept on going. I'm on the cross-country team. It's what I do."

"Cross country. Do you run track, too?"

"I used to, but I graduated last spring. This is my last season. My name's Jacob."

"Heather," she answered, though he hadn't asked.

She looked at him. He was thin as a rock star, without the cocaine-addict look. His hair was too long and curly. His eyes were direct. He wore a wool shirt open at the collar, showing a few wisps of dark hair at his throat. Faded blue jeans. Running shoes but no socks. Heather liked what she saw. Jacob would do. She could forget about her old boyfriend with a guy like Jacob.

"Listen, Jacob," she started. "If you're this tired, why don't you sit on the couch? I could sit there with you."

"Too tired to get there. The floor is good."

"People might step on you. I live a few blocks away. It's quieter."

Jacob considered Heather's offer for only a few seconds. Then he finished the beer, and stood. "Let's go," he said.

Heather woke the next morning to find Jacob standing at the foot of her bed buttoning his shirt. She crawled from the bed, wearing only a T-shirt and hugged him. Beneath the fabric his body was as hard and smooth as polished wood.

"You're up, early," she said.

"I've got to run."

"Do you want breakfast?"

"I'll eat later. I've got to run."

Heather held on. "Can I see you?" He wasn't like the boy she had lost, but he was good. She felt her need for him, but it bothered her to be pleading with him not to leave her.

"Sure." Jacob answered. "I'd like that. You want to get together tonight? What's your number?"

"Yes. Tonight." Relieved, Heather gave him her number.

Jacob left and loped home through the empty Sunday morning streets, three miles that didn't count in his training diary because they were run in street clothes, not running gear. When he got home, he ate a light breakfast, changed to his running clothes, stretched his legs for a half hour, and headed off along the banks of the Charles River for nearly two hours of steady running. The miles flowed from his legs as easy as honey. He finished tired but refreshed and called Heather.

"Hey Heather, this is Jacob."

"Oh, hi." She was just a little surprised that he called. Even though she had been with just one guy for a year, she remembered that it wasn't unusual for a girl to spend the night with a boy and never hear from him again. She was thrilled that he had called back and began to sense that there might be something special to their connection.

"So, Heather. We said we might want to get together today. Can I come over? Maybe let's go get a bite?"

"I'd like that," she said.

"I'll be over in a while," he said.

She hung up the phone, and got ready. And she waited.

Jacob watched the Patriots game on TV. Then he took the T back to Heather's neighborhood. The trolley took almost as long as it had taken him to cover the distance on foot in the morning, but he was too tired to run.

They went out to dinner and then returned to her apartment. Heather was embarrassed to have Jacob there, with Emily at home, watching them from across the living room. But Emily gave her space as she always did. She and Jacob were alone. At first, when they went to her bedroom, Heather thought Jacob might spend the night. But after they made love and dozed for a while, Jacob roused himself and got dressed again.

"Tomorrow will be an early day for me," he said. "I have to get up before seven."

"Don't go," Heather begged.

"I have to. But let's see each other tomorrow. Okay?"

"I'd like that, Jacob. I'd really like that."

After he left, Heather began to dream. Jacob was small, so lean and so fit. Unlike any other boy she had ever known. And she felt safe when he held her. She felt the strength in his taut torso, and in his legs with their thin cords of muscle. She believed she might already be falling in love with him.

Certainly the sex was good. She scolded herself. It was too soon after her old boyfriend had left her. But she couldn't wait to see him again.

Jacob still saw it as a game, just one more thing he did. Just one more woman. Heather was a diversion to him. She entertained him when he wasn't running. He doubted that it could last, but she was pretty, and he enjoyed sleeping with her.

They fell into an easy pattern, meeting each evening at Heather's apartment. Sometimes Jacob would show up weary and thin, holding a bag of groceries for Heather to cook for dinner. Sometimes he brought just a six-pack of Sam Adams. Most nights he ended up staying till nine, then leaving, always with the words about having to get up early the next morning. Other nights, particularly on the weekends, he stayed till the morning.

Heather had rarely talked with Jacob about his running. When they were alone, they talked about anything else. Jacob found her to be a release from his obsession. He wanted to talk about other things, about her English Lit classes, about her family. It was something to do to put her at ease before sex. They spent a typical evening together eating dinner, watching television or talking, and then going to bed.

On one of those evenings, several weeks after they met, Heather rolled toward Jacob in the bed, pulled the blankets up to her bare shoulder and said, "Tell me about yourself, Jacob. We've been together a long time now. Almost a month. But I don't really know you. What were you like as a little boy? What is your family like?"

Jacob laid back, bare chest above the blanket. "There's not much to say. I'm an only child. Not much of a family."

"You're an only child? Me too! My parents spoiled me rotten. They always took me everywhere they went. To the theater and to restaurants. They sent me to dance lessons, but they wouldn't let me date any boys till I turned sixteen. And then only boys they knew. I guess I just broke out of my shell my freshman year here. I must have dated a hundred boys as soon as I got out of my parents' house. But other than the thing they had about protecting me from boys it was pretty good. They gave me anything I wanted. So, you're an only child too. We've got a lot in common."

Jacob laughed and answered. "No, not really. My parents left me pretty much on my own. My father's a fisherman. He's gone for days at a time, and when he comes home he's too tired to do much but sleep. And my mom works the second shift as a nurse in a hospital. Most of the way through high school, I'd come home and cook my own dinner."

"Oh, it couldn't have been that bad."

"No, it wasn't really bad. I had all the freedom I wanted. I could do anything I wanted to as long as I didn't get into trouble."

"They must have gone to all your races and been really proud of you for your running. They did that, didn't they? My parents were at everything I did in school. Every play. Every concert. And I wasn't even very good. Not like you and your racing."

"Well, my mom got to some of my races. She must have gone to work late those days. And sometimes, my dad would get to a race on the weekend. But not much. Yeah, I guess they are proud of me. My dad would leave me notes on my pillow about my races. And cut out newspaper clippings and put them on the refrigerator."

Heather thought it over for a moment. "So, they are proud of you. You must feel pretty good about that."

"It's no big deal. I don't run for them. They keep all the trophies, but I don't really care. I run for myself. I run to beat the other guys. It's that simple. I don't care about what my parents or anybody else thinks. All I want is to win. And I almost always do. In high school I never lost a race after my sophomore year."

Heather was impressed. "And I'll bet you've never lost in college either," she said.

"I lost when I first got to college. I didn't know what to do about it, and I almost quit running when I started to get beat. Then I realized that the guys who were beating me were older and more experienced, and trained more miles than me. So I went out and began running more and more miles. And now I'm just about unbeatable again. No one is as strong as me at the end of a race."

"I saw a story about you in the college newspaper," Heather said. "I didn't realize I was hanging around with such a big star athlete. You're practically famous. Your teammates must be proud to be part of the team with you. And your coach."

"Really? I was in the paper? I didn't see it."

"Yeah, a picture and everything. They had a picture of you at the finish of some race."

"Who cares? I just run to win. I don't give a damn about the college newspaper. And the other guys on the team are slow. They goof around and chat with each other while we're out training. I run alone most of the time because they can't keep up anyway. And my coach doesn't know what to do with me. Just get me to the starting line and get out of my way. That's all he does. I had mono and missed a season when I was a sophomore. So I have this cross country season still eligible to compete. I live alone off-campus and I train alone most of the time. Then I show up for a meet and win. I don't really give a damn what the rest of the team or the coach thinks. Just as long as my coach gets me entered in the race. And as long as I win."

"I don't get it Jacob. You say you don't care if your parents come to your races, and you don't care about your team. But you're so good. I just don't get it."

"Then you need to come see me race. I have a race this weekend. It's in Franklin Park. We start at ten on Saturday, but you might want to get there a bit early to park and find a good place to watch. Go where you see the crowd. The race will run all over the park, around the golf course. But if you're at the start, you can see us get going, and we'll run past again near the finish, and then we'll be finishing right nearby. There's not much to see, but you'll finally see what I do. I promise to win for you."

Saturday was a chilly, foggy autumn morning, with the ground still wet from a nighttime rain. Heather walked over the muddy ground trying to keep her shoes dry. She stood alone, out of place in the crowds of athletes, and watched. Clumps of runners in nylon warm-up suits cruised by, running easily, getting ready for the race. She overheard some older men, coaches or officials she assumed, talking.

"Who looks good today?" one of them asked.

"Payne," answered another. "I can't see anyone touching him. He's in a world of his own."

Heather felt a small rush of pleasure when she realized they were talking about her Jacob. She scanned the crowd of runners looking for him. There must have been more than a hundred, from many colleges. She found his team, stripping from their warm-up suits and finally picked him out, a bit away from his teammates. The runners from all the teams gathered and spread across the starting line getting ready. Heather saw Jacob burst alone from the crowd, sprinting across the open field in front of the line. She was startled by the sheer speed of his tiny body. She watched him turn and jog back to the line and push in among his teammates to wait for the start.

An official made some announcements through a bullhorn. The starting line crowd became still, and for an eerie moment, everything was silent. After a gunshot, accompanied by the shouts of spectators, the crowd of runners blew across the meadow, arms and legs swinging, a bobbing mass of white shirts and many-colored shorts. They congealed, and began to stretch into a long, thick line of rushing bodies. The snake of runners climbed a short hill, rolled over the ridge, and was gone.

Minutes passed. Officials gathered at the finish area. Coaches walked past, holding clipboards and checking watches, talking quietly with each other. Heather stepped carefully across the wet meadow, trying to understand how to watch such a strange sport, where the athletes spent most of the time out of sight. She noticed a large digital clock on a scaffold and understood that the finish line was marked in chalk on the grass beneath the clock. Numbers clicked by on the clock counting the time the runners had been away. She saw the crowd moving to the edge of a path that came out of some woods not far from the finish area. She followed the crowd to the path and waited.

A few minutes later she heard an approaching auto horn, and shouts of spectators in the woods. A golf cart popped out of the forest on the trail, honking its horn, with a tight clump of five runners not far behind. Jacob ran at the front of the pack, his face intent, his brow slightly creased. The other runners ran in step behind him like a small platoon of soldiers marching quickly. Heather shouted Jacob's name as they flashed past, but he seemed not to hear her.

The runners passed behind the starting area, crossed the meadow again, and headed toward a short, steep hill. Even from a distance Heather could see a sudden shift in Jacob's running. A coach near her said, "Jeez, there goes Payne. Oh my God, there he goes!"

In a moment, he was clear of the other four runners. Then he was alone, with the space behind him growing stride by stride, second by second, as he sprinted up the hill. They topped the hill and were gone, out of sight again. Behind her crowds of runners were now passing by, following the course Jacob had run a minute earlier. Many of them were gasping, huffing for air. None ran with the easy grace she had seen when Jacob flew by.

In the distance, the golf cart honked as it approached again. It rose over another ridge and drove rapidly toward the finish, downhill through an open space roped off to hold back the crowd. As Heather watched from behind the rope, Jacob followed the cart over the ridge. He was alone. The golf cart pulled to the side, leaving Jacob rushing solitary across the wide space of the approach to the finish. He was across the line before any other runners came into view. Still running fast, he cruised to the end of the roped finish chute. His pursuers began to stream by, red in the face, scrambling against each other. Then crowds of runners began to pass, frantically sprinting to the end of their races.

Proud as she had ever felt for any boy she dated, Heather hurried past the crowd to the end of the finish chute looking for Jacob. She couldn't find him in the crowd of mud-caked runners staggering out the end of the chute. Mud was everywhere. The runners' shoes sucked at the muddy grass as they walked. Their legs were coated with water and mud to the knees, and they were all spattered with Dalmatian spots of mud front and back as high as their shoulders. They smelled of wet grass, earth, and sweat.

After several moments of looking through the crowd, Heather finally spotted Jacob, jogging still, coming out of the forest across the field, alone. She waved, catching his eye. He trotted up to her, grinning cockily.

"How about that?" He laughed. "Had all of them eating out of my hand the whole way."

Before he could say more to Heather, a group of reporters surrounded him. They held small recorders down to him, small as he was, and wrote in notebooks as they interviewed him. Heather stepped back and watched and listened as they interviewed him.

She noticed that, like all the other runners, Jacob's legs were streaked with mud up to the knees. But unlike the others, only his back was spattered with mud. It came to her suddenly that Jacob had never run behind anyone during the race, catching the mud their spikes threw back. The mud that spotted his back was from his own feet.

His body and face were still flushed red, and steam rose from his shoulders in the chilly air. She saw that he wasn't even breathing hard, though it was only a moment since he had jogged over to her. She listened to him.

"I just wanted to control the race from the start. The course was slippery, and I didn't want to be getting pushed around in a crowd."

A reporter asked another question. Jacob answered, "No, I never felt that the pace was fast. Not till I took it out with a half mile to go. I had a lot left at the end."

When the reporters were done, Jacob pulled on his warm up suit, covering his muddy legs. Heather gave him a small hug once the mud was covered. She could smell his sweat and the faint ammonia scent of burned adrenaline.

"You're good," she stated. "I had no idea. Were you ever behind in the race?" She wanted to confirm her guess about his mud-free front.

"No, not for a single step. The other runners are all assholes. If I'm behind them I have to be looking at their asses. When I'm in front they have to chase mine."

"That's disgusting."

"Yeah, well. Go talk to them. They're all assholes. And slow, too. Your guy is the fastest gun in the country."

Heather chose to let it pass. To continue the conversation she asked, "I looked for you after the finish. I saw you come back out of the woods. Where did you go?"

"I ran off into the woods after I finished."

"Yes, I know, Jacob, but why? The race was over. Why didn't you just stop? Weren't you tired?"

"Yes. But being tired's nothing. It passes. I just wanted a few moments alone after I finished."

"Why?" Heather was baffled. It was a strange, wet, muddy sport she was discovering. And Jacob was so clearly good at it. And he still seemed to be keeping most of it away from her. He was her boyfriend, and she wanted to know more about him and what he did.

Jacob looked around. He was alone with Heather. "Okay, Heather. Here it is. Don't ever tell this to anyone. I want them all to think it's really easy for me. It makes them concede races to me, makes them give up because they don't think they can beat me. If they think I can blow them away like I just did without even trying, it makes it easier for me the next time I race them. But it's not easy. It really hurts to run the way I do. And when I race, sometimes I get nauseous when it's over. I ran off to the woods to throw up where nobody could see me. And don't you ever say anything about that to anyone."

"I won't," Heather agreed. "But that's sick, Jacob. Couldn't you run just a bit slower and not throw up? Wouldn't it be better not to do that?"

"Why would I want to run slower? The whole point of running is to race. And the whole point of racing is to see how fast you can go. To see if you can win. So I throw up sometimes. It's no big deal. You can't imagine the things I've done off in the bushes in the middle of long training runs."

Foolishly, Heather asked, "What? What have you done in the middle of your training runs?"

"Let's just say that it's a long time between bathroom breaks when you're on a twenty-mile run."

"Oh Jacob that's disgusting! Let's change the subject."

"Yeah, but Heather. You saw me win. No one was close to me. What do you think about that?"

Heather weighed the two sides of his running. There was the mud, his nausea at the finish, the sweat. But, she conceded, he was fast. He was a winner. No one could run the way he did. And the body that had just won the race made love to her several nights each week. She would take the bad with the good and try to sort it out.

"Jacob, your team is getting on the bus. You've got to go."

"No, it's not a problem," he replied. "I run home after the meets. It's only a few minutes. Maybe five miles. It helps me shake my legs out after a race, and it keeps my mileage up. I'll see you tonight?"

"Sure," Heather answered, eager to get their relationship back into the familiar world of her apartment bedroom. "Stop over when you're ready to go out."

Driving back to Boston she passed Jacob, a tiny figure running alone on the margin of the Jamaica Way. He looked no different than any other jogger unless you were aware of the speed with which he covered the ground, even now at rest.

As the weeks passed, they settled into a routine that revolved around Heather's apartment. They spent all their free time there, living their lives as intimately as they could in the company of Emily. Emily moved quietly around them, giving them room.

The week before Thanksgiving, Heather and Jacob were sitting on the sofa in her apartment watching television and eating ice cream. Emily had conceded the living room and the couch to them and gone off to her bedroom. Heather decided to search for new sides to Jacob. She knew there had to be more to him and to their relationship than the physical chemistry they shared.

She began, "Jacob, I've never seen your apartment. Could we go there sometimes? I feel bad about always being here with you. It makes Emily have to stay out of our way."

"Does she mind, Heather? I haven't heard her complain. Is it a problem?"

"I don't know. She really hasn't said anything. But I think it would be easier if maybe sometimes we went to your place and let her back into the living room. I know she's giving us our space, but I want to be considerate. It is her apartment, too."

"And, it's yours too, Heather. What is it? Doesn't she like me? She's welcome to stay out here when I come over."

"Yes, I know. But she wants to give us some privacy. Some space. No, I think she likes you. She hasn't said she doesn't."

"Hey, she has the room to herself and the TV too, when we go to your room. Some nights she turns the TV up when we're in there."

"Yeah, Jacob, I wonder why she turns up the TV? Maybe she wants to make a bit of noise so she doesn't hear us."

Jacob laughed. "Don't ask for us to be quiet. I like noisy sometimes."

Heather let that topic drop but came back to the idea of his apartment. "Do you have any roommates, Jacob? What's your apartment like?"

"No, no roommates. I just have a small place. Over in Brighton on a side street at the foot of the Commonwealth Avenue hill. It's nothing to see really, and it's a mess right now. Maybe sometime we can go there, but not now."

"Okay, Jacob, maybe sometime later on." Heather changed the subject. "Something else, Jacob. Do you have plans over Thanksgiving vacation? It's next week. Are you going home? I know you live somewhere up on the North Shore. I'll be with my parents in Connecticut for Thanksgiving, but I could come back after that and come up to see you. Or if you would like, I would love to have you come down to Connecticut and meet my parents and see where I grew up."

"Jeez, Heather, what is this? First you want to come over to my apartment, and now you want to meet my parents and have me meet yours. What's this all about?"

It was the first time Heather had ever seen Jacob angry. She couldn't understand it, and felt herself flush, angry at herself, that she had somehow made him act this way.

"Oh, come on. I thought we could get together over Thanksgiving. We don't have to go to either of our parents'. We could just come back before the end of the weekend to see each other. It's going to be a long weekend, and I know I'll miss you."

"Back off, Heather. Don't push me."

Jacob stood up and grabbed his coat. "We've got a good thing here. Don't fuck it up by trying to make it into something it isn't. You can come to my apartment when I'm ready for you to come there. And we can meet each other's parents when the time is right. But this isn't it."

Without another word, he walked out, slamming the door behind him. Stunned, Heather sat on the couch alone. She felt numb. The television was still running, the laugh track from a comedy incongruous against her pain. Emily had heard the fight and came out to sit with her. She put an arm around Heather and said, "He's an asshole, Heather. You can do better."

"You don't know him," Heather protested crying just a little. "He can be really nice, and he's really a kind, gentle guy. He's always treated me right. You don't know him the way I do."

"I know what I see, and I see a guy who's using you. Forget about him. He probably won't even call again. But that'll be okay. You'll meet another guy, a better guy."

Heather stopped crying and answered firmly, "He'll call."

"Maybe, but if he doesn't, that's okay. You'll meet another guy. You'll be okay."

"He'll call," Heather repeated. But she really wasn't sure if she would hear from Jacob again.

Moments later he called. "Heather, its Jacob. Listen, I don't know why I did that tonight, why I said all that to you. I'm honestly baffled. It's never been a big deal to me before. I could easily have just walked out and never bothered to see you again. But I kept thinking all the way home that I made a mistake, made a fool out of myself. I don't understand why I did that back at your apartment. Even more than that, I don't understand why I'm calling you now to apologize. This is all new for me."

He paused, trying to figure out the next thing to say. Heather helped.

"That's okay Jacob. Let's give it some time tonight and maybe talk tomorrow about what to do over Thanksgiving. We can do whatever you'd like."

"Okay, yes, let's talk it out tomorrow. Maybe that's what the thing is though. I won't be around at Thanksgiving. I have a race down in Tennessee, and I'm leaving Thanksgiving night. I won't be back till Sunday. So I couldn't see you anyway. Here in Boston, or at my parents' or down at your place. And I'm a little nervous about the race. I sometimes get a little edgy before a big race."

"Okay. I understand," Heather said, though she really didn't. All she wanted to do was patch things up. To get things back where they should be. Back where Jacob came to her every evening and they made love.

She continued to soothe him. "We'll get together then, tomorrow night. And don't worry about the race. We can talk about that, too, if you'd like. But I'm sure you'll do fine. You'll win. You always do."

"Yeah, well this is a big one. Runners from all over the country. Kenyans, and other foreign guys and Americans running for colleges from everywhere. I might not win."

"Don't worry. And we'll talk tomorrow?"

"Yeah, tomorrow. And Heather, thanks for not holding a grudge against me for the way I acted back there."

"Not a problem, Jacob. I love you."

"Yeah, I love you too, Heather. Good night."

Jacob hung up. He paused for a moment, sitting on his couch and realized that it was the first time he had ever told anyone that he loved them. Not even his parents. It amazed him to have said it. It left him smiling quietly to himself, but just a bit scared. He pushed the thought from his mind. He had a race to get ready for.

In her apartment, Heather turned to Emily, gloating. "That was him. I told you he would call!"

"Yeah, I figured that out. And you caved right in and forgave him?"

"Yes, and he told me he loves me."

"*After* you told him you love him, or before you told him?"

"I don't remember. It doesn't matter anyway."

"Yes, it does matter. I still think he's an asshole and he's using you."

Heather and Jacob met the next evening. He took her to an Italian restaurant for dinner, the first time he had taken her out to a real restaurant since they met. They talked and laughed the way they always had. But he turned the conversation away from the race he had to run whenever Heather tried to bring it up.

Finally he said, "Look Heather, the race is a big deal. But it's something I've got to face alone. I'm alone out there when I'm racing. Just me and the other runners. And I've got to get ready alone in my mind. Right now I need to keep it inside. It fuels me. I feed on it when I race. I can talk to you about it later, maybe. When I get back. But not right now."

He called Heather Sunday night after Thanksgiving. "Hey Heather, it's Jacob. I just got home. Wanted to give a call and let you know I'm back in town, safe and sound. How was your holiday?"

"Thanksgiving was good. I missed you. How did you do in the race? Did you win?"

"Nah. Fifteenth. Just not my day. No big thing. That's it for me and college races. I'm all done. On to bigger and better things now."

"Like what?" Heather asked.

"Oh, I don't know. Road races. Marathons. We'll see. Can I come over tomorrow?"

And with that they resumed their old routine. Jacob continued with his grad school classes, and continued running as he always had, just without the college team. Heather continued meeting him most nights, watching television with him, sharing dinner and sex. They were as happy as they thought they could be.

Christmas vacation was approaching, and Jacob decided to allow Heather into one more small piece of his life. He started, "Listen Heather, you wanted to visit my parents' house back at Thanksgiving. Do you want to come up over Christmas? How about for a day sometime between Christmas and New Year's?"

"Oh, Jacob, that would be wonderful. And would you like to come down to Connecticut for New Year's Eve?"

"Sure. Okay, I guess. So let's pick a day when you can come up. We could meet in Boston at your place and I'll drive you up to my parents and my town."

Heather returned to Boston after Christmas. Jacob met her at her apartment late the morning of the next day. It took an hour for them to drive from Boston, north past the malls and restaurants, and on up the coast till they reached Gloucester. They went to his house, a small Cape on a side street several miles from the harbor.

"They're home. That's my dad's pickup in the driveway, and my mom's car's here, too. Let's go in and meet them and have some lunch."

Jacob parked on the street and they went in, Heather eager to meet his parents, Jacob awkward and anxious. His parents stood side by side, smiling. This was the first time Jacob had ever brought a girl home. They wondered if this was more serious than his usual short-lived relationships.

"Heather, I'd like you to meet my parents. This is my dad, Walter, and my mother, Eileen. Mom, Dad, this is my girlfriend, Heather."

Heather reached out her hand to them, gracious, as she had been raised. "It's so nice to meet both of you. Jacob is such a fine young man. You've raised a real gentleman."

Walter and Eileen shook her hand. Eileen began the conversation, "How long have you and Jacob been seeing each other?"

"We started seeing each other in the Fall. October, I think."

"Have you seen him run?" It was Walter. "Have you seen him race?"

"Oh, yes. He's pretty good, isn't he?" It was a statement, not a question.

"Here. Come with me, young lady. Let me show you his trophies."

Walter led her down the stairs to a paneled family room in the basement. Eileen followed, with Jacob reluctantly tagging along. A big-screen television and a wrap-around sofa dominated the room. But one wall was covered with a floor to ceiling set of shelves. The shelves were loaded with trophies, plaques, and framed sets of medals and ribbons. There were also framed newspaper clippings and photographs.

"Look at all this," said Walter. "And this is just the awards he got before his sophomore year in college. I don't know how much he's won since then. Or how much he's going to win before he's done."

"Dad, it's no big thing. I don't run for the trophies. I run to win. It's not that big a deal."

"Oh yes it is, son. Just look at all this. Do you know anyone who's won this much?" They'd had this conversation many times before. The proud father debating the son who had grown up alone, finding himself by outrunning everyone around him.

"I don't know. I don't keep track. I just pay attention to my times and what place I finish."

"And that's always first."

Eileen interceded. "Oh, Wally. We all know how good he is. Don't make such a fuss. Let's go upstairs and get some lunch and meet his young lady. Are you hungry Heather? Would you like a sandwich?"

"Please, that would be nice. Thank you." Heather and Eileen led the men back up the stairs to the kitchen. Together they prepared the sandwiches while Jacob and Walter sat at the kitchen table. While they ate, Heather told them about her classes.

"I'm an English major. Maybe I'll teach after I graduate. Maybe I'll go into journalism. I haven't decided yet."

"That's nice," Eileen answered. "I expect you'll make a fine teacher. Jacob's majoring in Physiology in grad school. He could coach or be a trainer, or a physical therapist. I know some people at the hospital where I work. I could probably get him a physical therapist job after he graduates."

"Mom, we'll cross that bridge later. Right now, I'm a runner. My coach has me hooked up with Nike. I can make a little money from them and I can win some races, make some more money, too. We'll see about the physical therapy thing later. Right now I run."

Walter stepped in. "Of course you do, Jacob. And if there's money out there, prize money, you'll win it."

"You're a fisherman, Mr. Payne?" Heather asked. "Tell me about that."

"Yeah, I fish for a living. I go out of Gloucester, usually. Small stuff, flounder and sole. I also do some lobstering. I don't want to go out for days at a time anymore, so I'm sticking pretty close to home most of the time. It's hard work this time of the year. Cold and bad weather."

Jacob added, "But Dad, you make good money, and we always had all the fish we could want to eat for dinner."

"Sure Jacob. I'm a big deal fisherman. But nobody's giving out trophies for catching sole."

They had barely finished lunch when Jacob grabbed their coats and said, "Come on Heather. Let me show you around my town."

"So soon? I've hardly met your parents."

"But I want to show you my town. Let's go."

At the door Jacob stopped. He clapped his father on the shoulder and gave his mother a kiss. "I'll call," he said.

"Well, all right, then. It was nice to meet you Heather. You take good care of Jacob for us." Eileen gave her a brief hug.

Walter stood back, stoic, but finally stepped forward. "Yes, Heather. It was good to meet you." He shook her hand.

Jacob and Heather walked to the car without a word. His parents were back inside with the door closed by the time they started the car. They drove through Gloucester with Jacob pointing out the sights; his high school, the track, covered with snow now, where he had trained and raced before college, the hospital where his mother worked, the harbor and the docks, and the big fish processing plants.

"Jacob, I would have liked to spend more time at your house. I want to get to know your parents better. Could we come back sometime? Maybe make a weekend of it. See a movie or go to dinner, spend the night up here?"

"There's not really much else to see up here, Heather. Gloucester's just a working fishing port. And sure, there's a movie theater and a mall nearby. They have those everywhere. But there's not really much to do here. And there's not really much else to know about my parents."

Jacob couldn't tell her about his feelings growing up. He understood that his parents had to work hard to make a living in a town like Gloucester. But he remembered many evenings coming home after winning a race, eager to tell them about it, but finding the house dark and empty. He knew it was a part of who he was, but it wasn't a part he could talk about. Certainly not with Heather.

Heather jumped right back in. "Oh, I think your parents are nice. Why did you get so quiet when your dad showed off your trophies? It was almost like you were angry, or embarrassed by him showing them to me."

"They're just trophies. I got my first medals in Junior High School. I figure if little kids can win them, they're really not that big a thing. But my dad gets all worked up about them."

"He's proud of you."

"Yeah, I guess. But I don't run for him. I run for myself. I've told you that."

"Still, I'd like to come up and spend a weekend up here. It could be fun."

"Sure, I can see it now. We've got three bedrooms in that house. One is my parents', one is mine, and the third they turned into an office sort of a thing. There's no bed in there. So what would we do? Sleep together right there in my parents' house? That won't happen."

"Okay, okay. I give up. But for New Year's Eve we're staying at my parents'. We have a spare bedroom. But I don't know if we can be together, you know, sleep together there either. I wouldn't want to do that with my parents there."

As Jacob and Heather drove into her town in Connecticut, Heather noticed him checking and rechecking the odometer on the car.

"What are you doing?" she asked.

"Checking the mileage at landmarks around your town. I'll be going for a run tomorrow morning and I want to know where I am and how far I run."

Heather sat silently for the rest of the trip till they came to her street.

"Turn here," she said.

"What's the matter? You seem upset about something."

"It's nothing. Here's my house on the right. Pull in the driveway and come meet my parents. Then we can settle in before the party tonight."

"There's a party?"

"Yes, with a bunch of my old friends. Emily will be there, too. We went to high school together."

"Swell. A party with Emily." Heather ignored his comment as they parked beside a double garage and got out of the car.

Jacob looked over the house. It was a large colonial set back at least a hundred feet from the street.

"Your parents must be doing all right," he stated.

"My father's in insurance. I guess he does okay. My mother doesn't work. Come on in."

They walked up some stairs to a wide side porch. Her mother opened the door, beaming.

"Heather! Welcome home! And you must be Jacob. Heather's told us all about you."

"Us?" Jacob asked. "I don't see anyone but you." It was not a good start and he realized it as soon as he said it.

"Oh, my husband, Heather's father, is in the den watching football. Come on in!"

She led them through the kitchen and down a hall. Then, taking their coats and bags, she left them at the door to the den. A large, gray-haired man sat on a leather sofa. He looked up, then extended his hand without rising.

"Hi, I'm Heather's father. And you're Jacob?"

"Who else," Jacob answered. Again an awkward reply and Jacob began to worry if he would make more mistakes as the day continued. Cautiously, he shook the big man's hand.

"Sit down, Jacob. It's some bowl game. Michigan or Michigan State is playing somebody from down south. I can never keep these teams straight. You like football?"

"Yeah, I watch the games. I follow the Patriots on Sundays. But I'm usually racing on Saturdays during the fall, so I miss most of the college games." Jacob felt like he was getting along better. Heather's dad seemed all right.

"I miss a lot of the college games, too. And I'm more of a Giants fan on Sundays. You want a beer, Jacob?"

"Sure."

"Heather, go get your young man a beer. I believe we've got some Heineken in the refrigerator."

Heather left to get the beer and Jacob was suddenly alone with her father.

"I don't drink, myself," he said. "But Heather told us you were a beer drinker so I stocked up for you. Do you like Heineken?"

"It's all right. I prefer Sam Adams. But I don't drink much. Just a beer now and again. I'm always in training."

"Yes, yes. She told us about your running. She says you're pretty good. I figured you'd be bigger, being an athlete. Stronger looking. You're not much bigger than Heather."

"Bigger's not always better. For a runner it's just more baggage to carry around."

Heather returned with two opened bottles of Heineken and saved Jacob from more conversation. She handed one of the bottles to Jacob, kept the other for herself, and squeezed in between her father and Jacob. As Jacob tipped the bottle back for his first sip, he saw Heather's father looking without pleasure at the bottle in his daughter's hand. He noted also that Heather seemed to enjoy the beer more than usual.

They sat without talking, watching the game and drinking the beer. Heather's mother was somewhere else.

The party they went to was almost as uncomfortable for both Heather and Jacob as the time they had spent with her parents. Emily kept her distance, as usual. Heather's other friends seemed excited to meet him, and their boyfriends tried to engage him in talk about football and college. None of the conversation seemed relevant to him, and none of them knew anything about running. He had nothing to say to them and they offered nothing of interest to him.

Heather and Jacob stayed until just past midnight, kissing as they watched television to see the ball drop in Times Square. They drove home through the cold, quiet streets.

Her house was dark except for a couple of lights left on in the kitchen and hall. "My parents aren't late night people," Heather explained. "They probably stayed up till midnight and then went right to bed. We should be quiet."

"Real party animals, aren't they?" replied Jacob. "But quiet's fine with me." He kissed her and went to his private bedroom alone.

The next morning was bright and cold with a pale blue sky. Heather came downstairs in her robe and found her parents in the den on the leather sofa watching a parade on television.

"Good morning," began her mother. "You and Jacob came in late?"

"Not that late. We were in by one."

Her father joined in. "Well, he's quite the sleepy head then. It's already eleven. You college kids all live on a different schedule than us old folks. What time do you expect he'll get up? We have some pastries for breakfast and a fresh pot of coffee. Does he drink coffee when he's in training?"

"He's always in training, daddy. And yes, he eats just about everything. But it's not like him to sleep late. I'll go see if he's awake."

"Heather, dear," her mother spoke up. "You really shouldn't go look in on him while he's in bed. It might give him the wrong idea about you. You wouldn't want him to think you're easy. You know what I mean. It might put thoughts in his head."

"I'll go get him up then," said her father. But as he stood, Jacob came across the porch to the kitchen door, dressed in his winter running gear: tights, a nylon jacket, gloves and a stocking cap. He was red in the face and sweating. He walked into the kitchen, traces of slush falling off his shoes onto the tiled floor.

"What a great way to start the New Year." He grinned. "You've got a beautiful town. A great place to run. Hilly, and beautiful roads."

"You went for a run?" It was Heather's father. "I didn't hear you leave. When did you go out?"

"I was up a bit after nine, and I poked around the house a while, then headed out just before ten. I tried not to make any noise so I wouldn't disturb you."

Heather's mother asked, "How far did you run? You've been gone an hour. That's a long time to run."

"An hour eight minutes to be exact. Probably twelve miles. I took it easy so I could look around and enjoy the morning."

"Why do you do it?" her father asked. "Why run? What are you running from?"

Defensively, Jacob pushed back. "I'm not running *from* anything. I'm running *for* something. Heather, I haven't told you yet, but my coach pulled some strings and got me in the Boston Marathon. That's in April. Most people have to run a marathon to qualify, but they accepted me because of the things I did during the Cross Country season."

"So that's what I'm doing," he directed the answer now to Heather's father. "I'm getting ready to see if I can win the Boston Marathon. Okay?"

"Oh well, I hope you do well in it," he answered. "But don't the Kenyans always win that race? You're still a college boy. Good luck then." He shook his head, almost laughing.

Jacob ignored the reply and went upstairs to shower. He and Heather left right after breakfast.

"So, that was fun," Jacob began during the ride home.

"Fun? You were rude to my parents. You had nothing to say to my friends. Ignored them most of New Year's Eve. What was fun about it?"

"I had a great run this morning. Beautiful. Clean air, and nice, hilly roads."

"I knew it!" Heather sulked, crossing her arms and leaning back against the car door. "I knew as soon as I saw you checking the miles around the town. That's all this was for you. A new place to run. You didn't care about meeting my mother and father. Or about the party and my friends. All you really cared about was going for a run in a new place."

"Yeah? So? I get a little tired always training on the same streets around Boston, starting out of the same place. This was nice. I don't get it. What's the big deal? So I went for a run while we were down here in Connecticut. Why get upset? It's no big thing."

Jacob turned up the car radio, and they drove the rest of the way home without talking.

Heather sat sullen next to him in the car, lost in her thoughts. He was a special person, she knew. And she was convinced that she must be in love with him. If she weren't, she rationalized, how could making love with him be such a powerful thing? But he still seemed distant so much of the time, so hard to reach, so hard to touch. There had to be more, she thought. There had to be more.

It was late January when Heather finally made her first visit to Jacob's apartment. They had returned to school after Christmas and learned that

Emily was planning a big party at the apartment. Jacob didn't want to go, and Heather wanted to be alone with him. Jacob offered to bring her to his apartment for the first time. They went out to dinner, and then put in a token appearance at Emily's party. After a short time they slipped out and went to his place.

Jacob was still a little embarrassed to let her see the Spartan look of his apartment. It puzzled him that he had never before cared what a girl thought of his apartment. With Heather it was different. He realized that, for the first time, he didn't want to scare a girlfriend away. He spent several hours in the days before Heather's visit, cleaning each room, with special attention given to the bathroom. He did his laundry. He bought new sheets and towels. He stocked his refrigerator and cabinets with bagels and cream cheese, things he knew Heather liked for breakfast.

When they got to his apartment he showed her around. "Here it is. It's not much, but it's enough for me. There's this room on the front of the building. It's my living room and dining room. There's a small kitchen here, and this is the bedroom and bathroom. And I have one more small room over there." He indicated one more room, behind a closed door.

He set out new candles and lit them. Then he put on a new CD; Norah Jones. He produced a tray of sliced cheese on crackers from the refrigerator. Finally, he took a new corkscrew and opened a bottle of wine. Heather sat back on the couch, watching his performance. When he was ready, he joined her on the sofa. They drank the wine, snacked on cheese and listened to the music.

"No Sam Adams tonight, Jacob?"

"No, I thought it was a big deal having you over, so I went for wine."

"And Norah Jones. I didn't know you liked Norah Jones."

"I heard it over at your place and figured you must like it."

"I do." She snuggled closer to him.

The next morning Heather woke late, rumpled, in the bed alone. She sat up as she heard the apartment door close. Jumping from the bed, she heard Jacob heading down the hall and stairs to the street below. She found one of his sweatshirts on the floor of his closet, pulled it on and ran to the front of the apartment. Looking out the bay window she saw Jacob, dressed in running tights, a heavy nylon jacket and a stocking cap, heading off down the street.

For the first few strides he ran stiffly, like a marionette. But gradually he assumed the normal fluid stride she had seen at his race. He ran through the deserted street between the parked cars and gritty snow banks, gliding over the salt-stained gray pavement. Moments later he turned the corner and was gone.

Heather checked the clock. Eight-thirty. She guessed he would run for a half hour. She put on a fresh pot of coffee, rushed through a shower, and dressed to be ready when he returned. She got a cup of coffee and went back to a chair by the bay window to watch for him. The half hour passed and her cup was empty. She got up for a refill.

To pass the time Heather began to explore the apartment. A table next to the sofa was covered with books on Exercise Physiology and several issues of Track and Field News. There was no other reading material. She went to the closed door to the spare room and opened it. On the floor she saw piles of warm-up suits and at least a dozen pairs of new-looking Nike running shoes; odd shaped shoes in colors she had never seen on most sneakers of ordinary people. There was a barbell with a couple of small-looking plates on each end. It didn't look heavy, but when she tried to lift it, she could hardly get it off the floor. She noticed a single Nike shoebox, the lid on, sitting in the corner. Lifting the lid she was stunned to see that it was filled almost to the brim with medals and ribbons. Carefully, she replaced the lid and returned with her coffee to the seat by the window.

An hour had passed when it began to sleet. "He should be back any minute," she thought. "He won't stay out long in weather like this."

Still she watched, sitting at the window with her third cup of coffee. Briefly, she got up, found the bagels and prepared breakfast for herself. At ten o'clock, with Jacob gone for an hour and a half, Heather began to worry. The sleet had picked up, mixing with rain and some snow. The street was getting icy. She got a fresh cup of coffee and paced back and forth by the window watching for him. There was still no sign of him.

At ten-thirty, exactly two hours after she had watched him leave, Jacob rounded the corner, running fast, dancing over the icy patches. Relieved to see him, Heather ran to the apartment door and opened it for him.

At least a minute later, Jacob came into the lobby at the foot of the stairs.

He climbed the stairs, holding onto the handrail and moving slowly like an old man, a sharp contrast to the speed and grace she had seen moments before as he finished his run. Ice coated his cap and clung to the creases of his jacket. The tops of his thighs in the tights were soaked and dark. Bits of ice lingered in his eyebrows, and beads of water tipped the whiskers in the lines of his cheeks. He was flushed red, his eyes, dark and sunken. He looked at her, touched her arm briefly, and then walked straight into the bathroom without a word.

Heather heard the shower running. She put a bagel into the toaster and got a cup of coffee ready for him. Minutes past and the water continued to run in the bathroom. Finally she went to the bathroom door and knocked.

"Jacob, are you all right?"

"Yeah."

"Can I come in?"

"If you want."

She opened the door. The bathroom was steamy. His running clothes were in a wet heap on the floor. She pushed back the shower curtain and found Jacob sitting on the floor of the tub with the scalding water running over his gaunt torso. His eyes were closed. "Too tired to stand," he said.

"I've got coffee ready for you," Heather offered. "And a bagel."

"Make that two bagels. And go heavy with the cream cheese. I'll be out in a minute."

Heather put the second bagel in the toaster and coated the first one with a half inch of cream cheese. A few minutes later, Jacob walked into the living room wearing a wool sweater, blue jeans, and heavy socks. "Thanks for the coffee and the bagel. It's good to have this waiting for me after a long run."

"Are you okay? You look awful." Perhaps this was the moment, she thought. He was tired and vulnerable. Maybe this would be the time for her to reach him. She could mother him and he would become hers.

"No, I'm fine. Just tired. I had a great run."

"Wasn't it cold? Shouldn't you have come in when the sleet and snow started?"

"No, once I get going it's not bad. Besides, I was a long way from home when the sleet hit. I had to keep going to get home, anyway. It only bothered me when I headed into the wind. The ice stings when it hits your face."

"But what if you'd slipped on the ice? You could have been hurt."

"I'm careful. And if I fell, I'd just get up and keep on running."

"This is an insane sport you're in Jacob. Don't you ever take a day off? Even on a day like this?"

"No. Some days when I'm really tired, I take it easy. Maybe just go for an easy ten-mile run. But every Sunday I do twenty miles at pretty close to the pace I plan to run the marathon. It's like my own special Sunday morning religion. Today, I went out to Watertown and came up the other side of the river back to Boston. I went a couple of miles beyond twenty today. I figure, somewhere on a day like this there's some guy I'll be facing in the marathon. And he's doing those extra miles. If I want to be able to beat him when I race him, I have to at least match whatever he might be doing in training."

"There's got to be an easier way. This is insane."

"Then I'm insane. I told you I take an easy ten mile run as my whole day's training every once and a while."

"There is no such thing as an easy ten mile run. Maybe you *are* insane."

"Heather, running's become easier for me than walking. More natural. It's what I do. It's who I am. It's all I am. It's me. Love me, love my running."

With that, Jacob stood, stiffly and took his plate into the kitchen, rinsing the bagel crumbs into the sink. "A run like today does beat me up, though. I'd like to take a nap if you don't mind. You're free to stay with me or go. Whatever you want."

Heather thought about her choice for a moment. She wasn't reaching him. He was gone again. "I think I'll head back to my place, then," she said. "Call me or come by tomorrow night when you're rested?"

"Sure. See you tomorrow." He was already in the bedroom and face down on the bed asleep by the time Heather had her coat on. She let herself out and drove back to her apartment through the icy streets, the sleet rattling on the windshield.

For the next few days, Heather felt an uneasiness whenever she was with Jacob. He was always tired. When they made love he was awkward, rushing to finish, then falling asleep. His body still was as taut as ever, but he seemed thinner. They talked little. He was sullen, not caring to hear about her classes and not wanting to talk about his running.

Things fell apart one evening in February. Heather and Jacob were sitting on the sofa watching television. Emily slumped in a chair across the room, reading. In the midst of the show, Jacob leaned down and took off his shoes and socks. Then he took nail clippers out of his pocket and began trimming his toenails. Emily got up quietly, exchanging a quick look with Heather, and went into her bedroom and shut the door.

When Jacob finished with the nails he started trimming a curl of dead skin off an old blister next to his big toe. The toenail clippings sat in a ragged pile on the carpet.

"That's it! That's enough! Jacob, what are you doing?"

"Trimming my nails. And fixing this old blister. My feet take a beating when I run, and I need to keep things tidy or I get more blisters."

"You call this tidy? Look at you. Sitting here on my sofa with toenails and dead skin all over the rug. And look at your toenails anyway. They're all black. Some of them are hardly there, and some are missing all together. Your feet are a mess. They're ugly."

"Yeah. That's the point Heather. If I don't keep the nails trimmed, they bleed, they turn black and they fall off. That's why I'm doing this. What's the problem?"

"It's a mess, Jacob. It's a mess and you're a mess for making it. Stop it and clean it up. This is just disgusting."

Jacob put the clippers away. Then he picked up the clippings and took them into the kitchen, dumping them into the sink. He came back and began putting his shoes back on when Heather said, "I think you should go tonight, Jacob. Let's get together for lunch or something tomorrow."

"Okay." Jacob was baffled. It would be the first time in weeks that they had been together but hadn't made love. "Where do want to meet for lunch, then? And when?"

"I don't know. I'll call you and let you know. Someplace we can talk. I'll call."

She kissed him briefly on the lips as he left, but he knew it didn't feel right. Too much was missing.

The next day before noon, Heather found a quiet table in the corner of a busy sandwich shop and called Jacob. He came in, his coat open, walking with a rolling gate that mimicked his running form. He flipped his coat over the back of the chair, gave Heather a brief kiss and a grin, and then said, "This is new. We don't usually meet for lunch. I think I like it. What's good here?"

"Not much, I'm afraid."

"Then why did you bring me here?"

"Jacob, we've got to talk."

Jacob felt a chill and a sinking in his stomach. Was she going to break up with him? Girls didn't break up with him. They never had. He always left the girls, not them leaving him. And when they did leave him, he didn't care. But he'd been with Heather for nearly five months. It seemed like a lifetime to him. He couldn't imagine her leaving him. He focused on her, his ears ringing, and waited.

"Jacob, you're a special boy. I might have loved you. I don't know. I really like you. And you know we're great together in bed. But I want more. I want someone to love me. To really love me and care about me and the things that matter to me. All you have is your running. And I have to tell you. I'm sick and tired of the running. It's eating you alive. It's sickening, and I just can't take it anymore."

"Oh, come on. I run. It's what I do. But there's more to me than that. I'm studying physiology. There's something. We have all kinds of fun together. You know that."

But even as he said it, Jacob couldn't think of a thing that mattered to him except his running. And Heather. She mattered, too. But he didn't know how to tell her that.

"Jacob, I don't think we can see each other anymore. I need time. I just don't think I can live with your running, and I need time to decide what to do next. Maybe we'll get together sometime later, but I don't think so. I just don't think I can deal with you and your running anymore."

"Okay. So then, where do we go from here?" He knew it was dumb question, but he couldn't think of another thing to say.

"Where do we go from here? I'm going to my one o'clock class. And you, I expect, are going to go out for a run somewhere. I don't really care anymore."

Heather stood and walked out, putting her coat on as she went.

Jacob sat alone, stunned, watching her as she passed the window on the street outside. The waiter came to the table. "Are we ready to order, sir?"

"Fuck you!" Jacob pushed passed him and hurried to the street. He looked in the direction Heather had headed, but she was gone.

He stood for several minutes, alone on the sidewalk, trying to figure out what to do next. Run. Heather had said he should go for a run. It made sense. He could always count on a run. It was a great time to think things through. He headed back to his apartment to get ready.

When he was dressed to run, Jacob looked out his front window to check the weather, though he had just come in from the street and knew it was cold. It looked gray and damp and icy, a typical winter day in Boston. Jacob considered the gritty reality of running through the dirty streets in the cold. He felt his weariness from the weeks of long miles he had run through the winter. Dulled, he walked back into his bedroom and fell asleep, dressed in his tights, jacket, cap, and gloves.

Jacob awoke several hours later. It was dusk. For a few moments he considered going out for his run even though it was getting dark. He had run after dark many times, and he knew the miles would be important to have behind him when he got to the marathon. Instead, he peeled off the running clothes and took a shower. Then he returned to his bed, and crawled under the blankets naked. He dozed again briefly and woke thinking of Heather.

She was gone. *No big deal,* he thought. *She's just another girl. There are many more. Plenty of them. And better looking, with better bodies. She can go to hell. I don't need her.*

But he kept thinking about her and finally called her cell phone. It rang until it went to her voice mail. Hearing the recording of her voice, Jacob began to cry. He had never felt that way before when he had left a girl. Or those few times when a girl had left him first he had never cried. He hung up and waited. A half hour later he called again and left a message. "Heather. Hi, this is Jacob. Listen. I'm sorry for whatever I did, but I'd like to see you and talk this through. Call me. Let me know when we can get together."

Then he waited. It was almost nine o'clock and he hadn't eaten since breakfast. He got dressed and cooked spaghetti for dinner; a full box of spaghetti and jar of sauce. It was a lot but he always ate heavily after a hard day's run. After a few bites he lost his appetite. He dumped the rest of the spaghetti into the trash and opened a bottle of Sam Adams. He took the bottle to the chair by the bay window and sat in the dark looking out at the street below. The orange glow of the street light shone on the dirty snow banks and parked cars. It was silent and nothing moved.

Jacob finished the beer and called Heather again. Emily answered on the second ring.

"Hi, Emily. It's Jacob. Is Heather there?"

"Yes."

"Can I talk to her?"

"No. She doesn't want to talk to you."

"Can I come over to see her? We need to talk."

"No. Don't come over. She doesn't want to see you. And she doesn't have anything else to say to you. And you've got nothing else to say to her to change her mind."

"Oh, come on, Emily. Give me a break. Put her on the phone. I've got to talk to her."

"Jacob, all she has to say to you is goodbye. That's that. And I agree with her. Don't call here again, and don't come over. Is that clear? Now, goodbye."

The line went dead.

Jacob sat for a while longer looking out the window at the street. Still nothing moved. He paced the small room and sat staring out the window some more. The world seemed empty outside and in. It was after midnight when he went to bed.

He woke up to a bright day. Blue sky and sunshine. A good day for a run. He showered and shaved and put on a pot of coffee. Then he sat by the window with a bagel and a large mug of coffee. Parking places were empty; people had gone off to work. He felt very alone, abandoned by his neighbors. And by Heather. Puddles were next to the crusted snow banks. Birds pecked at the sand in the street. Spring was approaching. And with spring, the marathon. It would be a good day to run. But still he sat.

Jacob looked out the window for an hour more watching the street below.

Then he prepared a tuna sandwich for lunch. He gulped orange juice, right from the carton, with the sandwich.

He called Heather again. The call went to her voice mail and he hung up. He needed to talk to someone. Except for the brief dialogue with Emily, he hadn't spoken with anyone in more than twenty-four hours; since he cussed at the waiter. And the conversation with Emily hadn't been good.

He called his parents' house. Walter picked up on the second ring. "Hello?"

"Hi, Dad. It's Jacob. Is mom home?"

"No, she's gone to work. What's up?"

"Nothing. Just wanted to call and check in. You're home?"

"Yeah. I got in yesterday. I don't go back out to sea for a few days, so I'm home. Jacob, you never call unless you need something. What's up?"

"Nothing. Just wanted to call."

"Your running going okay?"

"Sure. Great. Lots of miles."

"You'll be ready for Boston?"

"Yeah. I'll be ready."

"How far did you go yesterday?"

"Actually, I took the day off. I guess I needed the rest."

"You never take a day off. Are you hurt? Or sick?"

"No. I'm fine." Jacob paused. "Actually, I don't know. I think Heather and I broke up."

"Aww, Jacob. That's a shame. She seemed like a pretty nice girl. What happened?"

"I don't know, Dad. Maybe I was a jerk. I don't know. But I'm pretty sure she's gone. I don't know what to do."

"Is that why you didn't run yesterday?"

"I guess."

"Okay. Listen, son. Don't worry about the running for once. You need to sort this whole thing out. You want to come home for a couple of days and hang out here? Get some home cooking?"

"Maybe. No. I can stay here. But I guess I do need to think things through. What should I do, Dad? I don't know what to do. I don't know how to do this."

"Well, Jacob, son. I don't know if I have any great advice or wisdom for you. Your mother and I've been married for twenty-five years this coming June. It's been a long time since I had to figure out what to do when I lost a girlfriend. But I remember that it hurts. And I understand that you're hurting now. All I can tell you is that I understand. And I care. And your mother and I will be here for you. We always have been and we always will be."

"Thanks."

The two men sat for a few moments longer, miles apart, in silence on the telephone. Then Jacob started again. "Dad, I've never felt upset when I broke off with a girl before. It's never mattered before. How long does it take to feel right again?"

"I don't know. Maybe it depends on how long you were together and how much she meant to you. This Heather. She was special?"

"I don't know. Yeah, I guess so. Yeah. She was special. And she's gone."

"Yeah. She's gone." Walter thought about it for a moment, while the words sank in with his son. Then he asked, "No chance she'll come back?"

"No. I'd like to think I could convince her to come back," Jacob answered. "But I've been thinking it over, and I guess I really was a jerk. A dumb fool. All I did was run and hang out with her. I didn't do anything special for her, and I guess she got tired of the way I treated her. Of the way I am. I could change, but she wouldn't be there to see it. I'm pretty sure I screwed up with this one."

"Okay. Well, son, take your time. There will be another girl. But take your time. Stay busy with your classes and your running. Don't rush into anything right away with the next girl you meet. Don't go looking to find another Heather so you can make it right. The right girl will be there when you're ready. But Jacob, when you find her? Learn from this and treat the next girl the way she needs to be treated. Okay?"

"Okay, Dad. Thanks. It feels good to talk with you."

"Okay, son. Your mom gets home a bit after eleven. You want her to call you then?"

"No, I'll call you if I need to. But I'll be fine."

"Anything else I can do for you son?"

"No, Dad. I'm fine thanks. This has been good. Talk to you later."

"Bye, son."

Jacob hung up and sat for a few moments longer at the window. He felt good. He got dressed and went out for a run. He was more rested than he'd been in weeks, after the day of not running and the long hours of sleep. He rolled through the back streets to Boston College. Turning right he headed out toward Newton, running backwards along the Boston Marathon route. His mind was blank. The exhilaration of the run was all that he could feel. He thought from time to time about Heather. About Emily, too. And about the things his dad had said. But mostly he just ran, enjoying the strength in his legs. The speed. The air rushing past his body. It was cool, but not cold. A brilliant sun shone.

Heartbreak Hill, they called this part of the course. *An apt name*, Jacob thought. He noted that it was a half a mile long and steep. It was at the twenty mile mark of the race, a time when even the best runners would be starting to feel the fatigue. In the race everyone would be going up. Running out from Boston, he was going down the hill, and he flew, the pent-up energy from his day of rest, and the stored anger and despair driving him faster and faster. Two more downhills followed his descent of Heartbreak Hill. Energized, he tore down the hills and turned toward Wellesley.

He had never seen most of the early miles of the marathon, but he had checked a map. He knew the route, and he continued tracing the course in reverse. He had run more than an hour when he passed through the center of Wellesley. Next was Wellesley College. Though he wasn't yet tired, Jacob realized that he needed to begin to plan to turn back toward Boston and home.

Wellesley College, he thought. *An all women's school. Maybe the next girlfriend would be a student at Wellesley.* He turned into the campus.

College girls were on the road through the campus. Most didn't even notice as he charged past. Those who did looked at him like he was an intruder in their dorm. None of them smiled at him. He left the campus and turned in a direction that would take him toward Boston. In several minutes he found himself back on the Marathon route, retracing his steps toward home.

The tiredness began to settle on Jacob after nearly two hours of running.

He was in Newton and facing the decision of turning and going back up over Heartbreak Hill, or going straight to follow a flatter, more direct route homeward. Jacob chose sensibly, for the first time in months, and went straight. His apartment was still at least five miles away.

The repetition of hundreds of miles run at a fast pace had trained Jacob's body to maintain his speed. Tired as he was, he continued on toward home, clicking through the miles in just a bit more than once every five minutes. The joy he had felt with the speed at the start of the run was gone now. He felt trapped in his body, as though he were locked in a runaway train. It became more and more difficult to hold onto the pace, but a slower speed felt clumsy and unnatural. He had to keep going. There was no other way home.

Now he was hurting, his legs locking on him in mid-stride from time to time. His shirt inside his nylon jacket felt cold and was soaked with sweat. The world he passed through seemed hazy and remote. Jacob concentrated on his running form, thinking about each step. *It's such a simple thing, running. Take one step, then another, then another. You take more steps, faster and faster. Each step brings you closer to home. Enough steps and you get to where you're going.* Tired as he was, each stride had become a conscious effort. Still he raced on.

How can I be so tired? he questioned himself. *I didn't eat much yesterday. Or today really. And I didn't drink enough. I'm dehydrated and out of energy. Learn from this. Don't let this happen in the marathon. Prepare. Eat and drink next time.*

The marathon! Jacob calculated the pace he estimated he had been running, and checked the time. His pace and the time would give him an idea of the distance he had run. Fatigue blurred logic. The math finally came together and he figured he might have run twenty-three, maybe twenty-four fast miles. Ahead he could see St. Elizabeth's Hospital looming above the street. An intuition flashed through his head. He knew that he was on the edge of a significant moment; something special was about to happen.

It's nonsense, Jacob thought. *It's just the fatigue. Nothing special is going on. I need to stay focused on my stride. On my rhythm. I need to keep running. It's a mile from the hospital to my house. I'll make it home before I die. And I may have run just short of a marathon when I get there. Just get me home. One step, then another. Each stride gets me closer. Just get home.*

A crowd was at the bus stop in front of the hospital. As Jacob approached them a girl stepped from the crowd into the street. She shaded her eyes from the late afternoon sun as she looked up the street watching for her bus. She saw Jacob. She stepped back to give him room to run by.

Worn down as he was, Jacob saw the girl, lit by the sun. Dark hair. A smile that made him want to stop. Her eyes met his.

As he passed her, she clapped and cheered him on.

"Way to run! You look great! Keep going, you're doing fine!"

I'm doing fine? Jacob thought. *Way to run? I'm a mess. I'm just stumbling along. And I'm certainly not doing fine.*

He turned for a moment after he'd passed and looked back. The girl was back out in the street, but not looking for the bus this time. She watched him as he ran away. She waved, grinned after him, and then pumped her fist in the air, still smiling.

"Go!" she shouted. "Go!"

Jacob finished the run and checked his watch. The run had taken two hours and twenty minutes. He also noted that it was just a bit after four-thirty. He had passed the hospital a few minutes earlier. Thinking of the girl, Jacob made a note of the time and wandered exhausted into his apartment. A shower, dinner, and several glasses of cranberry juice restored him.

The next morning, he ran his wake-up five miles, slowly and sore from the long run the afternoon before. Then he went to his classes. Classes were usually something he did to pass the time till the afternoon run. Today he paid attention and took notes. Things were different now. He ate a proper lunch, making sure to drink plenty of juice. Then he waited for the time to go for his afternoon run.

He anticipated this workout more than most of his recent runs. It was the girl. He wanted to see her again, and he knew she would be at the bus stop shortly before four-thirty. He timed the run carefully, running a loop that brought him by the bus stop at the hospital at the same time he had passed it the day before. The crowd was there, waiting for the bus, but the girl wasn't. Jacob ran home disappointed.

He had just finished dressing after his shower when there was a knock on his door. Jacob opened it to his coach. "Hey, Jacob. Your dad called and asked me to stop by after practice to look in on you. Said you were having some troubles. Want to go grab a bite of dinner?"

"Sure, Coach." It was the first time Jacob's coach had been to his apartment. It was also the first time he and Jacob had shared a dinner.

They went to a steak house.

"How did you find my apartment?" Jacob asked. "I didn't know you knew where I lived."

"We have your address in our files. And your dad gave me directions. He was worried about you and gave me a call. You doing all right?"

"Yeah. Now. My girlfriend left me, and it messed me up for a while. I missed a day of training. I talked to my dad about it."

"Don't worry about the training right now. We can talk about that later. Besides, a day off now and then won't kill you. You can always make up the missed miles."

"Yeah, Coach, I think I did that. Made up the missed miles. I ran a hard twenty-five miles yesterday. Crashed at the end, but I made it. At least now I have no doubts about being able to finish a marathon. Hell, I just about did that yesterday in training."

"Okay. Good for you. But right now that's not that important. Talk to me about this girl. What happened?"

"I screwed up, coach. I didn't treat her right. I just didn't see it. And I didn't realize that she was important. I made a mess of it and I lost her."

The waitress came to take their order. She flirted outrageously with Jacob while he ordered his steak.

"Rare," she said, repeating Jacob's order. "You like it rare. Me too. I should have known that a guy like you would like it the way I do. You're rare, just like me."

Coach watched, amused. When she was gone with their order he said, "It looks like you've gotten over the girlfriend pretty fast. You going to ask this one out? I've never known you to be without a girlfriend for long."

"No. She's cute, and it's fun to flirt. But, no. My dad said to take my time. I'd know when the right one came along. So, I'm not going to waste my time chasing around. I'll wait until I know I've met someone special. And this girl's not the one."

He thought again of the girl at the bus stop. Her hair. The smile. Her waving and pumping her fist in the air. *"You look great! Keep going, you're doing fine!"*

Jacob and his coach ate their steaks and talked about his training, and the marathon. And they talked about girls. As they were driving back to Jacob's apartment, Coach said, "Jacob, I've never coached a guy like you before. You've got a gift. It's not just your speed or your tolerance for the training. It's the emotion you bring to your racing. It makes you more desperate to win than just about anyone. But that can't get into everything you do, the rest of your life. It's okay to channel that into your running. But you have to be careful not to let it hurt you in the other parts of your life. And be very careful not to let it hurt the people you care about and the ones who care for you."

Jacob listened without saying a word. He got out when they were in front of his apartment. Coach rolled down the car window. "There's not much else I can do for you as a runner, Jacob. I can't make you any better. You're as fast as I can make you, and have been for a couple of years. You've still got a lot to learn, though. About how to race. Till now, you've been able to just beat up on people to win. But where you're going, everyone's as good as you. To win with these people requires something more. Nuances. Subtleness. You need to be able to stay in tune with yourself, which you already do. But you also have to be able to read the people you're running with. I can't teach you how to do that. It requires an emotional sensitivity. It's like an art, and it can't be taught. Either you've got it within you or you don't. I suspect that you do have it, but you have to find that for yourself. But I'm available to talk any time you want someone to talk with. Keep in touch. Give me a call."

"I will, Coach. You can count on it. I will. Thanks for dinner."

The next day Jacob planned his afternoon run to go past the hospital at the start of the run, and to loop back again to finish by the hospital at the usual time. Approaching the bus stop from the opposite direction at the start of the run, he saw the girl standing in the street, her back to him watching for her bus. She heard his approaching footsteps, turned, saw him, and smiled.

"There you are," she said. "I looked for you yesterday." It was unexpected. Jacob couldn't imagine that she too, had been hoping to run into him again. He stopped, something he never, ever did during a run.

"I ran by at four-thirty. Same time as the day before, when I first saw you. You weren't here."

The other people at the bus stop stood watching them without saying a word.

"No. I get out of work at three. That first day I was late getting out. I'm Kate."

"I'm Jacob. How can we get together? I'd like to get to know you."

"I live downtown. Here's my number. Call me?" She slipped him a piece of paper.

"You know I will."

"Now go run, Jacob. But call me. Tonight?"

"Tonight," he answered with a grin.

Jacob zipped the paper with the number into his jacket pocket as he ran off. *She had her number ready to give me. She was looking for me. Wanted to meet me!* As soon as he finished his run he went into his apartment and called the number.

A girl answered. "Hello?"

"Kate, please."

"Speaking. Who's this?"

"It's Jacob. From the bus stop?"

"Jacob! The runner. I'm glad you called. How are you? How was your run?"

"Good. A little over an hour."

"Mmm. That's a long way. You must be pretty good. You looked fast when you went by that first day."

"That first day I was really tired. I was a wreck when you saw me. But that's no big thing. Listen, Kate. I don't know a thing about you except that you work at St. Elizabeth's Hospital. But I'd like to see you some time. I'd like to get to know you."

"And I'd like to get to know you too, Jacob. Should we get together?"

"Yes, I think we should. How? When?"

"Do you work?" Kate asked. "Are you in school?"

"I'm in grad school at BU."

"Okay. Since I've got a job, let me take you to dinner. Is that okay?"

"Sure. When and where?"

Kate made the arrangements. They met the next night at a seafood place in the Back Bay. They talked. Kate asked about his running. "Jacob, you seem to run a lot. An hour, you said, the day we talked at the bus stop, maybe that far also the day we met. Are you a serious runner?"

"Yeah, I guess," Jacob answered. "But tell me more about yourself." He had really never talked much with Heather, he realized, and rarely about anything that mattered to either of them. As little as he had talked about his running with Heather, he felt that running had dominated their relationship somehow. He was determined not to let that happen again with Kate. He wanted to get to know her, something he'd never really done with Heather.

"I grew up south of Boston, the oldest of six brothers and sisters," she said. "My mom died when I was twelve, and my dad worked to support the family, so I kind of became the mother for my brothers and sisters. I took care of dinner every night, and did the laundry and everything. And I still got good grades in school and played on the soccer team. When I graduated from high school, I went to college to study to be a pharmacist. But I commuted and still did things for my family when I got home."

Jacob listened. He thought of his own life, doing things on his own, only for himself. He couldn't imagine living a life surrounded by so many other people, all of them depending on him. "It must have worn you out to live like that," he said.

"Not really. And it wasn't like I had a choice. I wanted to become a pharmacist, and my father and my brothers and sisters needed me. What else was I going to do? I had to take care of things, and I had to study. So I did."

"And now you're a pharmacist at the hospital? Tell me about that."

Kate described her job. Then she added, "The best thing is that now I have enough money to get my own apartment. And my brothers and sisters are getting old enough to take care of themselves without me. Two of them have graduated from high school already and the rest are pretty grown up as well. So now I've got an apartment all to myself here in the Back Bay. You can't imagine how good it feels to come home at night and have the place all to myself. It's really great to be alone."

"I've been alone my whole life," said Jacob. "I'm an only child and my parents were always off working. I just about raised myself."

Kate seemed puzzled. "Weren't your parents there for you? Didn't you have friends hanging around? And your running. Weren't you on your high school track team? Maybe in college, too? Didn't you have a coach and teammates to turn to? There must have been someone. I can't imagine you could have gotten all the way through college and into grad school without people there."

"Well, maybe." Jacob thought it over. "My parents are pretty proud of the things I've done with my running. And I know my dad is concerned when things don't go well for me. And yeah, I ran in high school and college, and I had teammates, friends, and coaches. But I didn't really hang with any of them. I spent a lot of time on my own. Maybe too much."

"What do you mean, too much?" Kate asked.

"I don't know. Maybe I should have paid a bit more attention to the people around me. I got pretty worked up about my life at times. About my running."

Kate was puzzled. "I don't understand. What do you mean you got pretty worked up?"

Jacob paused, thinking of how to explain. If he said this wrong, he could begin his relationship with Kate right where he had ended with Heather. But he needed for her to understand. "Kate, listen. I'm pretty serious with my running. You can't imagine what it's like. I run an hour and half each day. I lift weights three times a week. I stretch every night. It's the most important thing in my life. If I let it, the running can take over everything. I'm trying to slow down and take some time for other things."

"You've also got grad school." Kate reached over and took his hand. "And you've got other friends, other things going on, right?"

"Well I should, but I don't really have many friends. And my grad school work is in exercise physiology. The only reason I care about it is because it helps me understand why I'm able to beat the other runners. I need to back off on the running a bit and get some perspective here. There really ought to be more to life than just running."

Kate stopped him. "Slow down," she said. "Are you a good runner? I mean, are you really good? Do you win a lot of races and all that?"

"You can't imagine. Yes, I'm good."

"How good?"

"There aren't many runners anywhere who can beat me."

"Then you should keep at it. You should run against the best runners you can find and see if they can beat you. The Boston Marathon's coming up in April. Why don't you enter the Boston Marathon and see how you do? They always get a bunch of good runners for the marathon, right?"

"I'm entered. That's why I'm running the way I am every day."

"How do you think you'll do?" Kate asked.

"I don't know. But I'm planning to try to win it."

"Then you go and do it, Jacob. You can get back in touch with your friends, and you can keep up with your physiology studies. There's no reason you can't do all that and run well, too."

"I don't know, Kate. It's not just that the running takes a lot of energy. It wears you down in other ways. It becomes all you do if you're not careful. It gets to be all you even think about."

"Then be careful. Jacob, I hung around with this kid in high school. My best friend, really. He was an amazing piano player, and he graduated and went to Juilliard to study piano. One year he came home at Christmas with a brace on his wrist. He had developed carpal tunnel syndrome from playing piano twelve hours a day for weeks on end. They made him take a month off and not touch a piano. But when the month was over, he played piano again. He's going to have a career in music, but he needed to get a little balance. He couldn't play piano twelve hours a day. That's all."

"Was he your boyfriend in high school? Do you still see him?"

"No, he was just a really good friend. And yes, I still see him. But this is my point. Here's what I've seen with him, and with some other people too, doctors at the hospital, other really successful people. Anybody who's really good at something probably has two things going for them. They have a natural talent for that thing, and they probably are just about obsessed with doing it. They love doing whatever their talent is. They do it so much they get to be really good at it. There's nothing wrong with obsession as long as you have some connections to other things, other people. Do you think you're a really talented runner?"

"I know I am."

"Then run. Just keep your head up and look around at things as you run past them."

"Yeah. That's how I met you, Kate."

"And isn't it nice that you did? So here we are having dinner together. Are you enjoying yourself?"

"Yes, I am." Jacob had to admit that it was the best time he'd had in months, maybe years. Kate was amazing. He began to relax.

"So, tell me then, Jacob. Why is running so important?"

"I like to win. And I can."

"Why is that so important to you?"

"I don't know. I was the smallest kid in school. Always picked last for playground games. Sat on the bench in Little League. But I always liked sports. Then I got to high school, and found track. And I was good. Nobody could touch me. It's important to me."

It was the first time he had really thought about this, his motivation for racing. He had never talked about it with anyone.

"What's it like? How does it feel to win a race? How do you outrun the others?"

Jacob thought it over. He had always just gone into races and beaten the other runners. He'd never really had to think it through before.

"Part of it is physiology. This part I've studied. My body is very good at pulling oxygen out of the air and getting it to my legs. That's the scientific explanation."

"Okay." Kate listened, intrigued by what Jacob said. "There's more?"

"Yeah. The rest is the stuff that maybe comes from all those times I was picked last on the playground as a kid. I've got a point to prove. To other people. Maybe to myself. I'm still not that big, but I've got a mean streak. A chip on my shoulder when I run. I believe I can hurt the other runners more than a prize fighter does to his opponent. And I don't have to lay a finger on them. There comes a moment in a race where everyone is hurting. That's when I attack. I leave the other runners with an awful choice to make. They can hurt a bit less if they give up and slow down, and that means they let me win. Or they can hurt worse and worse by staying with me. They always let me win."

"If the other runners hurt when they race you, don't you hurt, too?"

"Yes, but it's just fatigue. It's part of the game. It passes, and you're left with a win. It's not a big deal. I honestly don't know why other runners don't put themselves out there the way I do. Maybe a few do, but I still beat them. Maybe they just can't put up with the pain the way I do. I don't know. But I do enjoy winning races. I enjoy beating the other runners. Maybe a little bit is that I enjoy making them hurt."

Kate sat in awe, stunned by the placid, small man sitting across the table from her sipping an after dinner cup of coffee. He was so matter of fact as he described how he could hurt his opponents. How he liked hurting them.

"Your mean streak," she said. "I can't see it. You seem like such a gentle person."

"That's because I'm not running right now. I'm not racing."

"We met when you were running," Kate said. "You didn't look mean then. You even stopped and took my phone number."

Jacob laughed. "Sometime I'll take you to a race. Not now though, not yet. You'll see the other side of me then."

They stayed at the restaurant till closing. Then Jacob walked Kate back to her apartment. As they crossed Commonwealth Avenue he put his arm around her and she shifted closer. They continued walking in step, without speaking till they were at the steps to her apartment building.

"Can I see you again?" Jacob asked.

"Sure, I'd like that." Kate stood closer.

"I'll come by tomorrow at seven. It's Friday. We'll do something."

"I'd like that," she repeated.

He leaned forward, pulling her to him by the lapels of her jacket and kissed her. Just once. "Good night, Kate. See you tomorrow."

Then he was gone.

They were together each night for the next week. They spent some time out in Boston, but not at bars or clubs. They walked around the city, sometimes stopping for dinner or a cup of coffee. Mostly they just talked. About each other's childhoods, about their families, about music and religion. About Jacob's studies, and about Kate's work. Sometimes about Jacob's running.

Kate invited Jacob in to her apartment on their third evening together. He looked around the apartment. It was small but well-furnished and clean. He felt embarrassed thinking of the barren look of his own apartment. Kate brought out chocolate cake and more coffee. They ate and talked some more. And again, they kissed good night as he left.

What am I doing? Jacob asked himself on his way home. *Usually by the third date I'd be in bed with the girl. Sometimes on the first. Here I am not even making a move on her. I don't want to screw this up by moving too fast, but this isn't at all like me.*

At the end of the week, the night ended, as had now become their habit, with the two of them sitting together on Kate's sofa. They kissed, and after a few moments, Jacob's hand slid from her shoulder to her neck. And from there inside her shirt. His fingers found the strap of her bra, sliding it from her shoulder. His palm rested on the softness of her breast.

He heard her take a short, quick breath, and for a moment she let his hand remain. Then she carefully reached and took his wrist. Slowly she lifted his hand out of her shirt. She kissed his palm and looked him in the eye.

"Jacob, not now. It's not that I don't want to do something. But not now. I broke up with my old boyfriend not that long ago. I'm just not ready. I think we may have something really special here, and I don't want to move too fast and make a mistake."

"Okay. But Kate, we have something special. You know it. And I know it. Why not now?"

"If we do it before we're both ready, it would be a mistake. It could lead to a situation where our relationship was all about sex. I want more."

"So do I. But our relationship could grow to more. Having sex doesn't mean that won't happen."

"Jacob, I don't want to have sex. I want to make love. There's a huge difference. I believe that if we do it before the relationship is solid, we might never get anything more out of it. We're too good friends already for me to want to take that chance."

Jacob sat back and looked at Kate. "Are you angry with me? Was it a mistake for me to do that?"

"No, of course not. You've been a perfect gentleman. In fact, I was a little surprised you didn't do something sooner. But it's just not the time. Not yet. You're not upset with me for stopping you, are you?"

"No. It actually does make sense. It's been a long time since I had a girlfriend I didn't sleep with. I'm trying to figure out what I'm supposed to do."

"We just keep doing what we've been doing for the past week. I don't know. We'll know when the time is right."

"How?"

"I don't know. I knew when I saw you that first day at the bus stop that you were someone special. I just felt it. And I'll know with this, too."

"Yeah, that day at the bus stop," Jacob continued. "I knew something was happening, too. So, I've got to believe you that we'll know when the time is right."

"Kate, you mentioned an old boyfriend. You said you broke up with a guy not that long ago. Tell me about it. What happened?"

"There's not much to say. We were together for almost three years, all the way back to college. He wanted to get married, and he wanted me to quit my job and have a lot of babies with him. He was pretty well off and said I wouldn't have to work. I could just stay home and raise his babies."

Jacob watched Kate as she talked. He saw the light in her eyes. Her dark hair, thick around her shoulders. He listened to what she said, fascinated by the littlest mannerisms and the small things that shifted about her face as she spoke. Just watching her mouth was enough to distract him from her words. He thought for a moment of Heather, but found that he couldn't even remember the color of her eyes.

To stay engaged in the conversation, Jacob asked a question. "Why did you and he break up? You would have had a pretty easy life with him."

"Yes, easy maybe. But that's not always such a good thing. You should know that from the things you've said about your running and racing. I love my job. And I've spent my whole life till now raising a family. I didn't want to give up my job to raise his family. There's more to me than to be just a breeder and a housewife for some guy. Finally, it came down to this. I said I planned to stay with my job and wait a few years to have kids. He said that my job was a stupid waste of time. So I walked out on him. You're the first guy I've seen since him. And it's been six months."

Jacob mulled over what she said. He understood.

"So, Jacob. What about you? What about your past? Other girlfriends? Other loves?"

Jacob thought about Heather and the other girls he had known. "Lots of girlfriends, but I'm afraid I might never have been in love before." He caught himself just in time. He almost added, "before I met you."

He continued, leaving the thought unsaid, but sensing that she had picked it up. "I've always been able to find girlfriends, but I never really bothered to do much except sleep with them. I really was a mess for a long time. Never had a long-term relationship until this past year."

"What happened this past year?"

"I met a girl last fall. We dated till just a couple of weeks ago. I really treated her like a jerk, and she dumped me. We were together for nearly six months, which is the longest I've ever been with anyone."

"How did you feel when she left you?"

"It hurt. I'd never felt that before. And I didn't know what to do."

"How did you get through it?"

"I ended up talking to my dad. And my coach came over. Then I met you."

"Well, I don't want to be the 'rebound girlfriend'. But I do like being with you. Are you okay with where we are right now?"

"Yes, of course I am. And you're not the rebound girlfriend. You're just my girlfriend, and I happened to meet you right after my old girlfriend left me."

"Right time and right place. If you had met me a year ago, I would have noticed you. There would have been 'chemistry'. But we probably wouldn't have gotten together because I was engaged to that other guy. It's good we met when we did."

"Yeah, and if we'd met a month ago, it would have been the same for me. Chemistry, but no connection, because I was still with my old girlfriend."

The evening ended as they had all of the earlier nights, with good night kisses. And even without sleeping with Kate, Jacob felt better about the evening than he ever had with Heather.

They continued getting together at the end of each day. Every evening Jacob would come by. Some nights Kate would have dinner cooking. Other times she would have her coat on when he came to the door and they would go out to eat together. Sometimes they went to a movie. Sometimes they stayed in and watched television. It wasn't that different from the way it had been with Heather, but Jacob felt a different mood to their evenings. Always they talked.

At the end of their third week together Jacob offered, "Kate, I'd like you to see my apartment. I'll cook dinner for you for a change."

"That will be nice. Can I bring something?"

"Sure. Wine. Red. I'll make spaghetti. Tomorrow about six?"

He gave Kate the address. The next day he skipped classes to get ready. Between his morning and afternoon runs he cleaned the apartment, the first time in the two months since Heather's visit. He set out the towels he had bought for Heather, and made the bed with the new sheets, all the while knowing that he would probably not take Kate into the bed.

He loaded up a series of songs on his IPod, but deliberately left out Norah Jones. That was Heather's music. It would not be played tonight. He put on soft rock. Sarah McLachlan. Music he knew Kate liked. He went out and bought flowers for the kitchen table where they would eat.

He got the kitchen ready to cook the spaghetti, the best meal he knew how to prepare. He was ready. He waited.

Kate came in and surveyed the apartment while Jacob hung up her coat. She walked to the bay window at the front of the apartment and stood, hands on her hips, looking down at the street.

"I love this window," she said. "If I've got my bearings right, it faces East. If I lived here, I'd sit here in the morning with my coffee, catching the sun, and watching the street down there wake up. Do you ever do that?"

Jacob remembered the morning after Heather left, the day he'd run twenty-five miles. The day he'd met Kate. "Yes, I've done that. It is nice."

Kate walked around the main room and past the kitchen. Spaghetti sauce simmered on the stove. She peeked into the bedroom, then stepped back, giving Jacob a small smile. "And there's the bedroom," she said, moving on. "And what's behind this last door?"

"That's kind of like my private home gym."

Kate went in. She picked up the bar of weights, and hefted it briefly over her head.

"Heavy," she said, "but not too heavy. What do you do for a weight routine?"

Jacob replied, amused that Kate seemed to understand weight training. "I do several sets of basic drills. High reps, but you're right, not that heavy a weight. The point is to be sure that my arms will be strong enough to help me late in a race when I'm tired."

"Mmm," Kate said as she started to leave the room.

"Wait," Jacob said. "You missed something."

He scooped up the Nike box from the floor. "You asked a while back if I was any good as a runner."

"Yes," Kate answered. "And you said that you were."

"Well, look." Jacob took the lid off the box and began sifting through the medals. "There. That's a couple of years of racing. So yes, I'm good."

Kate lifted one of the medals out of the box and examined it. "Pretty," she said. "It's on a ribbon with a pin. Why don't you wear all of them on your jacket like a Pentagon general or something?"

"Come on, that would look ridiculous!"

"Yes, but then everyone would know you were fast. Listen, Jacob. The nice thing about your sport is that you look perfectly normal. You're not, though. You know it and I know it. But people can't look at you like they would look at a seven foot tall basketball player and just know that you were a special athlete or something. I think you're right to keep all the medals here in a shoe box. Or maybe you could take some of the prettiest ones and put them in a frame. And if you win the Boston Marathon, that one you really ought to show off."

"Hey, Kate, if I win the Boston Marathon, I'll give you the medal and you can wear it like a piece of jewelry on a chain around your neck."

They walked back into the main room of the apartment. Kate took another long look around.

"I like it here" she said. "It's very comfortable. Spartan, but comfortable. It's you, Jacob."

"I think I need pictures. The walls are too bare."

"Yes, pictures would add something. But you don't *need* them. They would be nice to have. Maybe we can check out some of the art galleries on Newbury Street sometime. We could pretend we're rich, and act like we were seriously going to buy something."

"Do you like art?" Jacob asked.

"Yes, but I still can't afford to buy anything but basic prints and photographs. No original paintings. Maybe someday."

"Okay, Kate. Here's an idea. My parents live up in Gloucester. On Cape Ann. I'm sure you know that Rockport is up there on Cape Ann, too. There are galleries all around Rockport. We could go up there so you could see where I grew up and meet my parents. And then we could go see the shops in Rockport. Maybe next Saturday."

"Don't you have to run?"

"Well, that's the good news. I've been checking in with my coach once a week to talk about my training. Coach has me starting to back off the miles this week. Boston is two weeks away, and he wants me to start getting rested. I'll only run about seventy miles this week, with a basic ten mile run on Saturday and another on Sunday. And then I take it really easy next week. It's like a vacation, almost. I could do my run first thing in the morning and have the whole day wide open for you."

"Okay! Let's do it!" Kate gave him a quick kiss and joined him in the kitchen to cook the spaghetti.

They drove to Cape Ann on Saturday. It was warm for early April with the sun shining.

"I hope it's like this for you next week for the marathon," said Kate. "I wouldn't want it to be cold or rainy on the day of the race."

"I would," Jacob explained. "I've been training all winter in the cold. My body's used to it. Heat can be a problem on a long run. So pray for a cool, rainy day with a tail wind from the west."

They stopped in front of his house. Walter was in the yard tending to the gardens. He stopped and wiped the dirt from his hands. Then he came out to the street to meet them.

"How you doing, Jacob? And this is your new girlfriend?"

Jacob let the "new" pass, as did Kate. "Yes, dad, this is Kate."

Walter shook her hand. "Nice to meet you, Kate."

Eileen came rushing from the side door. "Jacob! Hello! Welcome home! And who is this young lady?"

"Mom, this is Kate. I told you about her on the phone."

"Yes, yes. Come on in the house, Kate. Get yourself comfortable. Jacob tells us you work at a hospital in Boston. I'm a nurse in the hospital up here in Gloucester."

"Yes, Mrs. Payne, I work in the pharmacy at St. Elizabeth's." They all went into the kitchen.

"How did you meet Jacob?" Walter asked.

"He was out for a run and we met. Just one of those things."

"Well, young lady, you come with me and I'll show you what he's all about with his running. Come on down stairs. Let me show you his trophies."

Walter led Kate out of the kitchen. As she left, Kate gave Jacob a smile and a quick wink. He had warned her to expect this. Jacob stayed behind with his mother. When Walter and Kate were gone, Eileen said, "Jacob, be careful with this girl. It hasn't been long since you were with Heather. Don't do something too quickly with this one."

"Mom, I'm fine. We're fine. Great, actually. It just didn't work out with Heather, but this is different. Don't worry. Talk with her. Listen to her. You get to know her just a little and you'll understand."

"She is pretty, but you've always had pretty girls around. Heather was pretty, too. But there's more to it."

"Mom, I know. I really do know the difference. And it's so different with Kate. You've got to trust me with this. She's pretty special."

Kate and Walter returned from the basement. Kate went over to Jacob and gave him a hug. "You really must have been something," she teased. "You think you can still run fast enough to win any prizes?"

"We'll see in a week. Mom, dad, you're both going to be able to come to the marathon?"

"We wouldn't miss it." said Walter. "Are you ready?"

"Almost. Coach has me easing off the miles to get rested. He's got a pass so he can drive me out to Hopkinton for the start. You can ride out there with us if you get to my apartment early on race day. Kate's coming, too."

"We'll be there," said Eileen. "Just let us know what time."

Kate and Jacob had lunch. Then he showed her around the rest of the house. Finally, they were ready to leave.

"We're going to head over to Rockport for the afternoon," Jacob said to his parents. "But I'll call as soon as I know what time you should be in Boston next week to meet up with Coach and Kate and me."

"Well, Kate," said Eileen. "It was very nice to meet you." She gave a Kate a hug.

"Yes, it was," added Walter. "I'm sure we'll see a lot more of you."

"Yes, I've enjoyed it. Thanks for lunch. See you at the marathon next week."

Jacob gave Kate a quick tour of Gloucester, then headed out to Rockport. They spent much of the afternoon wandering through the shops and art galleries, holding hands. Late in the afternoon, they bought a bottle of wine and some bread and drove south along the coast. Several miles after leaving Cape Ann, Jacob turned onto a narrow road that wound down past some mansions to the ocean. There was a gravel parking area next to a small rock beach on a cove. Rocky cliffs, crowned with huge houses, guarded each side of the cove.

Jacob got out of the car and led Kate to some of the rocks at one end of the beach. They sat and Jacob opened the wine, pouring it into two paper cups. They sat with the wine and bread and watched the surf together.

"You're awfully quiet," said Kate.

"Thinking about the race."

"What about it?"

He sat silently for a moment looking out at the waves. She waited.

"Kate, listen. Remember that time I explained how I win races, and you said you thought I was too nice to hurt my opponents?"

"Yes." She paused, waiting to see what was on Jacob's mind, why he was so quiet.

"Well, you're about to find out where that mean streak comes from. It's not something I like. Something I'm particularly proud of. But I find an attitude somewhere that makes me be like that. I can feel it coming already. I get a bit nasty sometimes as I get near a big race. I don't know if you'll want to be around me. I can get quiet. Sullen, someone once said. Little things can set me off. If you want to leave, that's okay. Just be there after the race."

"I'm not going to leave, Jacob. Unless you want me to. And, yes, I'll be there after the race."

"No, I don't want you to leave. I just don't want to irritate you or make you see me at less than my best."

"It's all right, Jacob. Just let me know what I can do to help you these next few days."

"There's not much you can do. I have to run the race alone. I have to prepare alone."

"I'll stay away if you want, but I'd rather be with you through this. Would you like me to come by to spend time with you this week? Would you like me to cook for you next weekend before the race?"

"That would all be nice. Yes, please. Just please be patient with me."

"Of course."

"And understand that I might not win this race. I can beat just about anybody in college, but this one's different. Now I'm going to be racing grown men. Guys who've been running races like Boston for years. This is how they earn their living. You know how I said I can take guys and hurt them till they give up and let me win? A bunch of these guys might be able to do that to me. And I might not be able to do anything about it. These guys might be able to make me really hurt, this time."

Kate looked at him. She sat silently for a minute. Then she said, "Jacob, whatever you do, I'll still love you. If you win, that's great. That's fantastic. But I love you, whether you win or not. I hope you do win, but that's not why I love you."

Jacob took a sip of the wine. He thought about what Kate had said. That she loved him. He tossed a chunk of the bread to a sea gull, and stared at the waves.

"You love me? What's to love? You say you love me. Why?"

"Because you're you. Just the way you are. I can't explain it. It's just the way things are. And your running is part of who you are. Win or lose."

"It may not be pretty Kate. After the race, I might throw up. What would you do about that?"

"I'd wash your face. I'd give you a sip of cool water. Remember, I work in a hospital. I've seen worse."

"But you haven't seen me like that. I'm going to hurt myself next week. It's how it is when you race a marathon. When I finish, they tell me I may be too sore and stiff to get my warm-up pants on. I may be too tired to get out of my racing shirt and into a dry T-shirt. I'll be soaked in sweat. Up close it's not a very nice sport."

"If you're too sore to get into your warm-up pants, I'll help you sit down. Then I'll help you get them on. Listen, Jacob. I'm in this for the whole ride. I want to be with you, and I don't care if you throw up or get sweaty. Okay?"

Jacob looked at her. The setting sun caught her hair from behind. He leaned to her and kissed her. "Okay. Thank you. I think I might love you too, Kate."

He paused for a moment thinking about what he had just said. Then he kissed her again, and grinning, added, "Hell, I *know* I love you Kate."

The Boston Marathon is run on a Monday. It's Patriot's Day in Massachusetts, the day of Paul Revere's Ride and the start of the Revolutionary War. The weekend before the race is devoted to pre-race activities in Boston. Kate met Jacob at his apartment on Saturday after lunch and went with him to the Prudential Center to pick up his number.

Crowds of runners milled about, dressed like Jacob, in running shoes, blue jeans, a T-shirt, and a warm up jacket. Kate held his hand so she wouldn't lose him in the crowd as he hurried to the number pick-up area. Jacob walked without a word, pushing through the other runners. He was flushed, Kate noticed, and kept his eyes down, avoiding looking at the other runners. Lines of runners crept toward tables where volunteers checked names off lists and handed the runners their numbers. The runners also collected bags of promotional items, coupons to buy running shoes, running magazines, granola bars, juice boxes. The tables were marked with large signs: #101-500, #501-1000, #1001-1500. The numbers continued up to well past 10,000. The line of tables went beyond Kate's sight.

"Jacob, there are more than ten thousand runners entered. I had forgotten it was such a big race. Do you know what your number is?"

"Yes."

Jacob moved to the end of the room to a table that was set aside labeled "Elite Runners: 1 – 100." There wasn't a line at this table. Kate followed

Jacob as he darted up to the table, gave his name, showed an identification card, and got his bag and number.

"What's your number?" Kate asked.

"Eighty-eight."

"What's in the bag?"

"Junk."

They walked quickly away into the crowds, Jacob leading, Kate chasing after him. A grinning runner saw them leaving the Elite table and stopped them. He wore a clean, new pair of white Nikes, blue jeans, and a jacket with "Akron Road Runners" stitched across the chest.

"You just left the Elite Runner table," he said. "Who are you? Can I have your autograph?" He held out a pen and a Boston Marathon program opened to the first page of entries. Several names were scrawled on the page.

Jacob pushed past him, growling, "If you don't know who I am, you don't want my autograph."

The runner stood stunned as Jacob rushed off. Kate, embarrassed, followed.

A series of doors opened into a convention hall. A sign above the door announced that this was the entrance to the "Runners Expo." Jacob, head down, hurried past. Kate caught up to him and asked, "Do you want to go to the Runners Expo?"

"No."

"Why?"

"I had to hang out at the Nike booth there last night for an hour. I don't know why, except that I'm under contract with Nike. The booth was full of assholes like that idiot back there who wanted my autograph. It's just a hassle. Crowded and noisy. I can't deal with that right now. I don't need it. It's a big distraction and I don't need it."

They walked to the car in silence and drove back to his apartment with the radio blasting rock music. After one of the songs, the DJ came on and said, "Well, here we are rocking and running throughout the big marathon weekend."

Jacob turned off the radio. They finished the ride in silence and parked. Walking to his apartment, Jacob fussed, "The only place we can find to park is almost two blocks from my apartment. This is nuts! I have to waste all my energy walking all over Boston because there's no place to park. How am I supposed to race on Monday when I have to wear myself out with all this walking?"

Kate said nothing, but followed him into his apartment. She spent the day reading while Jacob napped and listened to rock music. Midway through the afternoon Jacob turned on the television. The Red Sox were playing the Yankees. "I hate the Yankees," he said. "How 'bout you?"

"I love the Red Sox. The Yankees are dead to me. They're nothing. Yankees suck."

"That's the spirit, Kate. Yankees suck. You like baseball?"

"Love it," she said. "I'm from Boston. Of course I love the Sox."

They spent the rest of the afternoon watching the game and talking about everything except the race. Then Kate fixed dinner; spaghetti again. Jacob had explained the theory of carbohydrate loading and how it might extend his ability to run before his energy was expended. While she cooked, Jacob went out and rented a movie. After the movie, they kissed and Kate got ready to leave.

"Do you want me to come over tomorrow morning or should I wait till the afternoon," she asked at the door.

"You want to come over tomorrow?"

"Of course. When?"

"Whenever you want. Early is good."

She was back by mid-morning on Sunday. Jacob was dressed in his running shorts and a long sleeved t-shirt. He was looking over a pair of thin running shoes. They looked more like ballet slippers than sneakers. They had a scant layer of cushioning on the bottom coated with a rubber skin that passed for a sole. The rest of the shoe was a delicate white fabric. The Nike stripe and the trim were neon red.

He slipped the shoes on saying, "I've worn these twice already. I need for them to be broken in so I won't get blisters tomorrow in the race. Now I'm off for my final training run. Five miles, Kate. See you in a few minutes."

Out the door and down the stairs he went, leaving Kate behind in the apartment. She watched from the window as he ran off, practically prancing like a show horse. She timed him, noting that he returned in twenty-seven minutes. He came into the apartment barely sweating, and not at all out of breath. Grinning, he walked up to Kate and gave her a bear hug and a long, wet kiss.

"Sweaty runners turn you on?" he asked. "You want some more of this?"

Kate answered. "First, you're hardly sweating. But yes, you turn me on. And yes, I want more. But not now. You need to save your strength, you know. I don't want to be the reason you finish second tomorrow."

"Well, maybe tomorrow then. After the race."

"Maybe. You're ready?"

"For the race? I'd better be. It's too late now to do anything about it if I'm not." He went to the kitchen and got a large glass of water. He was suddenly quiet again; sipping the water till it was gone, then refilling the glass. He sat down on the sofa.

"Kate, I'm scared," he said. He looked around the apartment and out the window, distracted and panicky. He wouldn't look Kate in the eyes.

"Why?" Kate sat next to him, but not too close.

"I don't want to lose, but I don't know if I can win. And I know it's going to hurt. I don't mind hurting if I win. But I don't want to go through all that and lose."

"Jacob, you run as hard and as fast as you can for as long as you can. And you come home to me, win or lose. I'll be there for you."

Jacob woke up before sunrise on race day. He showered. On a chair by his bed he had laid out his racing shorts and a shirt, the Boston University singlet he had worn for four years. He clung to the belief that he might be unbeatable if he wore the uniform in which he had won so many races. He dressed, then checked and rechecked a duffle bag he had packed with water bottles, a jar of Vaseline, toilet paper, extra shoe laces; anything he might need before the race started. He slipped on the nearly-new racing shoes. Then he sat on the chair by the bay window eating toast and jam and sipping a cup of coffee. The sun came up. He thought of Heather briefly and wondered if she was thinking of him and the marathon that would run so close by her apartment in a few hours. He watched and waited for Kate. And Coach. And his dad and his mom. Today he knew he needed them.

They all arrived a few minutes before seven. Jacob slumped into the front seat of Coach's car. Kate and his parents rode in back. They drove out along the marathon course, down the hills through Newton and into Wellesley. Jacob watched the road roll by, remembering his run six weeks earlier. The run he had done the day after Heather left him; the run when he had met Kate. After Wellesley, they were on roads he had never seen, through Natick and Framingham and on into the countryside.

Jacob began to panic. "It's too far!" he suddenly blurted. "Too far! I can't run this far. All the way back to Boston? It's too far. I can't do this. It's insane."

"Sure you can." It was Coach. "You've gone almost a full marathon several times in training. This is no different."

They continued on in silence. With less than a mile to go to the starting line, the road began to climb steeply into Hopkinton. "My God," said, Jacob. "Look how hilly it is out here."

This time Kate spoke. "Jacob, think about it. You run out of Hopkinton the other way. You'll be going down this hill, not up. You'll be flying."

"Kate, you don't understand. Up hill, down hill, it won't matter. I've never run twenty-six miles before. Not this fast."

"Are you worried you can't finish?"

"No, I know I can run twenty-six miles," he admitted. "But to race it? Against the guys who are here? That's a different story, Kate. The question isn't whether I can run twenty-six miles. It's a question of how fast I can do it. That's what scares me."

Police stopped the car, but checked Coach's pass and let them continue on into Hopkinton. The center was a classic New England village. White frame houses with black shutters surrounded a grassy town Common, shaded with old trees. A bronze statue of a marching soldier stood beside the Common, and next to the statue a wide, light blue line was painted across the road from curb to curb. "Boston Marathon Start" was painted on the blue line in yellow.

Orange plastic snow fencing and movable metal barriers blocked off the edges of the street back from the starting area down, over a hill and out of sight. Coach turned in behind a white church next to the starting area. A sign on the church announced that it was for "Elite Runners." A policeman and a man in an official's jacket checked Coach's pass again, and checked

Jacob's number against a list. "You can all stay till nine," the official said, "but only the runner can be here after that time."

They all went into a large room in the basement of the church. Jacob found a chair against the wall and sat down. Other runners milled about. Some lay on the floor, dozing or stretching. Others sat in other chairs. A few talked with each other, but the room was quiet. Jacob took out a water bottle and sipped a little. He looked at his mother. Then his father. Then Coach. Finally Kate. He took her hand for a moment, then dropped it, embarrassed suddenly in front of his parents.

"Well here we are," Jacob said. "Everything comes down to today. Today we find out where it's all headed."

Kate took his hand again and gave it a quick squeeze, then let go.

His dad said, "You'll do fine. Just fine."

His mom added, "We'll see you in Wellesley, and we'll be waiting at the finish for you. You know where to meet us?"

Coach offered some advice. "Don't even worry about that part, Jacob, just run your race. Like your dad said, you'll do fine. You run your race. On your pace. I'll meet you at the finish area, and get you over to your parents and Kate."

"We'll be at the statues of the horses outside Copley Place," said Kate. "If you don't see Coach, just come there. That's where I'll be."

Jacob took another sip of water. "I'm ready," he said.

They sat together for a while longer. Then it was time for Coach, Kate, and his family to leave. Coach shook his hand and gave him a small pat on his shoulder. "Give 'em hell, Jacob. Let them know who you are. Be proud and show them who you are."

His dad said nothing. Telling Jacob what he felt for him had never been easy. He gave Jacob a brief hug and turned to walk out to the car. His mom held onto him longer. She finally let go, saying, "Jacob, you go run. Make your dad proud." Then she too headed after Coach and her husband.

Kate looked at Jacob, gave him a smile, a long hug, and a kiss. "It's like we're sending you into surgery back at the hospital," she said. "Only you're so darn healthy."

"Be there at the finish for me, Kate. I need you there."

"Don't you ever doubt that Jacob." She gave him a final quick kiss. "I love you." Then she was gone.

Jacob returned to his chair, alone. He sipped some more water and looked around the room. The top hundred runners filled the space; Africans, Asians, Europeans, Latin Americans, Australians, a few Americans and Canadians. Jacob recognized the faces of several of them. He had seen them in his running magazines and on television during the Olympics.

The runners wore flimsy uniforms with the logos of running shoe companies. Some of the uniforms were national team colors. All of the runners' shoes were the freakish lightweight special shoes like the pair Jacob had received from Nike. Many of the runners were small like Jacob. A few were taller, but slight. All of them were impossibly lean; almost caricatures of athletes. Their legs were thin with small bunches of muscle high on the back of the calf, and long ropes of muscle along the thigh. Weight-trained sheets of scant, hard tissue covered their shoulders and chest, but their arms were pathetically lacking in any muscle.

The runners all had the direct eyes and the cold look of trained assassins, but none of them carried themselves with the gun-slinger swagger that Jacob had seen among so many sprinters at track meets.

Jacob got up to visit the bathroom and found himself waiting in line behind a Japanese runner he remembered watching in the Olympic marathon on television. *How strange*, Jacob thought. *I never stopped to think that even the best runners in the world would have to use the bathroom before a marathon.* Jacob had another revelation when it was his turn. The bathroom smelled as bad as bathrooms everywhere. The best runners, he realized, may be faster than most other people, but in every other way, they are absolutely average humans.

Jacob returned to his chair and checked the clock on the wall. 9:30. He had a half hour till the start. His legs felt stiff and leaden. He saw several of the Kenyan runners coming in from a warm-up run. *I don't want to tire myself out. But a short, easy run would probably do me some good. Get me rolling and shake things out a bit.*

Jacob went out and jogged slowly around the Hopkinton Common. Crowds were everywhere. Runners were walking up to the High School, nearly a mile away, where there were bathrooms, and the busses would take their warm-up suits back to Boston. Spectators pushed past Jacob. Television trucks with dishes high in the air lined the Common. The Common itself was filled with people. There were booths where the Girl Scouts sold cookies. The High School band played. A massage therapist had set up a tent and gave five minute massages to runners. A line of runners stretched back from the tent blocking Jacob as he tried to run. After five minutes of jogging, Jacob gave up and returned to the church and his chair.

He slathered Vaseline on the insides of his thighs, in his armpits, and on his nipples; places he knew that chafing might become a problem during the run. Another runner approached him. With signs and speaking a language Jacob had never heard, he made Jacob understand that he wanted to use the Vaseline as well. Jacob gave him the jar.

Jacob visited the bathroom one last time. Then he sat in the chair, feeling very alone, waiting. Finally, officials rounded up the Elite Runners and escorted them out of the church and to the starting line. It was still a cool morning, but sunny. Jacob wore an old sweat shirt over his racing uniform. When he got to the start, he peeled off the sweat shirt and tossed it into the crowd. There was no way to get it back to Boston. A spectator would think it was a great souvenir. As he tossed the shirt, for the first time, he really noticed how big the crowd was. Runners filled the street from edge to edge and stretched back in a solid pack beyond Jacob's sight. They were held back by a rope from the front space reserved for the elite runners.

On the sides of the road, spectators pushed against the orange snow fence and the metal barricades. They were packed so thick against the sides of the course that Jacob couldn't tell how many rows deep they went. Overhead, helicopters from television stations circled, their motors roaring above the noise of the crowds.

The band played the Star Spangled Banner. More runners pitched old warm up suits into the crowd. Jacob paced a bit, afraid to jog or sprint the way he usually did before the start of a race to get his legs moving. He saw some of the other elite runners darting away from the start, warming up, but he was afraid to waste the energy. The officials finally herded all of the elite runners together behind the pale blue line. There was a long pause.

His private demons began shrieking inside his head. *You can't do this. You don't belong here. Not with these runners. You're not good enough. Not fast enough.*

Jacob pushed the negative thoughts aside and focused back on the race course in front of him. *Downhill start. There will be pushing and shoving in the crowd. Protect yourself. Get out fast, but stay alert. Twenty thousand runners are here, but only a few dozen are really in the race with you. Get clear of the rest of them and settle into your pace.*

Still the demons screamed. Jacob remembered Heather for a moment. And her father, laughing. *Don't the Kenyans always win that race? You're still a college boy. Good luck then.*

Go to hell, Jacob thought. *I can win. It doesn't matter what country they come from. It's just a foot race. The first guy to get to Boston wins. Heather and her father can go to hell.*

The howling in his head continued. Jacob suppressed it now by thinking of Kate. Of the day they met as he passed her bus stop. Of their first kiss. And of how she had kissed him as she left him not so long ago in the church.

Be there at the finish for me, Kate. I need you there.

Don't you ever doubt that, Jacob.

Jacob stood on the line stripped down to just himself. The other runners crowded next to him, their heat pressing against him. He was alone.

The gun and a shout from thousands of spectators. Jacob flew away from the start, his arms out slightly to avoid being pushed by the other racers. Down the long hill out of Hopkinton he went, over a rise, then down some more towards Ashland. He saw a sign high above the crowds beside the road. "One Mile."

Jacob checked his watch. *4:39. Fast, but considering the downhill start, and the mass of runners pounding along behind us, that's good. Not too fast, but certainly fast enough.*

A large pack of runners formed. Jacob looked around, trying to count how many runners were in the pack, but there were too many. He guessed that there might be forty runners. The pack moved like a large animal with many legs. Jacob floated in the midst of the pack, being carried along somehow without effort, like a leaf in a fast-moving stream. His breathing was deep but regular and steady. He found a steady, fast rhythm and settled in for the long ride back to Boston.

The miles clicked by. The pack chased a squadron of vehicles; a large press truck covered with a pyramid of writers and cameramen, a smaller truck with a television camera and a digital clock on it. Several police motorcycles with their lights flashing patrolled the side of the road, pushing the crowds back from the runners' path. The pack passed five miles in a little over twenty-four minutes.

For a moment Jacob worried. *Too fast? If I'm too fast, too soon, I'll have nothing left at the end. Remember how you felt that day? The day you met Kate? Remember how drained you were? How dead your legs were? How hard it was to keep going? Kate! My God, Kate! Her face. Her voice. Kate! Not now. Think of her later. Focus on your running. Your pace, your rhythm, your breathing. Watch the other runners.*

Around Jacob the runners settled into their work. Kenyans chattered with each other at times in their strange language. Sometimes a runner would dart ahead of the pack, only to fall back into the group. Most of the runners stayed in their place in the fast-moving crowd. Sometimes one would move to the side of the road and fall back a bit before rejoining the pack.

They approached a water stop. Tables lined both sides of the road. Cups of water and sports drinks covered the tabletops. Past the water tables, many of the elite runners had special bottles set out; an assurance that they would get the drinks they were used to. The pack broke into two long lines as runners sought their drinks from the tables on the sides of the road as they dashed by. Jacob drank only water and scooped up a cup. He sipped it quickly, gagging as he tried to swallow while breathing. Moments after the water stop the pack reformed.

The pack swept past a small lake and climbed a short rise into Natick. Ten miles. A large digital clock clicked 48:24 as Jacob rolled by in the middle of the pack. It still felt easy. Jacob worried. *Too easy? But there's no turning back from the pace.* He looked around for a moment and realized that the pack was smaller, maybe twenty runners were still traveling together. Jacob took a quick look back over his shoulder. A short distance behind the pack were four runners. Farther behind them was another small crowd. A few more straggled along the road, falling behind the leaders. Jacob turned his eyes back to the front.

Approaching Wellesley, the course climbed a short hill. For the first time Jacob felt the effort of the pace. He was winded and huffing as they cleared the top of the rise, and his legs felt the work. But he pulled himself together in moments and continued rolling in the middle of the pack.

Ahead of him, beyond the press trucks, he heard a high-pitched wailing sound. The noise grew louder. Then they were into the noise. Hundreds of Wellesley College girls, the girls who hadn't even looked at him several weeks earlier, now stood close by the race course, screaming. They howled, shouting encouragement, Jacob believed, though it was hard to tell. They reached out, trying to touch the runners as they flew past. Jacob felt goosebumps on his arms, and the hair prickling on the back of his neck as he heard their keening. Then the girls faded behind the pack of runners. Still they screamed, the bedlam retreating into the distance. One of the Kenyans said something, and another Kenyan laughed shortly. Then it was back to the business of running.

The pack flowed through Wellesley Square. They were now covering the route that Jacob had run that day. *The day I met Kate. Kate will be at the fourteen mile mark with Coach and mom and dad. I need to see her. I need for Kate to see that I can do this, even if only for the first half of the race. I just need to see her.*

Jacob sifted to the left side of the pack to be in a position where he knew he could see Kate and Coach and his parents. He searched the crowds looking for them. On a slight downhill he spotted Kate and then the rest of them standing at the front of the crowd.

"Go Jacob! Keep going, you're doing fine!" Kate smiled at him and clapped.

"That's it, son," shouted his father. "Go get 'em, Jacob!" His mother beamed and clapped but said nothing.

Coach ran next to him for a few strides. "You okay?"

"Fine."

"Hang onto the pack. Let them carry you as long as possible."

"Yup."

"Give 'em hell, Jacob!"

Coach stopped. Jacob cruised on, drifting back to the midst of the pack. They flashed through the crowds in Wellesley Hills and tore down the hill into Newton. Suddenly, as they began the climb into Newton, one of the Kenyan runners burst away from the front of the pack. His arms flailed to the side and he appeared almost awkward, but he sprang up the hill, running impossibly fast.

Match his tempo!

Turn your legs the same rate as his!
Watch him!
Stick with him!
Jacob tried to match the Kenyan, but he couldn't.

A second Kenyan chased away from the pack after the leader. Then a third Kenyan, a tall, stilt-like runner moved away from the pack as well. Three other runners, not Africans, pulled free from the front and began to work their way after the leaders.

Don't panic! Jacob told himself. *Keep them in range! Maintain contact with them!*

They topped the hill and pushed on. The pack, now lacking the leaders, felt thinner. Jacob sensed that other runners had broken off the back of the pack. He resisted the urge to look back to be sure, but he counted only ten other runners remaining with him in the group that chased the six leaders. He locked onto the tall Kenyan, his eyes focused on his back, determined not to let him expand the distance between them.

As they turned the corner to begin the ascent of the second Newton hill, Jacob felt a stinging and a softness under the big toe on his right foot. *A blister. Nothing to do about it now. Just keep running.*

Jacob leaned forward, putting his head down and charged up the long hill. He crested the hill and looked up. He found the tall Kenyan and realized that he had lost a bit of ground, slipping further behind him on the climb. *Chase him! Get him! Don't let him get away!*

As they began the third hill, the blister burst beneath his toe. Jacob felt the wetness of the fluid inside his shoe. The sting was intense for several strides, but then it numbed. Jacob looked down and saw a small stain of blood on the side of his white shoe. *Concentrate! Maintain your stride. Plant your foot squarely on each step.* Jacob fought the instinct to land on the side of the foot to protect the torn blister. If he changed his stride, he knew he would slow down and fall behind.

Then they were into the fourth hill. *Heartbreak Hill. Not that long ago I ran down this hill. That was right after I lost Heather. She might be out on the course today, somewhere in Boston, a few miles ahead. She might be watching for me. I've come so far since that day. I really don't care if she's there or not. If she sees me racing by. It doesn't matter. I've got Kate at the finish. That's all that matters now.*

Kate's waiting at the finish. Get home to Kate!

Climbing the hill, the fragmented pack with Jacob fell apart completely. He found himself running alone. He passed the twenty-mile clock in barely more than an hour and forty minutes. Calculating quickly, Jacob realized that he averaged five minutes a mile, a pace that would give him nearly a two hour, ten minute marathon. *I can't let myself slow down. Maintain the pace! Get over this hill and race for home. Coach said that a marathon is a twenty-mile run and a ten kilometer race. I've done the twenty-mile. Now I've just got to race the ten K.*

Jacob felt curiously refreshed as he crossed the top of the final big hill and began the downhill past Boston College. He smelled cookouts and beer from the students who watched the race. He heard several shout out, some encouraging, some jeering at his Boston University shirt. He looked for the tall Kenyan, but couldn't see him up the road ahead. Other runners were there, though, and he chased after them.

Moments later, his body changed. The fluid style he had run with for so long was gone. Each step was an effort. His back ached. His shoulders felt clenched. His hips were tight, limiting his ability to stride out. His thighs and his calves felt cramped, twitching, and sore. The torn blister still stung, and he felt a second one starting beneath the big toe on his other foot.

Four miles to go. Do not slow down! Hold onto your form! Hold onto your rhythm! Hold onto your pace! Use your arms! Push off strong on each stride. Push from the hips. Drive off the toes. Go!

Jacob willed himself to chase the next runner ahead of him. On the side of the road, the crowd still lined the course, thicker now, clapping, clapping, the noise clattering around him. Jacob felt as though he was running through a tunnel. People and faces flashed by, and sometimes he heard his name called from the wall of people. But he was unable to recognize the faces or the voices.

Three miles! You're starting to let go. You're starting to slow down. Fight it, Jacob, fight it! A runner's moving up from behind you. Look at him. Hispanic, maybe? Mexican? I see fear in his eyes. I can take him. Go! Fight him off! Make him hurt! Break him! Oh, God, he's ahead of you. Hang on him. Stick with him. He'll pull you back into your rhythm. Back into your race. Get home to Kate.

Then the other runner was ten yards ahead. Jacob cracked, and the Mexican was gone.

Two miles to go. Jacob was frantic as he tried to keep his form and not lose more time, more places. His mouth was dry. His hands were dry. He had stopped sweating. The second blister popped. Jacob felt it almost as a perverse sort of relief. *At least now I don't have to worry about it breaking. It's done. Now I can just concentrate on my running.*

Approaching the final mile, Jacob raced along the edge of his Boston University campus. Crowds of faceless classmates shouted his name, helping him finish. As he passed the twenty-five mile mark, an official stepped from the checkpoint and called to him. "Go Jacob! You've come too far to let go now! Keep it up. Take it home!"

A policeman on a motorcycle circled and pulled in ahead of him as Jacob raced through Kenmore Square with a mile to go. The motorcycle obscured Jacob's view of the runners ahead of him, but it assured him of a pace for the final mile as he chased after it. Behind the metal barricades, deep crowds of people, fresh from the ball game at Fenway Park, streamed by, their noise pounding around him.

Jacob ran on instinct and fear now. His running, he knew, was ragged, but he was still covering the road as fast as he could. The noise seemed to recede, taking on a hollow quality as though he was under water. Jacob made a right turn, following the motorcycle up a slight hill, then a left. He looked down the final straight away. Far, far away, he could see the scaffolding at the finish. In front of him was the motorcycle, and beyond it he could see the Mexican runner, still pulling away, and passing the tall Kenyan. Jacob gathered as much speed as he could and pursued the Kenyan. The edges of his vision blurred and grew dark as he flashed down the middle of the wide, empty street. He was alone; no runners ahead of him close enough to catch, none behind near enough to catch him. On he dashed.

The finish scaffolding loomed, then, he was beneath it, finished. He stumbled to a walk, his hands seeking the ropes that lined the finish chute. Arms caught him. For just a moment his ears rang, and his vision blanked out. He heard someone ask, "Are you okay?"

"Yes."

He walked on, supported, to the end of the chute. His legs felt out of touch with his body. His feet seemed to flap beneath his legs. Someone wrapped a metallic plastic sheet over his shoulders to keep him warm. He staggered out of the chute and was escorted by two volunteers into a tent with a sign, "Elite Runners".

One of the volunteers, a man, helped him into a portajohn and handed him a plastic bottle. "For your drug test," he said. He held Jacob up until Jacob finally managed to fill the bottle. The urine was a dark red, orange. The volunteer labeled it and passed it to another volunteer who added it to a row of a ten or twelve other bottles. Most were also filled with dark, bloody urine. Jacob had read about this in his physiology class; extreme physical stress breaks down muscle tissue and blood cells and then passes them into the urine. Still, the look of the bottles, one of them his, concerned him.

As they came out of the drug-testing tent, Jacob suddenly felt nauseous. He slumped to his knees and vomited. Bile-filled water splashed onto the pavement between his hands. It made his eyes tear, but he felt immediately better, with the nausea gone. He heard a voice. "I'll take him from here."

He looked up. It was Coach. "You're okay. I've got you." He put an arm around Jacob, lifting him still holding the metallic blanket, and walked him carefully to the end of the fenced finish line paddock. "A few of your teammates are here to see you. No way were they going to let you run this alone."

"Who?"

"David, Colin, Peter."

"Good."

They found the gate at the end of the paddock and passed through. Jacob walked on stiffly and met his teammates. "Way to go, Jacob!" "Awesome, man!" "We knew you would do it."

"I lost guys."

"Are you kidding me? You kicked ass man. You were eleventh. Two-twelve, I think. Maybe two-thirteen. That's running, man! That's a great time!"

"Thanks, guys."

Coach stepped in. "Come on guys, give him some room. Give him some time. I've got to get him back to his parents and his girlfriend. They've got his warm up suit. I don't want him to tighten up."

The team pulled back. Jacob called to them, "I'll check with you guys tomorrow. I'll come down to practice and see you tomorrow. I appreciate your being here for me."

Coach led him away toward Copley Place, the statues of metal horses, his parents. Kate.

A block away the crowd roared as more and more runners finished the marathon. Small groups of spectators on the street, here, away from the finish, saw Jacob and clapped for him, knowing that he must have been one of the top finishers to be so far away from the finish already.

"Coach, what am I going to do? I'm a mess. I'm all salt and sweat coated, and I just threw up. What about Kate?"

"Don't worry about that. I think she'll love you just the way you are."

They crossed the street, walking slowly, painfully. Ahead, at the entrance to Copley Place, Jacob could see the abstract metal horses. Waiting beside the horses, he saw his dad and his mom. And there was Kate, watching him and beaming.

Coach led him to them. Jacob stood in front of them, feeling tears ready to start. He knew he was at a turn in the road. On his left were his parents. To his right, Kate. He turned to Kate and hugged her and held on.

He was home.

COMING SOON!

*Turn the page for a special preview of The Fairy Garden, to be published
Spring, 2020*

Fairy Garden

Elizabeth - Birth

Elizabeth squeezed her eyes tight to shut out the light. It was dark where she came from. It was quiet. She floated, embraced on all sides by her mother's pink presence. Suddenly, the water had left her and she was pushed, squeezed, thrust out of warm comfort into this cold, bright, awful place. Her head ached, pounding in pain after the pressure of the birth.

She flailed her arms and kicked her legs, newfound freedom, no longer contained, but frightening her with the possibility of falling. She breathed in and screamed in terror. Enormous hands cupped her body and her head, supporting her in the midst of cold space. She felt a sudden sharp pull at her belly as the cord was cut, severing her from the life she had always known. There was no pain. It was the finality of the cut that made her cry out again. She was alone in the world now.

A warm cloth slid softly over her body, new wetness, removing the old familiar coat. She was wrapped in heated fabric, confining her arms and legs. It felt good to be swathed like this, but it was not her home, not the warm, quiet place where she had always lived. She cried again, a despairing wail lost in the emptiness of this new space.

They floated above her, tiny lights amid the terrifying brightness. "She is beautiful," they chimed. "She is lovely. She is like we are. We must tell the others that she is here." No one heard them but the newborn baby.

"It will be all right, little one," the fairies sang, comforting her. "You will be happy in your new life. Your family will love you. They will care for you."

In her mind she sang a reply. "I want to go back. It was good. I was warm. I was never hungry. I was content inside my mother. I have to go back."

"You cannot," they told her. "You are here now. We will watch over you."

Overcome with exhaustion from her short journey, Elizabeth fell asleep.

Elizabeth – Age Thirty

Elizabeth sat at the black wrought-iron table on the brick-paved terrace holding a glass of red wine by its thin stem. It was cool in the shade of the oak and crepe myrtle that guarded the garden. She pushed her auburn hair back from her face and peered out into the dark foliage watching for her daughter Livvy, playing on the paths that wound through the garden. She couldn't see her little girl but she heard her singing.

The house and the garden were hers now, bequeathed to her in grandfather Papa's will. He also left a sealed letter for her. She recalled the moment when her brother Michael handed her the envelope saying, "The will says you get the house. Mom and Dad get half of Papa's investments. I get the other half. I'm sorry there's no money for you. Only Papa's house. You'll be okay, right?" Michael rested a reassuring hand on her shoulder for a moment, sincerely concerned for his younger sister.

"I'm fine. Everything is fine," she answered grimly.

No, it wasn't fine. It wouldn't be now that Papa was gone. But Michael didn't understand, nor did her parents. There had been so much loss in the past months. The house was all she had from Papa now, but it was all she would have wanted anyway. It was enough. She thought of Papa's letter.

Dear Elizabeth,

I know how much you have loved my house and my garden. Even when you were a little girl it was your special place. It is yours now. I understand that money would have been nice for you to have, but if I had left the house to anyone else in the family, they would have sold it.

Papa must have written the letter months ago. He didn't know that Lucas would leave her. Elizabeth hadn't seen that coming either.

Elizabeth looked back at the house behind her, at the French doors from the terrace which led into the living room, at the white columns supporting the roof that sheltered the half of the terrace closest to the house. It was a wonderful house, a brick colonial with more white-painted columns in the front. But it was the backyard, the garden that Elizabeth loved. Papa's backyard wasn't really a yard at all. It was a long, formal English garden, stretching behind the house, bound on all sides by moss and ivy-covered, weathered brick walls. The walls were high, too high for a child to see over, too tall for even an adult to climb easily. Oak, magnolia, and crepe myrtle trees hung over the whole garden. Brick-lined walks made of crushed white oyster shells separated beds of myrtle and pachysandra.

Spaced throughout the garden were three circular brick-paved junctions of the paths, rimmed with boxwood. Two, on either side of the garden, were banked with wrought-iron benches and dominated by statues of dancing children on brick pedestals; a boy at one end and a girl on the other. Real children weren't allowed to play in the garden—they might crush the flowers. Elizabeth remembered her childhood here, being permitted only to walk along the paths. She had the same rule in place now for Livvy, but Livvy, just like her mother when she was young, darted off the paths once she was out of the sight of grown-ups. The third circle, the largest, was in the center of the garden. A bronze armillary sphere, mounted on the top of a short column, consumed the middle of the circle. Verdigris stained rings, marking the cycles of the seasons and the time of day, formed a hollow globe. The metal rings were pierced by a narrow bronze shaft, tipped with a polished brass arrowhead, pointing due north.

Livvy danced into view on one of the paths. Elizabeth watched as the tiny girl pirouetted around the armillary with her arms stretched above her head. She was five and had the innocence of a child; every day was a new adventure. Livvy threw her arms wide and spun with her eyes closed, her face turned up into the springtime sunshine. Her long sundress, her choice of dress-up clothes for Papa's funeral, twirled around her body. Inside the wide-flung dress her narrow torso was as lean and lithe as a sapling. She sang a song, her voice melodious though the words were hard for Elizabeth to make out. Dizzy with the spinning, Livvy fell and sat, giggling on the grassy plot next to the white seashell path. When her balance returned, she stood. She leaned down and peered into the flowerbeds, holding her white-blonde curls back from her face. She began talking to herself, hovering over the blossoms. Then she straightened and walked deeper into the garden, still talking quietly, her child's voice sing-song. Like most children, she was living in a world of make-believe.

Elizabeth was concerned when she lost sight of her daughter. She worried what could happen to her baby unattended out there in the vastness of the formal garden. What if she fell and was hurt? What dangers lurked out there? No! Be logical, Elizabeth reminded herself. It will be all right. The garden is walled in. It's private and safe. Except for the fairies.

She relaxed for a moment. Still, it was unsettling. She had lost so much this past year. First, her husband Lucas, then her Papa, her grandfather. Both losses were unexpected. Don't troubles come in threes? She couldn't bear to lose Livvy too.

Elizabeth held up her glass, catching the sun. The wine was deep burgundy, tinted pink, orange, lavender, and purple where it washed the edge of the sparkling crystal glass. She swirled it, sniffed, and took a sip. This moment should be perfect, she thought, with the sunshine, the warmth, the wine, and Livvy dancing in the garden. It would have been wonderful to share this time with Lucas or Papa, or both. But aside from Livvy, she felt abandoned and alone now. Lucas had left her and now Papa was gone. She felt a fresh wave of the despair that had begun with Lucas. She willed herself not to allow tears. She reminded herself as she had done all day, and at the funeral, "Livvy needs me to be strong, now more than ever."

There was a stir of motion on the garden path, Livvy running up the path laughing. "Mommy, guess what?" She jumped up the brick steps from the garden one at a time and climbed, wriggling onto her mother's lap.

Elizabeth set her wine on the table, being careful not to spill. "What, Honey Bunny?"

"There's fairies in the garden!"

Elizabeth hugged her daughter. She remembered when she first discovered the fairies. She had been just about Livvy's age. She knew how special it made her feel to talk with the fairies, to dream about them at night. Maybe she had clung to her belief in the fairies too long. Maybe, she wondered, that belief had blinded her to the hard realities of life with Lucas. Elizabeth had always counted on the fairies to save her from dangers and hard times. There was no going back now, no way to turn back the clock, no way to bring back either Lucas or Papa.

Elizabeth turned to her little girl. "Really? Fairies? Tell me about them."

"There's all kinds of fairies. And you wanna know a secret?"

"Sure. What's the secret?"

Livvy squirmed closer, cupped her hand and whispered in her mommy's ear, her moist breath tickling. "One of them is named Olivia. Just like me. And she's my own special fairy."

"Really." Elizabeth said the word as a statement, not a question, her tone flat, emotionless. She looked across the white-painted railing into the garden. The garden was a beautiful place in the spring sunshine with the early flowers, filled with sounds and never-ending motion. She heard the hum of the bees and other insects. Birds sang, flying from tree to tree and hopping from branch to branch. There were butterflies and dragonflies. She saw no fairies. For years the fairies were there for her but now they were gone. For that she was glad. She'd had enough of the fairies.

"Yes Mommy. Really. There's Olivia and the Queen and a grumpy man-fairy called Thomas. They're the only ones I've met but I think there's more."

"Oh, I expect there are more. Do you like seeing the fairies out there?"

"Yes."

"Well, you go play. See if there are more fairies. See if they live in a castle."

"Okay." Livvy slid off Elizabeth's lap. Then she paused and leaned to her mommy, burying her face in Elizabeth's lap. "I miss Daddy," she mumbled. "And Papa too. But I want Daddy to come home."

"I know, sweetheart. But Daddy's gone to live somewhere else. And Papa passed away. You know they both love you. Papa's looking down from heaven right now watching you."

"I know." Her voice betrayed her sadness.

Livvy was a child with a child's resilience. She recovered quickly, pulled away and brightened. "Can I go play now? Do you think there are unicorns in the garden too?"

"I don't know. Why don't you go and see? Run along, Livvy. Go play and have fun."

Little Livvy hopped down the steps, one at a time, reaching her hand up on the stair railing. Then she ran back into the garden, her white sandals flying along the path. Elizabeth sat alone again, watching Livvy play. Seeing her imagine the fairies brought it all back to her. She had believed the fairies were real for years. Papa played along, making her believe he also saw them. Maybe he did believe in them; maybe he didn't. It didn't matter now that he was gone.

The fairies gave her the support she never could get from her parents. But where did believing in fairies get her? She began to feel angry reminiscing about what the fairies. If they were real, what had they done to bring her to this point in her life? Should she tell Livvy that the fairies weren't real, she wondered? After her experiences with the fairies, she didn't want her daughter growing up depending on them the way she had.

Out in the garden, Livvy leaned to the flowers again and began talking to the blossoms. The breeze brought her child's voice clearly up to Elizabeth. "Hello again, little fairy," said Livvy. "Where is the Queen?"

ACKNOWLEDGEMENTS

I have been working on these stories for several years. That they are now being published is due to the support of many people. I am grateful to all of them. Jeanne Johansen read the stories and believed in their value. Without her support this book would not have been published. Narielle Living, my editor, refined my original manuscripts and added just the right touches. This edition is being published by her company, Blue Fortune. So many of my family and friends have seen early versions of the stories and offered their suggestions. Though I can't mention all of them, several must be cited. Fellow New England authors Brian Schulz and Richard Tappan gave me direction and guidance. My writers' groups in Williamsburg, Virginia reviewed a few of the stories and offered suggestions. Most of all, my wife Debbie has seen me through the whole writing experience. She has given me encouragement, grammatical direction, and new ways to think about the development of the story lines.

About the Author

Peter Stipe enjoyed a long career that included time in education as well as work in Human Resource Development and Training for a variety of businesses. He has a Bachelor's degree in History from Boston University and a Master's in Education from Tufts. In addition to his writing, Peter is an accomplished artist, working with photography and in watercolor. He has photographs on display at the On The Hill Gallery in Yorktown, Virginia.

A competitive long distance runner for many years, Peter has completed numerous marathons with six finishes in the top fifty places in the Boston Marathon and participation in the 1972 U.S. Olympic Trials. A New Englander for most of his life, he now lives and writes in Williamsburg, Virginia.

www.ingramcontent.com/pod-product-compliance
Lightning Source LLC
Chambersburg PA
CBHW070944190726
48292CB00004B/1331